MONTH OF SUNDAYS

Visit us at www.boldstrokesbooks.com

By the Author

In Medias Res

Rum Spring

Lucky Loser

Month of Sundays

MONTH OF SUNDAYS

by
Yolanda Wallace

2012

CREDITS

EDITOR: CINDY CRESAP
PRODUCTION DESIGN: SUSAN RAMUNDO
COVER DESIGN BY SHERI (GRAPHICARTIST2020@HOTMAIL.COM)

Acknowledgments

I've been a fan of cooking shows like *Iron Chef, Top Chef,* and *Chopped* for several years, so I guess it was a given I would eventually attempt to write a novel with a chef as one of the main characters. I hope the manuscript that follows does justice to a profession I have long admired.

Thanks to the usual suspects—Dita for continuing to put up with me, my fellow authors for accepting me as one of their own, and Radclyffe, Cindy, and the rest of the Bold Strokes family for making the finished product look effortless. The biggest thanks, of course, goes to the readers. Thank you once again for supporting my work. I'll do my best not to let you down.

Bon appétit!

Dedication

Dita, I'm sorry I made you reach for the snacks
so often while you proofread this one for me.
Love you, though. Mean it!

CHAPTER ONE

"You've got to be shitting me."

Rachel Bauer took one look at the gorgeous blonde sitting next to her best friend Jane Mangano, turned, and fled. Thankfully, Jane was so engrossed in her conversation she didn't see her leave.

When Rachel had agreed to meet Jane and her partner, Colleen Lambert, for drinks at Maidenhead, she had agreed to just that. Drinks. A couple of rounds of draft beer, perhaps an import or two. Not a surprise blind date with someone who made a supermodel look like the Wicked Witch of the West.

She knew Jane was desperate to get her out of her apartment, the safe harbor she abandoned only for work and the occasional foray to the corner bodega, but this was too much.

In her self-appointed role as Rachel's social planner, Jane had made it her mission to force her to spend a night out at least once a month. To keep her spirits up before she turned into a recluse with a house full of cats. So far, so good. Her apartment was feline-free and her state of mind leaned more toward happiness than melancholia. Usually.

Jane meant well and Rachel appreciated her efforts, but sometimes she went a bit overboard. Like now. What was Jane thinking? When—*if*—Rachel ever made her way back into the dating scene, she intended to ease into it, not jump in with both feet. Spending even five seconds of face time with the blond goddess sharing a booth with Jane and Colleen would be like skydiving without a parachute. She didn't feel like being turned into a really bad version of Crêpes Suzette.

On a scale of one to ten, the blonde was a twelve on an off day. Even when she took the time to primp and shellac herself to within an inch of her life, Rachel usually felt like a six at best. Lately, she had been feeling more like a four. She had been stress eating since her breakup with her ex, packing twenty pounds on her sturdy five foot eight frame. Her self-confidence was at an all-time low while her weight was at an all-time high. Not the ideal time to meet someone new.

She squeezed past the patrons in the crowded tavern and headed for the door, intending to retreat to her apartment, slip into her pj's, and crack open a pint of ice cream—her preferred way to spend a Friday night.

She had been working nonstop since Thanksgiving, covering for coworkers who had back-ended their vacations to the latter part of the year so they could spend the holidays with their families.

With her love life nonexistent, work was everything to her these days. It had been for a while. With nothing and no one to go home to, she had spent the past eight months chained to her desk for twelve hours a day, eating too much junk food and drinking too much coffee. The extended hours had been great for her productivity and her bank balance but hell on her social life. What remained of her social life, anyway.

She had devolved into something of a hermit since her ex had turned her life upside down and walked out of it for what Rachel hoped was the last time. Her apartment wasn't filled with empty pizza cartons or discarded boxes of Chinese takeout, but it was starting to exude a distinct cave-like aura. Fitting. Because all she wanted to do when she walked in the door was grab a pint of ice cream, crawl into bed, and pull the covers up to her chin until the ache in her soul went away.

As she headed to the door, she wondered if she had enough ingredients in her refrigerator to make a truly decadent sundae. She wanted to slip into a sugar coma and put this near-miss behind her.

She had almost made her great escape when she felt a hand fall on her shoulder.

"Where do you think you're going?" Jane's familiar voice asked.

With a heavy sigh, Rachel turned to face the music. "Home. Where do you think? I didn't sign up to be a complete stranger's plus one."

"But you're here now. You might as well make the most of it."

"Why should I?"

Jane took a step back. "What are you so afraid of? That you'll actually enjoy yourself for once, or you'll lose your excuse?"

"My excuse?"

"The 'I'm still recovering from a bad breakup so I'm too wounded to give someone else a chance' excuse. You and Isabel broke up months ago. Isn't it time you moved on?"

Rachel narrowed her eyes. "That's for me to decide, not you." Jane's words held more than a hint of truth, but she wasn't ready to hear them yet. What were you supposed to do when your lover left you for someone else? What was the timetable for getting over something like that?

Jane threw her hands up. "Fine. I give up. Go home if that's what you really want to do. I'll come up with a reason for why you didn't show up tonight. I'll tell Griffin you had to work late or you were kidnapped by aliens or, better yet, you came down with a wicked case of the chickenshits and decided you'd rather barricade yourself in your apartment than spend time with your friends."

Rachel groaned in frustration. Jane was blatantly manipulating her, but it was for her own good, so how was she supposed to hold it against her? "One drink. That's it."

Jane flashed a rakish grin and began to steer her through the crowd. "You won't regret it; I promise."

"Don't make promises you can't..."

Words failed Rachel when she got a closer look at her date for the evening. Or was it the next thirty minutes?

"Rachel Bauer, meet Griffin Sutton," Jane said, introducing her to the stunning blonde who was staring at the display on her cell phone. "Griffin, Rachel."

Griffin, who looked vaguely familiar, stood up, put away her BlackBerry, and extended her right hand toward Rachel. A chunky silver bracelet dangled from her wrist. Rachel couldn't read the engraving. She was curious about the message, but not overly so. Her eyes slowly traveled up Griffin's long, lanky body and came to rest on her angular face. Her heart lurched painfully, preparing for the inevitable letdown. Her track record with blind dates left something to be desired. Why should this one be any different?

She could feel everyone at the table waiting for her to break the ice, but she couldn't think of anything to say. She felt like an awkward teenager. Her feet were rooted in place, her tongue glued to the roof of her mouth. She could barely breathe, let alone form a coherent thought. Fortunately, Griffin spoke first.

"Jane has told me so much about you," she said with a warm smile. Her voice, a husky contralto, was like honeyed whiskey. Her gray eyes met Rachel's and held them for a socially acceptable length of time. The expression on her face was open, non-judgmental. She seemed to see and appreciate Rachel for who she was and not who she wished her to be. Had Rachel dismissed her too soon?

Rachel shook Griffin's hand. Griffin's grip was firm and sure, two words Rachel couldn't use to describe herself at the moment. "I wish I could say the same," she said with a pointed glare at Jane. Although Griffin didn't appear to have an agenda, Rachel didn't think the same could be said for her so-called best friend.

Jane shrugged off Rachel's protests the way she always did when she was determined to get her way. When Griffin sat down again, Jane pulled Rachel into the booth before she could turn and disappear into the crowd a second time. "You really need to get out more." She wrapped an arm around Rachel's shoulder to prevent another escape attempt. "Griffin," she explained patiently as if she were talking to a small child, "is the head chef at Match."

"The place you've been trying to get into for months with no luck?" When Jane nodded, Rachel finally realized where she had seen Griffin before. Her face was plastered on the side of every bus, billboard, telephone booth, and subway placard in town. She wasn't easy to miss.

Match was one of the hottest restaurants in town. Open for less than three years, the waiting list for reservations was nearly that long. The critics for the *Times, Food and Wine,* and *Bon Appétit* had been raving. Not that Griffin didn't have her detractors. There were some who dismissed her as little more than the flavor of the month. Others wished the Orange County native would take her surfer girl looks, free spirit, and all-natural ingredients back to Southern California, where they felt she belonged. But her food seemed to be tipping the scales in her favor.

"How do you know each other?" Rachel didn't know the makeup of Griffin's social circle, but she knew Jane and Colleen's idea of fine dining was eating their takeout food off a plate instead of out of the Styrofoam box it arrived in.

"I picked her up," Colleen replied matter-of-factly, rearranging the items on the table to make room for the tray of hot wings the server had brought out. She had ordered a sample platter—twenty-five wings in five different flavors, ranging, by the looks of it, from merely spicy to almost deadly. "For a few minutes, she made me forget I was married."

"Don't worry. I made sure to remind her." Jane dug an elbow into Rachel's ribs. Zoning in on the hottest wings, she dipped one into a bowl of ranch dressing and took a bite. Rachel could smell the fumes from three feet away. "Have I ever thanked you for that night?" Jane asked Griffin with a wink. "Thanks to you, that was the best ride I ever got."

Colleen was a cab driver, so her pick-up line was supposed to be a joke, as was Jane's rejoinder about enjoying the ride, but the subject hit a little too close to home. Rachel hadn't ridden anything other than her hand in months and sometimes even it had the nerve to tell her it wasn't in the mood.

Pity party, party of one. Your table's ready.

Griffin sensed Rachel's discomfort. Or perhaps she could tell Rachel was about to bolt. Either way, she slid out of the far side of the booth and dragged Rachel out of her seat. "Come with me."

She placed Rachel's hands on her sides and covered Rachel's hands with hers, compelling her to follow. Rachel did, but at a safe distance. So she thought. When Griffin pulled up short to avoid bumping into someone, Rachel plowed right into her.

Her hands slipped off Griffin's sides and her arms wrapped around her waist. Her breasts pressed against Griffin's back. Griffin's hips molded against her stomach so perfectly it seemed the body parts were made for each other.

"Okay back there?"

Griffin reached up and brushed Rachel's cheek with her fingertips. The brief contact made Rachel's body come alive. She wanted to place her lips close to Griffin's ear and whisper naughty things to her while she rode one of her chiseled thighs. She wanted to watch Griffin's eyes darken as her hands slid across her skin. She wanted to know what Griffin sounded like when she came.

Her libido had been dead and buried for months. Where the hell did this wave of lust come from? Murmuring an apology, she gently moved Griffin away from her before her suddenly erect nipples bored holes in Griffin's back.

Maidenhead was always busy, especially on the weekends. Griffin made her way through the crowd, carved out some space for them at the anchor-shaped bar, and tried to get the bartender's attention. "You look like you could use a drink," she said after she ordered two flights of tequila.

"Gee, what makes you say that?"

Griffin grinned and gave Rachel's elbow a reassuring squeeze. Rachel mustered a smile that faltered the instant Griffin asked, "What's your porn name?"

"My what?" If the question was Griffin's version of an icebreaker, she must think Rachel was an iceberg.

"Your porn name. You take the name of your first pet and combine it with the name of the street you lived on as a kid. My porn name is Trixie Cerrito. My first pet was a Chihuahua named Trixie, and I grew up on Cerrito Avenue. What's your porn name?"

Playing along, Rachel joined the name of the goldfish she received for her sixth birthday with the name of the street she called home for eighteen years. "Puddles King."

"Sounds like you'd be limited to movies about golden showers, though I hear there's a growing market for that."

Griffin turned to check on the bartender's progress. Trying not to be too obvious, Rachel gave her a quick once-over. They were similar in height, but that's where their similarities ended. Even if Rachel gave her the extra twenty pounds she was carrying around, Griffin would still look ready to march down the runway. She wasn't model-thin, though. From the way she filled out her jeans, Rachel could tell she cooked as well for herself as she did for others, but at the same time, she was wiry and lean. Like she woke up every day at four a.m. to do a hundred crunches and go for a five-mile run. Rachel thought she could probably bounce a quarter off her abs—or her ass. The thought left her wishing she had some spare change in her pocket.

Griffin was neck-snappingly gorgeous so Rachel wasn't surprised she found her attractive. She was shocked, however, to find herself attracted to her. Her off-kilter sense of humor was a definite plus, but Rachel wasn't interested in a one-night stand, if that's what Jane had in mind when she set up the blind date. She wanted to get to know the woman behind the beautiful face and the hot body.

"I don't want to ambush you, which you must think I'm doing." Griffin shouted to make herself heard above the music and crowd noise.

Rachel was beginning to feel surrounded, but she thought that went without saying so she didn't say it.

The bartender, a sexy redhead in a white tank top and black jeans, placed the drinks in front of them. "*Blanco, oro, reposado,* and *añejo,*" she said, pointing out the various shots.

"In other words, one tequila, two tequila, three tequila, floor," Griffin said with a grin as she reached for a saltshaker. She turned back to Rachel. "I thought Jane gave you the heads-up about tonight."

"She didn't."

"Obviously not."

If she had, Rachel would have told her what she had been telling her for months: she wasn't ready to date yet. If ever.

"I'm sorry she didn't fill you in," Griffin continued. "I told her a few weeks ago that I've had one lousy date after another since I've been here, and she said she knew someone I ought to meet."

They took the first shot—the *blanco*—and it went down so smoothly Rachel believed the rest were going to be just as easy.

"I don't normally do blind dates," Griffin said.

"But desperate times call for desperate measures."

Griffin shook her head. "I wouldn't say that. I would say, though, that she was right about you."

Most chefs were champion schmoozers. Making a living doing a job predicated on making customers happy, they had to be in order to survive. But Rachel thought this one seemed sincere.

"What did she say?"

"She said you were the quintessential New Yorker."

"Meaning?"

"To me, New Yorkers are like Parisians without the sneer. You have the same sarcastic sense of humor and you both think your city is the greatest in the world. I love Paris, but I think New York wins based on diversity. You represent New York to me."

"So I'm something for you to conquer?"

"I prefer 'win over.'"

It was working. Griffin was effortlessly charming, and her quiet confidence held tremendous appeal. The woman was like catnip. Refreshing, exhilarating, and thoroughly intoxicating. Rachel could feel herself getting high.

"What else did Jane tell you about me?" Griffin recited Rachel's basic biographical information. When she didn't mention the dissolution of her relationship with Isabel Fischer, Rachel brought up the subject herself. "Jane didn't tell you I'm damaged goods?"

Griffin pulled up the sleeves of her fitted Ralph Lauren button-down shirt, then licked the back of her left hand and sprinkled salt on the wet spot. "She said your last girlfriend broke your heart and if I did the same, she'd rip mine out and feed it to me."

Rachel couldn't help but laugh. Good old Jane. Always looking out for her—even when she might not want her to.

"Go ahead," Griffin said, trying to keep a straight face. "Yuk it up, but I think she meant it."

"She did."

"Then I'll be sure to keep that in mind." Griffin raised her glass of *oro* and winked through the gold-colored liquid. "To second chances?"

"I'll drink to that."

They tapped their glasses, downed the tequila, and followed it with a bite of lime. Rachel slowly exhaled to try to ease the burn. It didn't help.

"If you don't mind me asking," Griffin said with apparent hesitation, "what did your ex do that was so heinous your friends are willing to threaten your dates with grievous bodily injury in order to avoid having history repeat itself?"

Unlike Griffin, Rachel didn't hesitate. "We were together for eight years, then she cheated on me and left me for another woman."

Griffin's tanned face grew pale. Mortification or a warning sign of similar behavior?

"Eight years is a long time. I don't think all of my relationships combined add up to half that time."

If Griffin's comment was meant to be facetious, it certainly wasn't delivered that way.

A player. I should have known.

"You don't believe in long-term relationships?"

"I believe in them, but I don't think I inherited the gene to be good at them. So I stick to what I do best."

"Which is?"

"Let's just say women who spend time with me leave knowing Disney World isn't the only Magic Kingdom." Griffin touched Rachel's forearm and laughed infectiously. "Did that make me sound like I was trying too hard or not hard enough?"

"The word 'coasting' definitely came to mind."

Griffin leaned toward her. Her scent—crisp and clean like a warm ocean breeze—filled Rachel's senses. Rachel knew she should back away, but she didn't. Instead, she moved closer. "I'd love it if you stayed," Griffin said, "but I'll understand if you don't."

When she pulled away, Rachel had to make a concerted effort not to follow her. Player or not, the woman had skills.

Griffin reached for the *reposado*. "What are you doing for New Year's Eve?"

"I don't know. I haven't planned that far ahead yet."

Griffin raised an eyebrow, but didn't point out that New Year's Eve was a little more than two weeks away. "I'm having a pizza party at my apartment that night."

It was Rachel's turn to raise an eyebrow. "I would have expected black tie and cocktails, not deep-dish pepperoni and Miller Lite."

"When I'm not at work, I like to keep things low-key." Griffin downed her third shot. Rachel followed suit. "If you're not doing anything, feel free to stop by." She reached for a cocktail napkin, borrowed a pen from the bartender, and scribbled something on the paper. She slid the napkin toward Rachel. "My address. In case you change your mind."

Rachel folded the napkin in half and slipped it into her pocket. She appreciated the invitation but was reluctant to accept it. Griffin struck her as someone who was easy on the eyes but hard on the heart. Their brief time together had done little to change that impression. Did she want to become the latest notch on Griffin's bedpost, or should she get out while the getting was good?

"I'll think about it."

Griffin looked at her, obviously sizing her up. Rachel wondered if she passed inspection.

"You're going to make me chase you, aren't you?" Griffin asked matter-of-factly.

Rachel twirled one of the empty shot glasses so she could focus on something other than Griffin's arresting eyes. "I doubt I'd prove much of a challenge for you. I'm not very fast on my feet."

"You could have fooled me."

Rachel forced herself to meet Griffin's gaze. She hadn't trusted her heart to anyone since Isabel broke it. If she gave Griffin a chance, would she have the time of her life, or would she set herself up for another fall?

"One can never have too many friends, Rachel. Perhaps I can be yours," Griffin said with none of her previous bravado. Rachel sensed a vulnerability about her that added to her considerable charm. Griffin nodded at Colleen, who was frantically waving them back to the table.

"Your wings are getting cold," Rachel said, giving Griffin permission to leave.

"If there are any left," Griffin said with another grin.

As much as she hated to admit it, Rachel liked the cheeky chef with the killer smile. But, then again, wasn't that the point of this whole affair?

Oops. Poor choice of words.

"Are you staying?" Griffin asked hopefully.

Rachel shook her head. Staying wasn't in her best interests—or Griffin's. She had too much thinking to do. "No, I think I'm going to take off."

When Griffin handed Rachel the final shot of tequila, her bracelet caught the light and Rachel could clearly see the words etched into the metal. *Don't let reality get in the way of your dreams.*

Rachel drank the *añejo*, and the room started to spin.

"It was a pleasure meeting you. I hope we see each other again soon." Griffin extended her hand. "And I hope the second time is less traumatic than the first."

Griffin flashed a disarming smile, and Rachel nearly changed her mind about leaving. But, sticking to her guns, she said her good-byes and finally slipped out the door. On the street, she buried her hands in the pockets of her coat in an attempt to ward off the cold, but it was no use. The chill she felt had nothing to do with the frigid temperatures. Her pilot light had gone out when Isabel walked out on her. Tonight, she had felt the flame begin to flicker back to life. When she had held Griffin in her arms, the flame had turned into a wildfire.

As she headed to the subway, she wondered if she were about to get burned.

CHAPTER TWO

Griffin tossed her keys on the console table in the foyer and hung her coat in the closet. "Better luck next time, old friend." Normally her good luck charm, the black leather jacket seemed to have lost its magic. The blind date Jane and Colleen had arranged had been awkward at best. Rachel had been interested in her, if her body's reaction to their accidental collision was any indication, but her interest had quickly faded.

She acted like she couldn't get away from me fast enough. Is she still too haunted by memories of her cheating ex to move on, or did I forget to take a shower this morning?

She sniffed her shirt to see if she smelled like the fifty servings of Chilean sea bass she had dished out tonight. The CK One she always wore was mixed with something else. Something bold but not overpowering. Rachel's scent. She closed her eyes and breathed her in.

She was usually attracted to hard-driving Type A personalities. Women who were headstrong and so confident they bordered on cocky. Women she could compete with, butt heads with.

As one of her former instructors loved to say, "Steel forges steel." She needed someone who kept her sharp. Clingy, emotionally needy types blunted her edge.

So what was it about Rachel that excited her so much? She was nothing like the women who usually found their way into her bed.

The others were like ghost chilies—so hot she couldn't enjoy the flavor. Rachel was like a bell pepper—sweet with a hint of spice.

Griffin remembered looking into Rachel's warm brown eyes. Eyes the color of hot chocolate and just as comforting. She had never needed an introverted counterpoint to balance her sometimes forceful personality, yet she was definitely attracted to one now. Was she drawn by the challenge of cracking Rachel's tough protective shell or the fact that Rachel seemed to have absolutely no idea how sexy she was? Rachel was shy and reserved, which made her even more alluring. Yes, she was a little heavy, but Griffin liked women with meat on their bones. And Rachel had curves for days, even if she insisted on camouflaging them under ill-fitting clothes like the shapeless sweater and baggy Chinos she sported tonight. Griffin would love to see her in something that showcased the voluptuous body she was trying to hide. The body that had molded itself to hers for a brief, tantalizing moment.

She remembered the feel of Rachel's hands on her hips. Rachel's arms around her waist. Rachel's full breasts pressed against her back. She could have ended the contact much sooner than she did, but she had lingered, longing for more.

She turned on the record player and continued to the kitchen. The phonograph needle hissed and popped as it slid through the well-worn grooves of her favorite album, adding another layer of sound to the trailblazing jazz played by Charlie Parker, Miles Davis, and Max Roach. She grabbed a beer out of the refrigerator and returned to the living room to read the thirty-page contract her personal assistant had delivered while she was out.

Two months ago, she sent in an audition tape for *Cream of the Crop*, a cooking competition/reality show that attracted hundreds of applicants each year and was watched by millions of viewers each week. A few days ago, she discovered she was one of eight contestants chosen to appear on the show. If she performed well, she could prove that female chefs were as talented as their male counterparts and they didn't need to rely on their looks to be successful, two stereotypes she and her peers often struggled to overcome.

She longed to prove herself against the best of the best, but she didn't want to put her life on hold to do it. If she agreed to do the show, she'd have to leave the restaurant in the hands of her sous chefs for three weeks. Her team was good, but she didn't know if they were ready to take the heat without her around to douse the fires. Match was on a roll. Momentum, once lost, was difficult to regain.

She took a sip of her beer and leaned back on the sofa. She closed her eyes and tapped out a staccato rhythm on her blue-jeaned thighs. The music washed over her. At its best, jazz was like aural sex, lifting her spirits, relaxing her body, and freeing her mind. Tonight, she desperately needed to come.

She hadn't become a chef for the attention. She had done it because she loved to cook. She was as ambitious as anyone in her profession, but unlike her celebrity counterparts, she didn't want to have her face plastered on the cover of her own monthly vanity magazine or hear her name bandied about on *Entertainment Tonight*. She simply wanted to make good food and have people enjoy it.

The two hundred fifty thousand dollar check and prestigious magazine spread awarded to the winner of *Cream of the Crop* were tempting, but she wanted to claim an even bigger prize. Winning the show could help her earn the respect of her peers, an honor that had eluded her for far too long.

She read through the contract, wincing each time she came across a clause she didn't like. When the show began filming in June, she and the other contestants would be sequestered in a spacious Central Park apartment, where they would be deprived of all contact with the outside world for three long weeks. No cell phones, computers, or TVs. Their every move would be filmed by a camera crew or shadowed by a stringer from the show.

Before they reported to the set, they would be sworn to secrecy, unable to tell anyone they were involved with the program or spill any of the behind-the-scenes secrets until after the winner was crowned during the live finale in August.

She looked at the last page of the contract. At the line on which she was supposed to sign her name.

"Do I really want to put myself through this?" she asked, thinking out loud. She weighed her reasons for going on the show against her reasons for staying put. "I don't have a girlfriend, my family's in California, and work will be there when I get back. What have I got to lose?" She rolled her pen between her palms like a dice player hoping to roll a lucky seven. "If I lose early, my critics will rake me over the coals and I'll never hear the end of it. But if I win, it will feel so good to say, 'I told you so.'"

She signed the contract.

❖

"Good evening, Fernando."

The concierge on duty looked up from a copy of a Spanish-language newspaper and returned Rachel's greeting. "How was your evening?"

"Let's go with interesting."

"In a good way?"

"I haven't figured that part out yet."

Rachel crossed the lobby and headed to the mailroom. Orderly rows of locked steel boxes lined the walls. Her box was full but didn't contain anything she wanted. Just the latest round of bills and a couple trees' worth of catalogs. Nothing said the holidays like a boxful of retail therapy. She tossed the catalogs into a nearby recycle bin and returned to the concierge desk.

With the end of the year rapidly approaching, tax season was about to kick in to gear. Rachel was going to be up to her ears from now until the following April. Some clients came to her with their supporting documentation neatly organized in color-coded notebooks. They were the easy ones and, in her mind, the most boring. She preferred the filers who showed up with shoeboxes overflowing with dog-eared receipts. Sifting through the mess to see what she could keep and what she needed to ignore made her job more difficult but more fun as well. She enjoyed the challenge.

Besides, accounting wasn't as cut-and-dried as it was perceived to be. From those boxes of disorganized receipts, she could re-create a year in people's lives, one scrap of paper at a time. What could be better than that? Oh, yeah. Having a life of her own.

Fernando and his wife, Montserrat, were two of her early birds. Each year, they made a beeline to her office as soon as they received their W-2s from their respective employers. They left her their paperwork, she phoned them if she had any follow-up questions, and she produced their completed return as quickly as she could.

"Montserrat brought me some of your information this morning. If all goes well, I should have your return ready the same day you provide me with your W-2s."

Fernando's eyes lit up at her news. According to Montserrat, the couple planned to use their refund to book a trip to Madrid to visit relatives and were eager to get the money in their hands so they could start searching the Internet for cheap flights.

"That's fantastic, Miss Bauer." Fernando's thick eyebrows, which often seemed to move independently of each other, furrowed into a uniform line of concern. "But at the risk of offending you, please allow me to say I think you work too much. When was the last time you did something *you* wanted to do? When was the last time you had a…how do you say?" He motioned for her to provide the phrase he couldn't come up with.

"A Me Day?" she said.

"Yes. When was the last time you had one of those?"

She tapped her utility bills against the edge of the desk. "Too long."

"Then why don't you take the weekend off? You could see a movie. Perhaps go to the park. Maybe invite a nice lady out to dinner?"

His grin was infectious. His enthusiasm was, too, but she was too tired to catch either.

"We'll see." She bade him good night and headed for the elevator. Before the doors closed, she heard him call Montserrat and relay the news that their travel plans could begin in earnest. As the elevator car rose to her floor, she felt her spirits sink even further than they had when she left Maidenhead.

She felt completely and utterly alone. Before tonight, she thought being alone was enough for her. Now she wasn't sure. Seeing Jane and Colleen together made her remember how much she enjoyed being part of a couple. Being half of a whole. Would she ever experience that feeling again?

She unlocked her apartment door and stepped inside. "Honey, I'm home." Her voice echoed dully off the Spartan interior.

She lived in Long Island City in a building across the river from Manhattan. Most didn't know the building by name, but by sight. It was the tall orange edifice next to the red neon Pepsi-Cola sign. Many TV shows and films featuring New York locales normally used the area for scene-setting exterior shots.

Isabel kept their old place, a duplex on the West Side. They were supposed to get a brownstone in Brooklyn, but they could never find one that suited both their tastes. Rachel's new digs were a good thirty minutes away from the city—twice that when the Midtown Tunnel was clogged. Most days she took the train. It was cheaper and less of a hassle.

In need of comfort—the kind that came in a cardboard carton with Ben and Jerry's emblazoned on the side—she kicked off her shoes and padded to the kitchen. She reached into her back pocket and pulled out the cocktail napkin Griffin had given her. She ran her fingers over the unfamiliar script. The words slashed across the paper like knife cuts. Griffin's invitation piqued Rachel's curiosity. She was tempted to attend the party if only to see how many A-listers she could spot before she lost count. If she did decide to go, would she walk into the fray alone or drag a friend along for moral support? A decision for another day.

She used a Betty Boop magnet to affix the napkin to the front of the refrigerator. Then she pulled a pint of Cherry Garcia out of the freezer, grabbed a spoon from the cutlery drawer, and prepared to dig in. The first bite was exhilarating, but as the sugary frozen treat slid down her throat, it didn't taste—or feel—as good as it normally did. The second bite was just as unrewarding. She was so far gone nothing could reach her.

She finished the ice cream not because she wanted it but because it was there. When she swallowed the last treacly spoonful, she felt full but unfulfilled.

If I want answers, I'm going to have to look somewhere other than inside my refrigerator.

She tossed the empty container in the trash and rubbed her bloated belly. "That's it," she said after unleashing a very unladylike belch. "Enough's enough. On Monday, I start spending lunch at the gym instead of my desk."

She said the same thing at least once a week, but this time she told herself she meant it.

Needing to decompress, she headed to the living room, turned on a twenty-four hour sports channel, and watched the scores scroll by. When that didn't work, she headed over to the window and stared out at the city. In the distance, the iconic metal exterior of the Chrysler Building was bathed in bright white light and the top floors of the Empire State Building were lit up in red and green. The clouds around them were an odd battleship gray, threatening to bring snow but not yet living up to their promises.

Her apartment building was quiet. Almost unnaturally so. She felt like the only tenant in residence.

She turned off the TV and sat in the dark, listening to the silence.

The next thing she knew, the sun was coming up and she hadn't been to bed yet. The ringing telephone tore her away from her ruminations—thoughts of her old flame and questions about the sexy chef with a firm grip and a taste for tequila.

Assuming the caller was Jane wanting to know why she didn't stick around last night, she took her time answering. She picked up the phone on the fourth ring just before the answering machine would have kicked in.

"Hey," Jane said. "How was your Rocky Road?"

"It was Cherry Garcia and it was awesome, thanks," Rachel said, stubbornly refusing to admit her evening had been less than satisfactory.

"If you say so. Be honest. How mad at me are you?"

"On a scale of one to ten, this one goes to eleven."

"You can't blame a girl for trying."

"Oh, I think I can find a way."

"Damn. You really are pissed."

"I think I have reason to be, don't you? The least you could have done was tell me what you had planned. Then I wouldn't have looked like a complete idiot in front of a total stranger."

An incredibly hot stranger.

"If I had told you Griffin was going to be there, would you have agreed to meet up with us last night?"

"Probably not."

"See?"

"Regardless, I would have appreciated having the opportunity to make an informed decision."

"If you don't stop being so logical, I'm going to have to start calling you Mr. Spock instead of Rain Man. Okay, cross my heart and hope to die. I promise not to set you up on any more blind dates."

"I'll believe that when I see it."

Jane chuckled. "You know me too well."

"Thank you for trying and thanks for caring, but I've sworn off relationships for the immediate future and I'm seriously considering making the condition permanent."

"You know what's going to happen, right? Now that you've sworn off women, you're going to meet the love of your life."

Rachel flashed back to the night before. "Maybe I already have."

"Who, Griffin? I'm not surprised. And you're welcome, by the way. After you left, she kept going on and on about you. About how different you are from anyone she's ever met. Being unaffected by celebrity must have its advantages. Women fawn all over the girl and she barely gives them the time of day. You ignore her and she's chomping at the bit to see you again."

"Is that why she invited me to her New Year's Eve party?"

"She did what? Color me green with envy. All the big names are going to be there. I don't know how you snagged the invitation or what you said when you two were having shots, but whatever it was, you must have made quite an impression."

Rachel replayed her conversation with Griffin but couldn't recall saying anything especially witty or incisive. Perhaps Griffin enjoyed a challenge as much as she did. Or was she looking for a pet project? If that was the case, she had better look elsewhere. Rachel didn't feel like being anyone's guinea pig.

"What do you have planned for today?" Jane asked. "Colleen wants me to paint the spare bedroom and I'm desperate to get out of it. Give me a reason."

"Sorry. I don't have anything exciting on tap. I'm going to clean my apartment, clean out my refrigerator, and watch an *I Love Lucy* marathon on TV."

"I'll be right there."

CHAPTER THREE

Rachel's stomach growled as soon as she opened her apartment door. Jane had a bucket of caramel popcorn under one arm and a bag of chocolate-covered potato chips under the other. Colleen was carrying a two-liter bottle of soda. Rachel turned her back on the mouth-watering junk food and returned to the task at hand.

"I'm joining a gym tomorrow," she announced as she headed to the kitchen. "Who's with me?"

"Not me," Jane said, closing the door. "I don't do manual labor."

She and Colleen made themselves at home in the living room, where they curled up on the couch and watched Lucille Ball do pratfalls in a vat of grapes. Colleen put her head in Jane's lap and Jane buried her fingers in Colleen's auburn hair.

They were so cute together. They had been a couple for nearly twenty years and married for the past six. They had met as freshmen at Vassar and had been an item ever since. They were truly each other's soul mates. Filled with love, their life together was nearly perfect. The only thing missing? The baby they were desperate to have. They had been trying for five years and had spent a fortune on in vitro fertilization treatments with no luck. They had experienced their share of false alarms but no pregnancies. Lately, Jane had begun to bring up the subject of adoption, but Colleen was steadfast in her determination to carry a child to term. To deliver a little miracle that was tangible evidence of the love she and Jane shared.

Rachel could hear her own biological clock ticking. The sound grew louder every day. Isabel hadn't wanted kids. She said her life was complete without them. Rachel felt otherwise. One more thing upon which she and Isabel hadn't been able to agree to disagree. Arguments over the issue had added more tension to their already strained relationship and may have contributed to its abrupt end.

Was Rachel supposed to apologize for wanting to be a wife and mother? Not a chance. She just hoped she'd eventually be lucky enough to meet someone who shared her desires.

Jane leveled her light blue eyes on Rachel. Her black hair was flecked with gray, lending her a distinguished air that her juvenile sense of humor often eradicated. Like a character in a gross-out comedy, she was endlessly amused by fart jokes. "Are you joining a gym because you want to or because you're trying to land Griffin Sutton?"

"I'm not trying to *land* anyone. I want to get back in shape for me. No one else."

"And the thought of making Griffin's eyes bug out of her head doesn't provide any extra motivation for you?"

Rachel's heart skipped a beat at the suggestion, but Griffin was out of her league. She was like the inspiration photo you took to the salon when you wanted your stylist to give you a new haircut—a fantasy desired but rarely achieved.

"The only carrot on a stick I need is the thought of being able to climb four flights of stairs again without having to take a break at the halfway point."

"So that's why you stopped coming to visit," Colleen said with a wink.

She and Jane lived in a fourth floor walk-up on the Lower East Side. Jane was an investment banker on Wall Street. The spate of scandals that had struck her profession had clouded her once rosy financial future, forcing her and Colleen to cut expenses. They sold their place on Park Avenue last year in favor of smaller, more affordable digs. Their new apartment was adorable, but the stairs leading to it were proving too taxing for Rachel's over-stressed knees.

Colleen looked up at Jane. "I'm stuck in a cab all day, but you could do it, babe." She poked a finger in Jane's midsection. "You're always saying you want a six-pack. Here's your chance."

"You said you loved my Buddha belly."

"I love every inch of you, sweetie." Colleen gave Jane a placating kiss to soothe any hurt feelings. "Even though I spend all day driving around the city, I can run circles around you. If we're ever lucky enough to have a baby, are you going to have the energy to chase after a two-year-old?"

Colleen's emerald eyes were so soft and nurturing Rachel was sure Colleen would make a wonderful mother. At the moment, those eyes were missing the positive energy Colleen was known for. Rachel wondered if the years of frustration had finally taken their toll. Jane picked up on it, too.

"Not *if*," she gently corrected her, brushing a finger across the tip of Colleen's button nose. "You mean *when*, don't you? *When* we have a baby, I'm going to run rings around both of you."

"That's a sight I can't wait to see."

Jane bent to press a kiss to Colleen's lips then turned to Rachel. "Looks like you've got yourself a workout partner."

"Sweet."

Rachel began to pull all the calorie-laden treats from her refrigerator.

"Damn, you *are* serious," Jane said when Rachel tossed two pints of mint chocolate chip ice cream and a box of Klondike bars into a trash bag.

"From now on, it's frozen yogurt, fresh fruit, and celery sticks." Rachel reached for the frozen Snickers.

"Give me one of those before you force me to go cold turkey."

Rachel underhanded her one of the decadent treats. Jane nearly took it down in one bite. Then she let out an orgasmic moan. "Mmm, that's better than sex."

Colleen smacked her on the arm. "Speak for yourself."

"I didn't mean sex with you, babe. Nothing's better than that."

She dipped her index finger into the ice cream-filled center of the frozen Snickers and slowly slid it between Colleen's parted lips. Then it was Colleen's turn to provide sound effects.

ANDA WALLACE

ne grinned and pointed at the TV. "Maybe later. It's time for
the Vitameatavegamin episode."

chel checked the expiration date on a box of frozen pizza.
Even though the contents were still good, she tossed the container
anyway. She quickly finished cleaning the refrigerator, took the bag
to the trash chute down the hall, then crashed on the couch with
her friends. Wrapped up in Lucy and Ethel's zany adventures, she
laughed her ass off and forgot all about her problems. In short, it was
a perfect Saturday afternoon.

ou *are* coming to our Christmas party next weekend, aren't
you?" Colleen asked as she and Jane prepared to leave.

he party's covered dish. If a professional chef is going to eat
my food, I want her to sample something other than bean dip or a
half-assed salad."

'm not angling for a date, Jane. Scout's honor." Rachel
crossed her heart and held up three fingers for emphasis.

oo bad. Sadly, no, she's not going to be there. She has to
work. Sunday is her only day off. It's part of her deal. She practically
had to sell a kidney in order to meet us for drinks Friday night. Then
you had to ruin it by turning tail and running. Now don't you wish
you had stayed?"

chel avoided answering the question by asking one of her
own. "How many people are you expecting?"

n uneven number. That means it's going to be all couples
except for me. Why do I have to be odd woman out?"

38 •

"In other words, I need to make a dish substantial enough to feed an army. Or I could cheat and pick up a brisket from the deli on the corner."

"Do it and die." Jane pointed a warning finger in her direction. "Homemade means homemade."

"Fine. I'll make the white chili you love so much."

Jane licked her lips in anticipation. "Extra jalapeños, please."

"Do that and *I'll* kill you," Colleen said. "This one may love jalapeños, but they don't love her."

"I know. I was her roommate in prep school, remember? I always had to open a window after she ate Mexican food."

Jane threw her hands up. "Hey, *she*'s right here and she can hear you."

"We know, honey," Colleen said. "That's what makes it more fun. See you Saturday night, Rach?"

"I'll be there. Without the extra jalapeños." She gave each of them a hug. "See you Monday, gym rat," she said to Jane's departing back.

Jane flipped her the bird before she and Colleen turned the corner.

Rachel closed the door and took a look around. Her hermit's cave exhibited a lightness it hadn't possessed a few hours before. Though her cleaning jag had helped, she thought the different mood she was noticing was more a reflection of the change taking place inside her than a testimony to the power of Windex.

For the first time in a long time, she felt like herself again. And that felt pretty damn good.

CHAPTER FOUR

On Monday morning, Griffin awoke to the sight of snow falling outside her window. She lay in bed and watched the fresh flakes blanket the city. Although the temperature outside was below freezing, her room was a comfortable sixty-eight degrees. Resisting the temptation to burrow under the covers and catch another forty winks, she tossed the comforter aside, put on workout clothes, and went for a five-mile run. Bitterly cold air pricked her lungs with each step. Snowplow drivers were out in force, their thick layers of clothing a far cry from the swimsuit-sporting beachcombers she was used to.

You're a long way from Newport Beach, baby.

She finished her run in front of her favorite grocery store, a hidden gem a few blocks from her apartment that sold the best fresh produce outside of the commercial markets.

"Good morning, Mr. Li."

Li Fong, the store's owner, broke into a broad grin. Laugh lines creased his weathered face. His impish grin and slight stature made him look like a teenager trapped in an eighty-year-old's body. "Good morning, Griffin. How are you today?"

"Hungry."

Like Old Mother Hubbard, her cupboard was bare. She filled a basket with enough fresh fruit and vegetables to replenish her supply and placed the carrier on the counter.

Mr. Li began to scan her purchases. "Did you enjoy yourself at dim sum yesterday?"

"Yes, I did. Thank you for inviting me." She patted her stomach. "I don't think I've ever eaten so much in my life."

Everything had tasted so good she hadn't been able to stop at one serving.

"Dim sum is about being together. That makes tea more important than the food. Tea, unlike a meal, cannot be rushed."

"I'll remember that. Thanks, Mr. Li." She paid for her purchases and walked home as the morning commuters began to make their way to the subway.

In her kitchen, she poured granola into a bowl, then added sliced peaches and two heaping tablespoons of vanilla yogurt. Her P.A. let himself in as she was shoveling the last spoonful into her mouth. He had two steaming cups from a nearby coffee shop in his hands. He offered her the one in his left.

She wrapped her hands around the warm paper cup and inhaled the cardamom-infused aroma of the chai tea inside. "If you were a woman, I'd kiss you."

"If you were a man, I'd let you." Tucker Croft set his latte on the counter and pulled a Day Planner from the depths of his messenger bag. "Give me your CrackBerry."

She dutifully turned over her smartphone. "What do we have on tap this week?" she asked as he updated her schedule and programmed electronic reminders.

He referred to the Day Planner. "This morning, you're doing a segment on the third hour of *Today*."

"On what? Remind me."

"Healthy, budget-conscious alternatives to traditional calorie-laden holiday meals. Tomorrow, you're taping a segment on New Year's Eve cocktails for *Good Morning, America*. Thursday, you're being interviewed for a profile in *Gourmet Magazine*'s Chefs and Restaurants section. Friday, some accounting firm has booked its holiday party at Match, which means you'll be cooking for fifty bean counters in pocket protectors and cheap suits."

Griffin grinned. "Not cheap. Budget-conscious."

"If a suit costs less than four figures, that spells cheap in my book."

"Not everyone shops at the Prada store, you fashion whore." Tucker's dark blue designer sweater and matching corduroy pants were paired with blue-and-cream colored leather saddle shoes. "Speaking of which, I think I'm paying you too much."

"For the amount of work I do, you're not paying me enough."

She placed her dirty dishes in the washer. "Do I have anything fun planned for this week, or will I be working nonstop?"

"You're invited to a holiday party Saturday night, but unless you can reschedule, you're going to be pulling a twelve-hour shift that day."

"Who's throwing the party?"

"Jane and Colleen are having a potluck at their apartment. You're familiar with potlucks, aren't you? They're what people like me who can't afford people like you to cater their events refer to as dinner parties."

"You're too young to be so cynical."

"But it explains why you keep me around."

She wondered if Rachel would attend Jane and Colleen's party. Rachel was Jane's best friend. Her presence would not only be expected but required. Griffin would love to see Rachel again to see if the sparks she'd felt when they met were real, but Saturday night was one of the restaurant's busiest nights. There was no way she would be able to get away.

Tucker returned her phone. "Jump in the shower while I try to find something telegenic amongst the ready-to-wear dreck in your closet." He wrapped his cashmere scarf around his neck and clapped his hands like an impatient dance instructor. "Hop to it. The limo will be here soon."

She pinched his bearded cheek. "What would I do without you?"

"Suffer," he said with a dramatic sigh. He rummaged through her closet in the master bedroom while she headed to the bathroom to get undressed. "Where's your *Cream of the Crop* contract?"

She raised her voice so he could hear her through the closed door. "On the coffee table in the living room."

"Have you signed it yet?"

"In blood. There were so many pages to initial I was feeling anemic by the time I finished." She tossed her workout clothes in the hamper.

"With the amount of money the producers will be paying you, you'll be able to drop by the blood bank and buy a few pints. I'll take the contract to the studio on my way uptown. When do you get to find out who else is in the cast?"

"The first day of filming."

"Is there anyone you don't want to see?"

"No one I'm afraid of competing against, if that's what you're asking."

"No, that's not what I'm asking. You know how reality show casting directors are. They look for types. The hero. The heel. The saint. The troublemaker. The powers-that-be might be looking to crown the best chef in America, but they want to guarantee there'll be plenty of drama along the way."

"If they expect me to be a drama queen, they're going to be sorely disappointed. I don't want to fill a role. I want to win."

❖

It was Rachel's week to pick up the pastries. Even though she no longer allowed herself to partake, she couldn't shirk her responsibility. Her coworkers would mutiny if she walked into the office empty-handed—or bearing rice cakes instead of bear claws.

She rode the elevator carrying a duffel bag in one hand and a bright pink box from her favorite bakery in the other. The duffel bag contained workout gear and a change of clothes for her planned trip to the gym. The box was filled with every fattening delicacy known to man—doughnuts, fritters, knishes, muffins, and cheese Danishes, to name a few. The smell of sugar and fried dough made her stomach growl. Two floors from her office, she was tempted to hit the elevator's emergency stop button and inhale a cruller. She gritted her teeth and kept her eyes focused on the floor indicator above her head. By the time the elevator doors opened, she had broken out into a cold sweat. Who knew resisting temptation could be such hard work?

She headed to the break room and was mobbed before she reached the door.

"Way to go, Bauer," Mike Andrews said. "I knew there had to be a reason we were keeping you around."

He bit into a cherry-filled doughnut in a way that made her mildly uncomfortable. She didn't know why the bosses kept *him* around. He hit on all the female employees, his work was sloppy, and he was always the last one in the door each morning and the first one out of it each afternoon.

"Glad I could help." Turning down the cheese Danish he offered her, she grabbed a bagel and headed to her desk.

"Don't you want some cream cheese with that?"

"No, plain's fine."

She locked her duffel bag in the bottom drawer of her desk and booted up her computer. She took a bite of her bagel while she waited for the computer's processing system to do its thing. Still warm, the bagel was perfectly cooked with a crunchy crust and a soft interior, but without lox and cream cheese, it was tasteless. She forced the first half down while she shuffled through the pile of tax returns in her inbox. She liked to tackle the more difficult returns at the start of the day when all her synapses were working as they should. She saved the easier ones for the afternoon when the post-lunch crash set in and she could barely remember two and two equaled four, let alone which page of the tax code applied to her client's needs.

"Turning over a new leaf?" Etta Simms, the office manager, took a seat on the edge of Rachel's desk.

"How could you tell?"

"New girlfriend?" Etta pointed to the remaining half of Rachel's bagel, then pinched off a small piece of her apple fritter and carefully placed it in her mouth, being careful not to smear her MAC-covered lips.

"Etta, you know you're the only girl for me."

"I'll tell Lawton you said that." Etta swung her shapely milk chocolate-colored legs back and forth and giggled like a schoolgirl. Even though she was a dyed-in-the-wool heterosexual, she obviously loved it when Rachel flirted with her. Rachel obliged her every chance she got. Lawton was Etta's husband of thirty years, though no one could recall ever laying eyes on him. Rachel often teased Etta that the wedding photo on her desk wasn't hers but one that came with the frame.

"When do I get to meet your mystery man, anyway?"

"Are you coming to the holiday party on Friday?"

"It's being held here at the office, isn't it?"

Etta pursed her full lips. "You don't read your e-mail, do you? This year's party is being held at an actual restaurant." She stretched her neck to see over the walls of Rachel's cubicle. "We don't want a repeat of last year," she said in a conspiratorial whisper. Rachel must have looked lost because Etta tried to prompt her memory. "Remember I walked in on Mike Andrews getting busy with one of the interns in the supply closet? The sight of his flat white ass doing it doggy style put me off the position for weeks."

Rachel shuddered involuntarily. "Thanks for putting the image into my head."

"Of Mike and the intern getting their freak on or me and Lawton doing the same thing?" Rachel blushed furiously, and Etta let out a throaty laugh. "I do what I can, girlfriend." She slid off the desk and smoothed the front of her fitted skirt. "Lawton and I are going to see you Friday night, aren't we?"

"Which restaurant?"

Etta put her hands on her ample hips. "Girl, you really need to start reading your e-mails." She commandeered Rachel's mouse and quickly located the mass e-mail she had sent out two weeks before asking everyone to set aside Friday night for the company holiday party.

Rachel had saved the date but hadn't retained any other pertinent information like time, venue, or dress code. She read the e-mail again. Her mouth fell open when she saw where the party was going to be held.

"Match? Our company party is going to be at Match? How did you manage that?"

"I made the reservation even before last year's party ended. No matter what the cost, I was not going to risk seeing Mike Andrews's bony ass again."

"You're my hero, Etta. I bow before you."

She bent and kissed Etta's hand. Laughing, Etta tapped Rachel's shoulders with a number two pencil. "Rise, my knight, and serve your queen." She spun Rachel around to face the computer screen. "In other words, get to work."

Rachel did as her queen commanded, but she couldn't concentrate on the task at hand. Her stomach was doing flip-flops. She couldn't tell which prospect excited her more—seeing Griffin again or finally being able to taste her food. It had to be the latter. The former was more unnerving than thrilling.

What if Griffin had been only humoring her the night they met? What if she had been only paying lip service when she told Jane and Colleen she wanted to see her again?

Whether she meant it or not, she'll see me on Friday. Then I can judge for myself.

❖

Griffin familiarized herself with the layout of the revamped studio kitchen at 30 Rockefeller Center before her segment began. She and one of the three anchors had been granted ten minutes, enough time to make a spinach salad but not nearly enough time to demonstrate the proper way to roast a turkey.

"Are you ready to shine?" Aggie Anderson asked as a makeup artist touched up her face. Griffin knew Aggie's given name was Augusta, but in much the same way Katherine Couric had morphed into Katie to appeal to the bleary-eyed masses, Augusta had become Aggie.

"I'm as ready as I'll ever be." Griffin rolled up the sleeves of her chef's coat. Its burgundy color was so rich she reserved the coat for TV appearances. She saved the white ones for work.

"You're not nervous, are you?" Aggie adjusted Griffin's clip-on microphone. "I saw the segments you did with Matt and Ann last year. You were a natural."

"They make it easy."

"I'd rather make it hard." Aggie smiled in mock apology when the back of her hand pressed against Griffin's breast.

From the moment Griffin arrived on the set, Aggie had watched her every move. She was cute in a way most television reporters were—attractive but nonthreatening. If Ann Curry, Robin Roberts, or Diane Sawyer were hosting the segment, Griffin might have trouble keeping her mind on the task at hand. As it stood, she didn't think she'd have any problems concentrating. Aggie was trying way too hard, putting her off instead of turning her on. If she learned to take her time and let Griffin come to her, it might be a different story.

Griffin grabbed Aggie's wayward hands. "Slow down. I'm not going anywhere. You've got me as a captive audience for at least another ten minutes."

Aggie's eyes glinted. "What if I want to hold you captive for longer than ten minutes? Could that be arranged?"

Griffin tapped her chest, reminding Aggie their microphones were live. Everyone in the studio could hear their conversation.

Aggie covered her own microphone with her hand. The look she gave Griffin could have melted steel. "Why don't we pick this up later? Come over to my place tonight for a drink. I mix a mean margarita."

"Sugar the rim and I'm all yours."

Aggie slowly licked her lips. "I like the sound of that."

The floor director held up a hand to get their attention. "Places. We're on in five, four, three, two…"

He pointed to the lead camera. The red light went on. Aggie flashed a brilliant smile as she stared into the camera lens.

"And we're back. The holidays are right around the corner. You know what that means. Family dinners that are high in fat and calories. Our guest today, noted chef Griffin Sutton, is here to take some of the guilt out of overindulging." She caressed Griffin's shoulder. "At my house, traditional Christmas dinner consists of turkey and stuffing, mashed potatoes, green bean casserole, and sweet potatoes loaded with brown sugar and marshmallows." Her hand slid down to Griffin's lower back. "Can you offer me some healthier alternatives so I won't have to waste a New Year's resolution on trimming my waist?"

"I'd love to." As Aggie's hand continued to roam out of camera range, Griffin pointed to the traditional meal choices and their low-calorie substitutions. "Instead of turkey and stuffing, try herb-roasted turkey breast. Instead of mashed potatoes loaded with butter and sour cream, combine sweet potatoes and Yukon gold potatoes for a savory medley. Like you, I have a weakness for sweet potato casserole, but maple root vegetables satisfy my craving for something sweet and alleviate the guilt."

"If your family's anything like mine, you grew up with a mother who kept reminding you to eat your green vegetables. Now you're saying some vegetables are bad for me?"

Aggie finally reclaimed her wandering hand, but her smile indicated she didn't plan to hold it—or herself—in check for long.

"Not the vegetables themselves. The way they're prepared."

"What about green bean casserole? Green beans are low in fat, aren't they?"

"Yes, they are, but the rest of the casserole's traditional list of ingredients—French fried onions, sour cream, canned soup, and pre-packaged cheese—certainly aren't."

"What do you suggest as a viable alternative?"

"Sautéed kale or, my personal favorite, spinach salad."

Griffin glanced at the floor director to see if she needed to speed up or stretch for time. He gave her an okay sign, which meant she was right on schedule. While Aggie made small talk, Griffin toasted some almonds, combined them with fresh spinach and dried cranberries, and tossed the ingredients with a light vinegar and oil dressing. Then she plated the dish.

Aggie grabbed a fork and helped herself to a sample of the finished product. "Mmm," she said as her eyes rolled back in her head. "Now that's the best thing I've had in my mouth all day. Griffin Sutton, thank you for joining us today."

"My pleasure."

Aggie turned to the camera. "When we come back, our film critic will review this week's new offerings. Stay with us."

Griffin smiled into the camera until the red light extinguished itself.

"And we're out," the floor director said. "Great job, ladies."

Griffin lifted her arms as a technician stepped forward to remove her microphone and battery pack. Tucker handed over her coat and gloves. When she headed for the elevator, Aggie followed her.

"See you tonight?"

"My dinner break's at eight. I'll see you then."

She wondered if Aggie's invitation came with a two-drink minimum.

"Let's go to the store, Tuck," she said as the elevator doors slid shut. "I need to pick up some sugar."

❖

"Are you ready for this?" Jane asked.

"No, but let's do it anyway."

Rachel and Jane selected a gym located halfway between their respective offices. After perusing the gym's menu of services, they paid for two basic memberships and signed up for a variety of classes that varied from spinning to yoga to weight training. By the time they were done, their bodies should look like a cross between a cyclist's, a gymnast's, and a bodybuilder's. Sounded painful. Rachel couldn't wait.

She and Jane left the safety of the locker room and headed upstairs to find the beginners' yoga class. Dressed in baggy shorts and loose T-shirts, unlike the spandex-sporting students sharing space with them, they stuck out from the rest of the class. For instance, they referred to themselves as students while their classmates called themselves practitioners. Apparently, yoga was a practice and not an exercise. Who knew?

They decided to start with yoga first, saving the more difficult classes for later in the week. As far as Rachel could tell, yoga was just stretching and breathing. One she did when she got out of bed each morning, the other she did without even thinking about. How difficult could it be to combine the two?

Less than five minutes into the class, she had her answer.

The instructor's name was Fernanda Gil. A bubbly Brazilian hard body who looked like she weighed ninety pounds soaking wet, she led the class through a brief warm-up.

"Okay, let's get the blood flowing and pump some energy into those bodies," she said brightly. Her Portuguese-accented voice carried throughout the overheated room even without the small microphone clipped to her ear.

Taking deep breaths, Rachel raised and lowered her arms several times and performed something called a sun salutation. Her muscles responded favorably to the stimulation and Jane unleashed a loud "Ahhh" when her iffy back popped as if Colleen had just spent fifteen minutes walking across it.

Rachel and Jane shared a look and flashed each other a thumbs-up sign, silently agreeing that this workout thing wasn't going to be as bad as they initially thought.

Then the pain began.

Downward facing dog bit Rachel in the butt and the plank position made her want to find one to walk off of.

Blossom, Fernanda's assistant, wandered around the room giving extra attention to those who looked like they needed it. Halfway through the class, she stopped working the room and planted herself next to Rachel's mat. For some moves, namely the warrior poses, it took both of them to manipulate her body into position.

Rachel didn't know whether to feel embarrassed because she was so uncoordinated she required extra help or because Blossom's hands on her body were the most action she had received in months.

By the end of the class, she was drenched in sweat and her muscles were shaking from exhaustion. Jane wasn't much better off.

"Why did I let you talk me into this?" Jane asked as they limped toward the showers.

"Because you're as crazy as I am. And I must be certifiable if I'm willing to subject myself to being seen naked in a group shower."

"This feels like high school all over again, doesn't it? Except instead of being surrounded by hot cheerleaders, we're surrounded by hot trophy wives. Then again, some of the bottle blondes encircling us could be the same girls but twenty years older." Jane took an appreciative glance at the eye candy scattered around the room. "Nice work if you can get it."

Rachel told Jane her big news to take her mind off their surroundings.

"Guess whose holiday party is going to be held at Match Friday night?"

"How did you swing that?"

"Two words: Etta Simms."

Jane shook her head in amazement. "I'm going to have to lure her away from you one day. How much are they paying her over there?"

"Not enough, I'm sure, but if you steal her away from me, I might not speak to you again."

"Considering the miracles the woman works on a daily basis, I think I'd risk it."

"Thanks, buddy. I love you, too."

"What are you going to wear Friday night?" Jane asked after they dried off, dressed, and prepared to return to work.

"The dress code is business casual, but I'm sure the outfits will range from jeans to black tie. Or, since we're talking about accountants, from gray suits to Sansabelt slacks."

"Colleen has to work that night. I'm available if you need a plus one."

"And you're offering out of friendship, not because of the free meal, right?"

Jane's broad grin let Rachel know she knew she had been busted.

"Sorry. I already told Etta I'd be coming stag."

"I'm sure Griffin will be happy to hear that."

"You think so?"

Jane looked at Rachel out of the corner of her eye. "Are you fishing for compliments or looking for reassurance?"

"Am I that obvious?"

"Let's put it this way, you're a hell of a lot easier to read than *War and Peace*." She gave Rachel a hug when they parted ways at Park Place. "Are we spinning tomorrow or hitting the weights?"

"Let me see how much pain I'm in tomorrow morning and I'll let you know."

Rachel picked up a turkey sandwich from a nearby deli and headed back to the office, where she polished off the three-bean salad she had ordered as a side dish. By the end of the day, she had put a serious dent in her inbox and her brain was still firing on all cylinders.

Maybe there were benefits to healthy living after all.

CHAPTER FIVE

The day after her first trip to the gym, Rachel woke up so sore she could barely move. Spinning made it worse, weight training even more so. By the time Thursday rolled around, however, her body had adjusted to her new routine and she had dropped almost seven pounds. Her self-confidence rose as the number on her bathroom scale fell.

After work, she braved the crowds of last-minute shoppers and headed to a department store to buy an outfit for her company party. She was tempted to buy an ugly Christmas sweater, but she doubted if anyone but Etta would be able to tell she was being ironic instead of genuine. She settled on a white silk blouse and a pair of black slacks. To make sure no one would confuse her for a member of the wait staff, she threw in a sequined red vest she confiscated from a clearance rack.

Closer to home, she stopped by the salon she often frequented and got her hair cut. She said she wanted a trim, but her stylist convinced her to try something different. Several passes of the clippers later, most of her hair was lying on the floor and she was sporting a fashionable new 'do that nearly made her unrecognizable even to herself.

Etta's friendly face was the first familiar one she saw when she walked into Match on Friday night. The greeter directed her to one of the private banquet rooms. Etta, resplendent in a beaded black dress, was standing outside the entrance. A tall man in a charcoal gray pinstriped suit stood by her side. Etta introduced him as her husband. With his razor-thin pencil moustache, soul patch, and elegant mien, Lawton looked like a jazz musician, but Rachel remembered Etta telling her once he was a retired mechanical engineer.

"You *do* exist."

"You're the second person who has told me that tonight," he said in a voice as deep as Barry White's. "I'm beginning to sense a trend."

"It's a pleasure to meet you," she said as they shook hands. "You're a lucky man."

"Yes, I know. She reminds me every day."

Etta took Rachel by the shoulders and looked her over. "I love your hair like that. Are you going to keep it short?"

"For a while." Rachel rubbed her hand over her closely-cropped hair. The curls she used to hide behind were long gone. "It's time I learned to walk without crutches."

"Whatever you're doing, keep it up. You're looking good tonight, baby girl."

"Thank you."

She hoped Etta wouldn't be the only woman here who thought so.

❖

Griffin chugged a bottle of water. She could already tell the evening would be a test of her endurance and her patience. She had placed Erica Barrett, her assistant chef, in charge of the house, freeing her to take care of the private party in the banquet room. The sous chefs were divided between them, most supporting Erica as she tended to the main diners, the rest helping her cater to the needs of the gaggle of accountants she was about to introduce herself to. If that weren't enough, the reporter from *Gourmet Magazine* who had interviewed her for nearly three hours on Thursday had decided to shadow her at work to "add context" to the story.

I'd better clean up my language tonight unless I want to be painted as a tyrant.

While the reporter watched her, she observed Erica. Though only two years removed from culinary school, Erica was preternaturally poised and exhibited tremendous promise. Griffin didn't think it would be long before she was fronting a restaurant of her own. Tonight, however, she was being forced to deal with a chef's worst nightmare—a hard-to-please customer. Griffin watched as the third medium rare steak Erica had prepared for table six was returned to the kitchen.

"Looks like we've got a Theresa Testi," headwaiter Paul Lacey said. Theresa Testi was the secret name the staff used to refer to difficult female customers. Thomas Testi was her male counterpart.

Erica's shoulders dropped when Paul placed the plate in front of her. Griffin didn't want her to lose confidence, but she didn't want to swoop in and bail her out. To get the experience she would need as a head chef, Erica would have to solve the problem on her own.

"Chef?" Erica's plaintive voice drifted across the room. She spread her arms. "I don't know what to do. The first one was too rare, the second one was too well done, and this one is—" She turned to the equally harried Paul, who was carving out a path between the dining room and the kitchen. "What's wrong with this one?"

Paul pursed his lips as if he were trying not to smile. "Too hot."

"Who does this chick think she is, Goldilocks?"

Griffin held up a hand as she checked on the progress of the entrees for the private party. "If it were me, there are two ways I would handle it: slap a raw steak on a plate and serve it to her or drag her to the kitchen and tell her to cook it herself."

The reporter scribbled in his notebook.

Erica turned to Paul. "Is she cute?"

"Does a politician know how to lie?"

Erica pulled an aged rib eye out of the meat locker. "Then get her back here ASAP."

Griffin smiled like a proud parent. *My job here's done. I've got work to do.* She pushed through the swinging doors that divided the kitchen from the house.

❖

Rachel entered the banquet room, mingled with a couple of coworkers, and waited for the festivities to begin. With no assigned seats, people grabbed spots wherever they could and saved places for their friends. Assuming Etta the social butterfly would wait until the last possible moment to sit down, she reserved seats for her and Lawton. They joined her when senior partner Dean Edelman headed to the front of the room.

Dean launched into a lengthy speech welcoming everyone to the party and recapping the year, but Rachel couldn't take her eyes off the woman at his side.

Griffin looked stylish, even though she was dressed for work. Her blond hair was swept away from her face and held in place by a flame-covered bandanna knotted pirate-style. Her white chef's coat looked freshly pressed and surprisingly free of stains, given what a madhouse the kitchen must be. Her low-slung jeans hugged her ass and corded thighs, making her long legs look even longer. Her feet weren't clad in the comfortable tennis shoes or airy Crocs Rachel expected, but a pair of well-worn motorcycle boots.

Dean thanked Etta for planning the party and asked her to stand and be recognized. Etta stood and waved. Her actions drew Griffin's attention to their table. When Griffin smiled at her, Rachel thought she was going to spontaneously combust.

"Thank you for gracing us with your presence tonight," Griffin said when Dean finally ceded control of the microphone.

Rachel told herself Griffin was addressing everyone in the room, but it felt like Griffin was talking only to her. She hung on to every word.

"My staff and I will do our best to make your evening a memorable one. For the sake of expediency, we won't be offering you our full menu, but I think the limited one we have created for you offers enough variety to satisfy all tastes. When the wait staff comes to take your orders, please make your selections for all three courses at the same time. Otherwise, we could be here for a while. You see these people all day. I don't think you want to spend all night with them, too."

"She means you, Mike!" someone called out.

Everyone laughed at the private joke but quickly quieted so Griffin could continue.

"To begin, you have three choices of salads: Caesar with romaine lettuce and cornbread croutons; spring mix with grilled vegetables and a warm bacon vinaigrette dressing; or house with arugula, grape tomatoes, red onions, cucumbers, and your choice of dressing. For your main course, we're offering prime rib au jus with new potatoes and green beans, barbecued salmon with ginger rice and wilted spinach, or, for the vegetarians in the house, eggplant parmesan with polenta and roasted garlic bread. To finish, bourbon bread pudding with caramel sauce, chocolate-drizzled profiteroles, or mango sorbet."

"One of everything, please!" Meredith from the secretarial pool yelled. Wasn't she the former intern who had spent quality time in the coatroom with Mike at last year's holiday party?

"A woman after my own heart," Griffin said. "My staff and I are here to serve you. If you have any questions or any problems, please don't hesitate to find me. Enjoy your evening."

She excused herself to return to the kitchen. God, Rachel loved watching her walk. She moved like a jungle cat, an intriguing blend of grace and power. Walking toward her, Griffin looked like a cheetah stalking her prey. *I suppose that makes me dinner.*

"Love the hair," she mouthed to Rachel as she passed her table.

"Do you know her?" Etta asked.

"We've met, yes."

"Oh, is that what they're calling it these days?"

"Remember what I've always told you, Etta. You're the only woman for me."

"Mmm hmm. Something tells me my name isn't the one you're going to be calling out in a few hours."

❖

Griffin cleared out of the way as the wait staff descended on the banquet room like a crowd of locusts. She returned to the kitchen with a renewed sense of purpose, barely cracking a smile when she saw Erica flirting shamelessly with the picky eater from table six. She always put pressure on herself to make each meal unforgettable. Now it was doubly important.

Rachel was here. And she looked incredible. Not just physically. She had lost a few pounds, but that wasn't what had captured Griffin's attention. Rachel's defenses were down. Her eyes were open, unguarded. The wary expression she had worn when they were introduced was gone. Had she shed the emotional burden that had been weighing her down? Griffin couldn't wait to find out.

She rolled up her sleeves and went to work. The second chance she had longed for had arrived.

❖

The food appeared relatively quickly despite the large number of people in the party and the even larger number of people in the restaurant itself. Rachel ordered the house salad, salmon, and sorbet. All were the best she had ever tasted. Based on the reactions of everyone around her, her opinion was a common one.

Raucous applause greeted Griffin on her next visit. "My compliments to the chef." Dean raised Griffin's arm over her head like a referee signaling the winner of a prizefight.

She basked in the applause, but she looked tired. Her formerly pristine chef's coat was dotted with various sauces, making it look like the early stages of a Jackson Pollock painting. Rachel couldn't imagine how grueling an evening she had experienced. Saturdays must be even worse.

"How do you do this for untold hours a week without getting burned out?" she asked during Griffin's return trip to her table.

"Because I love what I do."

Etta and Lawton were working the room, which meant she and Griffin had the table to themselves.

"Dinner was amazing. But I'm sure you've heard that more than once tonight."

"Just because I've heard it before doesn't mean I don't want to hear it again."

Griffin drank from a large bottle of mineral water. Rachel's Manhattan looked sinful in comparison.

"I'm sorry you aren't going to be able to make it to Jane and Colleen's tomorrow night."

"I'm going to be there."

Rachel did a double take. "I thought you had to work."

"I had a change of plans. After last night's shift, my assistant chef requested Sunday off to visit family so we switched days. I have tomorrow off instead. I can't think of a better way to spend it than with friends. Old ones and new ones alike." She gave Rachel a pointed look. "I e-mailed Jane and Colleen my RSVP this morning. Didn't they tell you?"

"Of course not," they said simultaneously.

"What are you bringing?" Rachel asked, knowing that no matter what dish Griffin brought, everyone else's would pale in comparison.

"I haven't decided yet. I have to look through my list of recipes and find one that seems most fitting. What about you?"

"White chicken chili."

Rachel hoped she'd get lucky and Griffin would say she felt the same way about white chicken chili that most people did about liver or Brussels sprouts. Then she wouldn't have to worry about insulting her superior taste buds.

"I *love* white chicken chili."

Wrong answer.

"It's my favorite comfort food. Do you make yours spicy or mild?" Griffin asked.

"I prefer spicy. Jane does, too, but no one else seems to agree with us."

"You're like me. The hotter the better."

For some reason, Rachel didn't think they were still talking about food.

"What time do you get off tonight?" she asked. Even though they were drifting into uncharted territory, she was enjoying the journey too much to cut the trip short.

"We stop serving in about an hour, but I could probably clear out before then if I heard an offer that was tempting enough. What do you have in mind?"

"I think I owe you a drink."

"Actually, you owe me several, but who's counting?"

Rachel circled the rim of her glass with her fingertip. She needed to ground herself to keep from reaching out and sliding her hand up Griffin's leg. "Are you always this effortlessly sexy?"

Griffin smiled and her fatigue seemed to disappear. "I think it goes along with the profession."

"Yeah, you lucked out on that score. I got screwed. There are hundreds of sexy things you can do with food. Numbers? Not so much."

"I don't know. Put a slide rule in your hands and I'm sure you'd find a way to attract my attention."

Slide rules were used for multiplying and dividing, not adding and subtracting. Rachel didn't have much use for them in her line of work, but she was too busy enjoying the pleasant image in her mind's eye to say otherwise.

"Meet you out front in five minutes?"

"Sure."

Rachel finished her drink, then handed her ticket stub to the clerk manning the coat check counter. Griffin joined her a few minutes later wearing a black leather jacket, a navy blue cotton shirt, and a fresh pair of jeans.

"Shall we?"

"Where would you like to go?" Rachel didn't want to pay a return visit to Maidenhead. The popular bar was bound to be both too noisy and too crowded to hold a real conversation. If they remained where they were, they'd be able to hear each other, but Griffin would be bombarded by so many well-wishers they wouldn't have a chance to talk.

"There's a new place in Greenwich Village. B&B, I think it's called. Have you been there yet?"

"No, but I've heard great things about it."

"So have I. Care to see if they're true?"

Griffin offered her hand. Rachel's heart skittered in her chest and she forced herself to remember what Griffin had said the night they met. She had mentioned the F word, not the L word. She had said she thought they could be friends. She hadn't said anything about being lovers.

She took Griffin's hand.

I'll take what I can get.

Outside, Griffin whistled for a cab like a seasoned pro.

"Where ya headed?" the cabbie asked.

"B&B."

"Got it." The cabbie input the club's name into the GPS attached to his dashboard and cranked the meter. Humming along to the Bollywood soundtrack blasting on the CD player, he didn't attempt to make conversation. Twenty minutes later, he parked in front of a crowded nightclub, announced the price of the fare, and sped off as soon as he was paid.

"I think it's safe to say our ride won't be featured on an episode of *Taxicab Confessions*," Griffin said, referring to the erstwhile late-night HBO reality series populated by actual taxi riders who willingly spilled their secrets, sexual and otherwise, to their overly chatty cab drivers while being filmed by hidden cameras. "But if there's something you want to tell me, feel free."

Rachel followed her inside the velvet ropes into the darkened club. "I don't know you well enough to start telling you all my secrets." She opened her eyes wide to help them adjust to the dim light.

Similar to a now-defunct bar that featured beds instead of tables and chairs, B&B offered the same comfy seating arrangement while adding an extensive breakfast-themed menu to the mix. "Ready for Breakfast in Bed?" a series of well-placed print ads inquired.

"Would you like to get to know me better?"

Griffin's directness took Rachel by surprise. She nearly tripped over a group of people enjoying cosmopolitans and eggs Benedict on a mattress nearby.

"If I tell you everything up front, there wouldn't be anything left for you to uncover. Where's the fun in that?" She narrowly avoided another header. *Way to make an impression. She's going to think I've forgotten how to walk and talk at the same time.*

"Are you saying I should peel you like an onion or a grape?"

Griffin took her hand—probably to prevent her from doing a face-plant before they reached their destination. Rachel latched on for dear life.

"What's the difference?" She was surprised to find herself capable of rational thought. She hadn't felt this drawn to someone since…well, never.

Griffin led her to an empty mattress in the back of the bar and waited for her to get settled in before she sat (okay, *lay*) next to her. "The difference is when you peel a grape, you have to do it slowly, sensually, and very carefully. When you peel an onion, every time you think the job's done, you pull back another layer. Getting to the center takes longer than you think it should."

"How long do you think it would take for you to get to my center?"

Griffin laced the fingers of her right hand through the ones on Rachel's left. "It would probably take me a month of Sundays, but I'm willing to put in the time if you are."

"What are you proposing?"

"One date each Sunday for the next…" She paused while she did the math in her head. "Seven and a half months. I get to know you while I peel the onion one layer at a time. I woo you, not with my body but with my mind. Something, I have to say, would be a first for me."

"What do I get out of the deal?"

"A trip around the world without ever leaving New York."

"How do you plan to do that?"

"That's for me to know and you to find out." Griffin's right thumb slowly slid against the space between Rachel's left thumb and index finger. Back and forth. Back and forth. The movement was as sensuous and hypnotic as a snake charmer's *pungi*. "Do we have a deal?"

A month of Sundays. The expression was as quaint as the idea that Griffin would like to spend thirty days—no—thirty *Sundays* courting her instead of trying to get into her pants right away. The thought simultaneously intrigued and frightened her. Intrigue won out.

"Deal."

"Where would you like to go first?"

Rachel leaned forward until her lips were no more than a breath away from Griffin's. When Griffin's gray eyes darkened, Rachel moved past her mouth and close to her ear. She could hear Griffin's breath quicken. She could see her pulse beating at the base of her throat, its rhythm matching the insistent pounding between Rachel's legs. "Surprise me."

"Gladly." Griffin's free hand slid across the nape of Rachel's neck, raising goose bumps on the sensitive, newly exposed skin. Her lips parted.

Rachel's heart trip-hammered in her chest. Was this really happening? Was Griffin Sutton, the sexiest woman she had ever met, about to kiss her? She watched Griffin's lips move inexorably closer to hers.

"May I bring you something to drink?" the waitress asked.

Rachel ordered a Manhattan, Griffin a bourbon on the rocks. Griffin looked around as if waking up from a dream. Rachel knew the feeling. She looked down. The fingers of Griffin's right hand were still wrapped around hers. Perhaps the dream didn't have to end.

"What's your favorite childhood memory?" Griffin asked.

Rachel reflected on family vacations, school recitals, and outings with her friends. All of them had been enjoyable in their own right, but they had paled in comparison to the Sunday afternoon excursions on which she and her parents used to embark.

"When I was a kid, I loved going to open houses with my parents. Every Sunday morning, my mother would scour the real estate supplement in the newspaper. She'd find listings in upper crust neighborhoods we could never afford to live in, then the three of us would put on our Sunday best, jump in my dad's Buick Regal, and drive around looking for realtors' signs. We'd tour all these houses we had no intention of buying, then have lunch somewhere and fantasize about what it would be like to live in the places we'd visited."

"Which one would you have loved to live in?"

"If I tell you, you have to promise not to laugh."

"Cross my heart."

"You have to keep in mind that I was ten."

Griffin squeezed her hand. "I promise I won't laugh."

Does she make everyone feel this special or just me?

"It was a seventies-style bachelor pad with mirrors on the ceiling, wall-to-wall shag carpeting, and an honest-to-God bear rug in front of the fireplace." She stopped when Griffin began to guffaw. "You promised you wouldn't laugh."

"I'm not laughing. I have something in my throat."

"Yeah, I think it's called mirth. What's your favorite memory?"

"Every year for the Fourth of July, my family would have a clambake on the beach. Each of us had assigned roles. My brothers would dig the fire pit, my father would gather the rocks to line the bottom of the pit, my mother and I would collect seaweed to place between the layers of food, and my grandparents would 'supervise' the entire affair. My favorite is the one we had before my brother Kieran left for college because I knew that was the last one we'd have while we all lived under the same roof. We still have the clambakes, of course, but they aren't the same. Because when the food's gone and the fire's out, we head off in different directions. We don't pile into a wood-paneled station wagon and go back to the same house."

"I'm sensing a theme. Food and family are a part of everything you do."

"It's true. I'm nothing without either one."

"Then why are you single?"

"If I knew the answer to that question, I don't think I'd be single."

"Can you see yourself being married with kids some day?"

Griffin pulled back. "I get the feeling if I say no, it could be a deal breaker."

"Not necessarily."

"If I squint real hard, I can see myself being married. A mom? Not so much. I love children, but I don't want one of my own. I'd rather be the fun aunt who takes the kids to the beach, teaches them to surf, and takes them home, not the mom who has to get them off to school every morning and stay up half the night worrying each time they get the sniffles." Griffin sipped her drink. "You look disappointed."

Rachel felt that way, too.

"Did I give the wrong answer?"

"The truth is never right or wrong. It just is."

And sometimes, the truth hurts.

CHAPTER SIX

Rachel arrived at Jane and Colleen's place an hour early so she could help with any last-minute preparations. She wanted to pat herself on the back for managing to climb the four flights without breaking a sweat, but her arms were too full to accomplish the feat. She had been working out for just a week and she wasn't even halfway to her goal weight, but she felt better than she had in months.

She banged on the apartment door with her elbow, being careful not to spill the contents of the Crock-Pot in her hands. Jane let her in and ushered her to the kitchen, where Griffin was conducting a master class on the fine art of preparing the perfect pot roast.

"The secret is to caramelize the meat first. Season it, put it in an oiled Dutch oven, and brown it on both sides on medium-high heat for about four minutes. That seals in the flavor."

Colleen and a few early arrivals were gathered around her. They hung on every word. Colleen's boss, Dieter Bock, and his boyfriend, Kevin Reynolds, were part of the crowd. Kevin studiously took notes as if Griffin would be giving the guests a pop quiz after dinner.

I'd better pay attention unless I want to get left behind.

"Where can I plug this in?" she whispered, indicating the slow cooker. After Jane cleared some counter space between the toaster and the electric can opener, Rachel plugged in the Crock-Pot so the white chicken chili could heat through.

Griffin winked at her as she continued her lecture. The playful gesture made Rachel as giddy as a teenaged wallflower whose crush on the most popular girl in school had just proven mutual, but her giddiness was offset by the fact that she and Griffin didn't want the same things out of life. She wanted to meet someone and settle down. Griffin enjoyed playing the field.

It's a good thing we're just friends.

She leaned against the counter and listened in as Griffin finished her impromptu cooking lesson.

"Set your oven for three twenty-five, add beef broth, the vegetables of your choice, and *voilà*. Three hours later, you have a roast so tender it practically melts in your mouth."

The more Griffin talked, the more Rachel hoped the wonderful aroma emanating from the oven was the pot roast she was teaching everyone to prepare.

Dieter rubbed his hands together. "I can't wait to try it."

Kevin arched an eyebrow. "You must mean hers, not yours. *You* could probably figure out a way to burn water."

Dieter playfully swatted Kevin's butt. "This is true, but you didn't marry me for my cooking."

The comment prompted a spirited—and ribald—conversation about size comparisons between "real" and latex members that raised the temperature in the room by several degrees.

"Small, medium, or large?" Dieter asked Griffin.

"Put it in terms she can understand." Kevin turned back to Griffin. "Carrot, cucumber, or eggplant, Chef *Girl*-ardee?"

"Fuck you, Kevin," Griffin said good-naturedly as everyone shared a laugh at her expense.

"Only if you're packing nothing less than a cucumber," he shot back. "You can save the carrot sticks for the salad bar."

Rachel waited for the laughter to die down. She topped off Griffin's glass of chardonnay, hoping the extra alcohol would loosen her tongue. "You haven't answered the question. Carrot, cucumber, or eggplant. Which is it to be?"

"It depends on if I'm giving or receiving." Her suggestive look made Rachel's stomach turn cartwheels. "What about you?"

Rachel could feel everyone else's eyes on her, but the only ones she wanted on her were Griffin's. Those beautiful steel gray ones that captivated everyone who gazed into them, herself included. Her, especially? Her desire for Griffin—to see her, to talk to her, to be around her—was growing by the minute. How long would she be able to hold it in check?

"You know what they say: sometimes it's better to give than to receive."

Griffin's eyes twinkled devilishly. "If we're flexible enough, we can do both at the same time."

Kevin fanned himself with his notebook as if he were a Southern belle in desperate need of shade. "I don't think this conversation is what Clement Moore had in mind when he wrote '*Twas the Night Before Christmas*."

"Christmas is two days away," Colleen said. "So technically, this is the night before the night before Christmas."

Kevin waved one hand dismissively. "Semantics."

Other guests began to arrive and the small apartment quickly filled with people. Griffin's pot roast was the runaway winner for favorite dish. Surprise, surprise. Rachel's chili, however, finished a close second. Griffin ate most of it herself, helping herself to two large bowls.

"This is fantastic." She stared at the remnants of her second serving like a fortune-teller reading leftover tea leaves. "You've crafted a wonderful mélange of flavors."

"I've never had a mélange before," Jane said.

"That's the *only* thing you haven't had, lover," Colleen said. She shook her head when Jane offered her some of her favorite Riesling.

Rachel noted the group's resident sommelier had limited herself to ginger ale all evening. She hoped Colleen wasn't coming down with something. Half the people she knew had colds or viruses or both. Not unusual for this time of year. If Colleen had become the latest victim of an already brutal winter, it would explain why she wasn't her normally perky self when she and Jane came to visit on Saturday.

"Do you mind if I guess the ingredients?" Griffin asked.

"Be my guest." Rachel was confident Griffin wouldn't be able to tell all the components she used simply by tasting the finished result. She had left out the jalapeños at Colleen's request, but she had practically emptied out her spice rack to make up for their absence. If Griffin identified even half the items she had thrown in, she would be mightily impressed.

Griffin dipped her spoon into the bowl and swirled the soup around her mouth as if she were at a wine tasting.

"Chicken, obviously. Chicken broth." She paused as if her taste buds were recalibrating. "Northern beans—dried, not canned. Garlic—no, garlic *powder*. Green chilies. Cumin. Onions. Oregano. Cayenne pepper. Olive oil. Cloves. Monterey Jack cheese. And paprika for a bit of heat. How did I do?"

Rachel gaped at her. "I kept waiting for you to leave something off the list, but you didn't miss a thing."

Jane unleashed an appreciative whistle. "Talk about a talented tongue. What other tricks does it do?"

"You'd be amazed."

The rest of the guests moved on to another topic of conversation, but Rachel couldn't let the previous one go.

"How *did* you do that?" she asked Griffin as they moved to the couch.

Griffin looked casual yet elegant. Her pleated tuxedo shirt and pinstriped bow tie were paired with frayed jeans and canvas tennis shoes. She sat with one long leg folded underneath her. Her other leg rested against the outside of Rachel's knee. When Griffin stretched one arm across the back of the couch and leaned toward her, Rachel felt hemmed in. But in a good way.

"Easy. I installed hidden cameras in your apartment. I've been watching every move you've made for days."

She was clearly joking, but the thought of Griffin seeing her in her most unguarded moments made Rachel blush. Griffin's gaze was too intense. Like the feeling you get after great sex when one more touch would bring not pleasure but pain. Rachel already felt in over her head. She tried to deflect Griffin's attention before she was completely overwhelmed. "If you've been watching me, you must be bored out of your mind."

"Quite the opposite. I'm fascinated."

"Why?"

"From what I hear—and from what I've seen for myself—you have a lot of great qualities. You're smart, you're funny, you're loyal to your friends."

"You make me sound like a golden retriever."

Griffin pressed forward. "You're also sexy as hell, even though you don't seem to think so."

"Fifteen pounds ago, maybe."

Griffin put a finger to Rachel's lips. "I didn't meet you fifteen pounds ago. I met you last week. And I think you're sexy right now."

Rachel wanted to draw Griffin's finger into her mouth and suck on it like a lollipop. Then she reminded herself she had given up sweets. "I think you need to get your eyes checked."

"My eyes are fine." Griffin lowered her hand until it came to rest on Rachel's leg. Rachel could feel the heat even through the thick fabric of her corduroy pants. "Every time I have a conversation with you, you always find a reason to put yourself down. I'd love to know why."

"Why do I prefer self-deprecation to self-aggrandizement?" Rachel shrugged. "It's easy. It's expected. It's what I'm used to."

"Then perhaps it's time you got used to something else."

Rachel wasn't ready for this conversation. No way. No how. She liked spending time with Griffin, but after the comment she made in B&B about not wanting kids, Rachel thought it best if she didn't get too involved with her. They could meet for lunch or dinner each Sunday like they planned, but as friends, not potential lovers.

As she tried to keep from wondering how being friends with benefits would work, she noticed a *Cream of the Crop* marathon was playing on TV. She jerked her chin at the screen. "I adore that show. Are you familiar with it?"

Griffin was noncommittal, her expression uncharacteristically muted. "I've seen a couple of episodes, but I wouldn't call myself a fan."

"I would. It's one of my guilty pleasures. I'm not sure what I'm addicted to more—the food porn or the contestants' histrionics. You should try out for it."

"Why?"

"I'd rather watch you compete than the arrogant assholes who think they're the best thing since sliced bread."

Griffin smiled. "How do you know I'm not an arrogant asshole, too?"

"If you were, I think you would have shown your true colors by now."

"So you trust me?"

"In my experience, it isn't in my best interest to trust beautiful women."

"I don't quite know how to respond to that. Should I thank you for the compliment or work even harder to gain your trust?" Griffin answered her own question. "I think I'll do both."

When the party finally began to break up, Rachel offered to clean the kitchen while Jane and Colleen entertained the last of their guests. Griffin joined her. In her element, Griffin rolled up her sleeves and took control. "I'll rinse and you'll load?" she asked, filling half of the double sink with warm water.

"Yes, chef."

Griffin flicked a dish towel at her, but Rachel could tell by the playful glint in her eye that she enjoyed being teased. *Note to self: tease her more often.*

They quickly found a rhythm. Griffin scraped dried food into the garbage disposal, rinsed a dirty plate or dish, and handed it to Rachel so she could load it into the dishwasher. Then they did it over and over again.

"What are you doing for Christmas?" Griffin asked.

"I don't have to go back to work until Tuesday, so after the obligatory family dinner with my parents on Christmas Eve, I'm going to put my feet up and enjoy the long weekend. Unless, of course, I give in to temptation and head to the office. I get more work done on the weekends when no one's around and the phone isn't ringing off the hook. What about you? What are you going to do before you cook dinner for all us poor slobs who are too lazy to do it for ourselves?"

"Cook lunch for people who can't afford a decent meal."

"What do you mean?"

"My family feeds the less fortunate every Christmas and Thanksgiving. Even though I haven't been able to be with them this year, I've tried to keep the tradition going. For Thanksgiving, I convinced Kathleen and Ava to open the restaurant for lower-income families. We're going to be closed on Christmas Day, so I'm going to head up to the Bronx. A friend of mine runs a soup kitchen up there, and I offered to help her serve meals to the homeless."

"Is it too late to change my answer? Way to make me look bad." Rachel nudged Griffin with her hip to show her she was being only mock serious. Griffin nudged right back.

Drop-dead gorgeous and a sense of humor. Talk about the total package. Well, almost.

Griffin had a lot of good qualities, but before tonight, Rachel would have sworn the only thing she took seriously was her job. Her passion for cooking was so great any woman in her life must feel like a mistress. Rachel wasn't up for another round of feeling second best.

She placed a serving platter in the dishwasher. "When I make my New Year's resolutions each January, I always resolve to donate my time to a worthy cause instead of dropping a check in the mail and writing it off on my taxes, but I never do."

"No time like the present. I'm sure Piper would be ecstatic if I brought an extra set of hands." Griffin fished her cell phone out of her pocket and thumbed through the screens. "If you give me your number, I'll give you a call on Sunday and we can head over. It's going to be a long day. Maybe we could meet for breakfast first."

Griffin's voice sounded matter-of-fact, but when she lifted her eyes, they shone with what appeared to be excitement. Rachel bit her lip to keep from smiling. *It's breakfast, not a date,* she reminded herself. As she and Griffin exchanged numbers, she felt herself getting lost in Griffin's eyes. *Not a date, but close enough.*

"Do you have any plans for the rest of the night?"

"Not really."

"I know a really cool jazz club in the East Village called Avenue C. The house musicians are out of this world and recording artists often drop in for late-night jam sessions. Last year, Wynton Marsalis and Wendy Harrison got into a cutting contest that went on for hours."

"A cutting contest?"

"Think of it as a musical game of H.O.R.S.E. The same rules apply—anything you can do, I can do better."

Rachel preferred classic rock to any other musical genre, but she couldn't turn down the chance to see a woman take her licks in a profession dominated by men—and spend more time with her new friend. "Do you think Wendy might play tonight?"

"If we ever get to the bottom of this pile of dirty dishes, maybe we can find out."

The pile seemed to be getting larger instead of smaller. Rachel made small talk to take her mind off how much work remained.

"I think I read somewhere that you're part of a large family. Is that true?"

Griffin scrubbed the baked-on remains of an entrée off the bottom of a casserole dish. "I'm the youngest of six and the only girl. I grew up with five brothers who tortured me relentlessly but wouldn't hesitate to kick the ass of anyone who even looked at me sideways. It was the perfect preparation for learning to deal with critics."

"What do your brothers do? Besides defend your honor, that is."

"Kieran's the oldest. He's a pediatrician. Ryan is a general contractor, Pearson is a bicycle cop, Duncan is a graphic designer, and Logan is a realtor."

She blew a stray lock of hair out of her face. When it didn't stay, Rachel reached out and tucked it behind her ear. For a brief moment, Griffin pressed her cheek against Rachel's palm. Rachel resisted the urge to grip the back of Griffin's head and pull her closer. To bury her face in the side of Griffin's neck and feel her pulse pounding against her lips. To slide her tongue across her skin.

"Of course," Griffin said, returning to the task at hand, "I've had the perfect revenge."

"How so?"

"Between them, my brothers have nine kids."

"Enough to field a baseball team."

"A softball team, you mean."

"All your brothers' children are girls?"

"Every single pink-outfit-wearing, tiara-sporting, *Hannah Montana*-loving one of them." She handed Rachel the casserole dish. "Jane tells me you're an only child. What was that like? Was it lonely?"

"Not at all. I have a ton of cousins, so I never lacked for kids my own age to play with. Because it was just the three of us, my parents and I had a close relationship when I was growing up. Coming out to them was the scariest thing I've ever done."

"Why?"

"Because I didn't know how they'd react. I grew up in the burbs. As we all know, no one is gay in the burbs. Or at least that's what it feels like when you're a teenager trying to find your way in the world. Homosexuality was never a topic of conversation in my house. Politics? Yes. Sports? Yes. Traffic on the L.I.E.? Definitely. Gayness? No way. But when I fell in love for the first time and it was with a girl instead of a boy, my parents didn't bat an eye. They were incredibly supportive. I shouldn't have been surprised. They've always been there for me every step of the way. The only subject we ever disagreed on was Isabel. I should have seen the writing on the wall when they were adamantly opposed to her presence in my life, but—"

Griffin rested a sudsy hand on her arm. "Don't beat yourself up for being human. We all have at least one bad relationship we wish we had never entered into."

"Yeah? What was yours?" She couldn't imagine Griffin crying over a broken heart. Breaking one? Definitely.

"My toxic relationship began when I was in culinary school. When I met Veronica Warner, sparks flew in every conceivable way. The competition was cutthroat and the two of us were always at odds. In the kitchen, all we did was try to top each other. In the bedroom, all we did was argue and have makeup sex. After a while, it became impossible to tell one from the other. When I first arrived on campus, I told myself I was there to learn, not chase girls, but I didn't listen to my own advice. If I had, I wouldn't have gotten a figurative knife in my back."

"Did Veronica switch the salt and the sugar during pastry week?" When the muscles in Griffin's jaw tightened, Rachel immediately regretted her attempt at humor. The subject seemed not just sore but downright painful.

"There's man law and there's chef law. You don't steal another chef's recipe or take credit for a dish you conceived together. Ronnie did both."

"What happened?"

Her expression as turbulent as a storm-tossed sea, Griffin dried her hands on a dish towel.

"It all comes down to a matter of integrity," she began at last. "When we were in school, we used to spend all day learning classic techniques. At night, we were free to improvise. We'd take established recipes and put our own spin on them or try to come up with recipes of our own. We were all intent on finding a signature dish, one that the minute you taste it, you know it could have been prepared only by a particular chef. Or, in our case, a pair of chefs.

"One night, we came up with an idea for a dish, went into the test kitchen, and tried it out. Vegetable lasagna with truffles and portobello mushrooms. It turned out great and everyone loved it. We joked about heading to the nearest patent office to trademark the recipe—we'd put both our names on it because we had come up with it together—but we didn't follow through. At least, *I* didn't.

"The practical part of our final exam was preparing a three-course meal. Appetizer, dessert, entrée. I challenged myself and tackled Julia Child's infamous beef bourguignon, one of the more difficult dishes to make because of the time and effort that goes into preparing it properly. Veronica said she planned to make an original dish, but she wouldn't tell me what. When she presented her three courses to be scored, the entrée looked familiar but the name didn't. The dish we had created had become something called Magic Mushroom Lasagna."

"I can't believe she took sole credit for something you came up with as a team."

"Believe it. And now it's her signature dish. She's even copyrighted the name."

"I don't think a dish qualifies as intellectual property, but she stole from you nevertheless. Isn't there a law against that? A man law not just a chef law?"

"Even if there were, I'm not interested in suing. I don't care about the money or the credit. I just want her to respect me, and she refuses to do that."

Her face reddened with anger, Griffin leaned against the counter. Rachel could practically see the steam pouring out her ears.

"What gets me," Griffin continued, "is she's always saying I'm not creative and I'm not original, but *I* helped her come up with the dish that separated her from the pack. I helped her get where she is, and she acts like I don't deserve to be there, too."

"Maybe she fears you. Have you thought about that?"

"What does she have to be afraid of?"

"You. She was better with you than she is without you. You're better on your own than you were with her. Maybe she can't handle that. Where is she now?"

"She stayed in Los Angeles and I moved here. Part of me wanted to stay and challenge her for the title of best chef in southern California, but coming here represented a huge opportunity for me, and I would have been crazy to turn it down. I wanted to live and work in this city. I wanted to prove I was on par with the best chefs in the world. That remains to be seen, but I think I'm on my way. Plus I sleep better at night knowing there are three thousand miles between us."

"What would happen if there weren't three thousand miles between you?"

Griffin's eyes darkened. "It would probably be the start of World War III."

"Hey, you two," Colleen called out. "If you're done with KP, come in here for a sec."

Rachel started the dishwasher. She and Griffin headed to the living room, where Colleen stood in front of the Christmas tree.

"Jane and I always open our presents on Christmas Eve," Colleen said. "Since it's after midnight, it's technically Christmas Eve." She selected three brightly wrapped gifts of various sizes and passed them out. "One for you, one for you, and one for you. Don't open them all at once. Open them one at a time. I want to see the looks on each of your faces. You first, Griffin."

"But I didn't bring anything."

Griffin attempted to return her gift, but Colleen wouldn't allow it.

"Sure you did. You brought the best pot roast I've ever eaten. Now open your present." Her eyes were shining and her cheeks were awash with color. The ginger ale must have helped. Or was playing Santa responsible for her apparent turnaround?

Griffin tore into the wrapping paper. The plain cardboard box underneath revealed no clues to its contents. She opened the box and slowly reached inside as if she were afraid of what she might find. She pulled out an apron that looked like a cocktail dress and a pair of elbow-length pot holders designed to look like opera gloves.

"You can use them for cooking or role play. That's entirely up to you," Colleen said.

"I vote for role play."

"My kind of girl." Jane held out her hand for a fist bump.

"Your turn, Rach."

Using Colleen's enthusiasm as a guide, Rachel opened her present with gusto. Her box contained a gag gift, too, though not one as stylish as Griffin's. Hers was a leather-bound organizer with several pre-filled entries.

She flipped through the pages. She understood the entries for Jane's and Colleen's birthdays and anniversary, but the one for July 25 had her stumped. "Kiss and cry," it read.

Colleen seemed to notice her confusion. "All will be revealed in due time." She turned to Jane. "Your turn, lover."

Jane's present was the smallest of the three, the box about the size of a pen case. Jane untied the red bow wrapped around it and flipped the box open. Rachel craned her neck to see what was inside. Judging by the expression on her face, Jane's gift was no gag. "Is this for real?" she asked, her voice choked with tears.

Colleen nodded, her eyes starting to glisten, too.

"Oh, babe."

Jane kissed Colleen and pulled her into her lap while Rachel scrambled to get her hands on the box. Peering inside, she saw two pregnancy tests. The indicator on one sported a bright blue plus sign, the other read Pregnant.

Rachel piled on the happy couple for a group hug. "How long have you known?"

"I've suspected for a few weeks, but I didn't want to get my hopes up again," Colleen said. "I took a home pregnancy test on Monday. When it came back positive, I took two more. Okay, five more. I made an appointment with my OB-GYN the next day and she confirmed the results."

"Why didn't you tell me before now?" Jane asked.

"I wanted to make this Christmas the best one ever."

"You already have."

Jane puddled up again. Rachel felt herself beginning to do the same. "I'm so happy for you guys." She gave Jane and Colleen another hug and kiss. "Congratulations."

"We were hoping that if this day ever came, you would agree to be our child's godmother," Colleen said.

"This is a lifetime commitment we're asking you to make," Jane said. "We wouldn't do it if we didn't think you were in it for the long haul. Are you game?"

Jane and Colleen each extended a hand to her. Rachel took their hands in hers. "You don't have to ask me twice."

"Any child of mine is bound to be a handful," Jane said.

"No shit," Rachel said, laughing through her tears.

"You'll need backup." Colleen squeezed her hand. "We're going to ask Dieter and Kevin to be godfathers. Between the three of you, I know the baby will be in good hands."

"You can count on me."

Rachel wiped her streaming eyes. She couldn't have been happier if the baby on the way were hers. The way things were going, being a godmother might be as close as she'd ever get. Would it be close enough?

❖

"This is perfect, thank you."

Griffin slipped the greeter a twenty for seating her and Rachel so close to the stage. Rachel, obviously still buzzing from Jane and Colleen's unexpected news, practically floated to her seat. Griffin could feel the excitement pouring off her in waves. She couldn't blame Rachel for being over the moon. She felt the same way each time her brothers announced another little Sutton was on the way, but she didn't plan on making a similar announcement herself. Her career was going too well to put it on hold.

"Any time. Would you like to see our wine list?" the waiter asked.

"No need." Longing for a taste of home, Griffin ordered a bottle of Napa Valley's finest.

"Coming right up."

"How do you always manage to be seated at the best tables?" Rachel asked.

Griffin tapped the side of her nose with her index finger. "It helps to have connections."

"Can your 'connections' get tickets to *The Tempest*?"

"I doubt it." The all-female version of Shakespeare's classic play was the hottest ticket in town. The entire run had been sold out for months, ticket sales spurred on by the presence of Academy Award-winning actress Helen Mirren reprising the role of Prospera she originated on film. Griffin put Rachel's request in her memory bank but didn't hold out hope she'd be able to make a withdrawal. But if she could, she might earn some serious brownie points.

Time to put Tucker to work.

She looked around the club. All the tables were filled. The booths, too.

Every time she came to Avenue C, she felt as if she were walking into a time machine. Vintage concert posters and album covers adorned the walls. Interspersed between them were autographed photos of artists who had graced the stage. Billie Holiday, Ella Fitzgerald, Duke Ellington, Charlie Parker, John Coltrane, Miles Davis, Thelonious Monk. What she wouldn't give to have been able to see those legends perform live.

The house band took the stage. Rachel applauded enthusiastically instead of snapping her fingers. A rookie mistake. She was instantly apologetic.

"I'm sorry I'm so weird."

"It's okay." Griffin rubbed her back to take away the sting of embarrassment. "I like weird."

Rachel surprised her by voicing her inner thoughts. "I like you."

"I like you, too, Puddles."

Rachel laughed softly at the private joke. Griffin wanted to hear the sound again.

"I hadn't pictured you as a jazz fan," Rachel said.

"It's in my blood. My grandfather used to own a jazz club in Los Angeles. The first integrated club of its kind."

"Used to own? Who's the current owner?"

Griffin shrugged. "Grandpa sold out during the sixties when acid rock took over and jazz lost its popularity. The place has been through several incarnations since then. Today it's a comedy club, but I don't know whose name is on the lease. I'd love to buy it back one day and return it to its original roots as a haven for up-and-coming musicians and a hangout for established artists."

"Why don't you?"

"Because my business manager says restaurants and nightclubs are bad investments. I know he's right, but sometimes you have to follow your heart."

The waiter brought the wine and two glasses. Griffin took a preliminary sip and nodded her approval. The waiter filled both glasses and left to attend to customers at another table.

On the stage, the drummer laid down a furious solo. His sticks moved so fast Griffin was surprised they didn't catch fire.

"I think you were almost as excited about Jane and Colleen's news as they were," she whispered when the stand-up bass player took center stage. Wendy Harrison, her trumpet tucked under her arm, stood waiting her turn.

Rachel slid her chair closer to hers so they could continue their hushed conversation. "They've been trying for a baby for years. I've shared every setback and disappointment with them. I'm ecstatic to be able to share the culmination of something they've struggled so mightily to achieve."

"I have to add another accolade to your growing list. Smart, funny, loyal, sexy, *and* loving. You're going to be a great mother."

"You mean godmother, don't you?"

"No." Griffin ran her hand through Rachel's hair and rested her palm on the back of her neck. "I've never met anyone with a heart as big as yours. Any kid would be lucky to be able to call you Mom."

Tears flooded Rachel's eyes. "Thank you," she said, her voice breaking. "If my kids need surf lessons, I know who to call."

Griffin draped her arm across the back of Rachel's chair. "I'm your girl."

❖

Rachel didn't want to go back to her empty apartment after the last set ended at Avenue C. She wanted to go home. Jane and Colleen's news was too good not to share. She said good night to Griffin outside the club, then headed to her parents' place.

It was nearly three when she rang the bell. Despite the late hour, flickering light filtered through the front window. The TV was on in the living room. No surprise there. Her mother was a notorious night owl. Her father, on the other hand, usually fell asleep as soon as the eleven o'clock news ended. He was probably snoring soundly in his armchair, waiting for his wife of forty years to wake him and tell him it was time to head up to bed.

Rose Bauer drew back the curtain and peered out the window. Her hair, a halo of salt-and-pepper curls, framed her heart-shaped face. Her cautious eyes softened when she saw Rachel. She let the curtain drop and unlocked the door. She poked her head outside and looked around.

Rachel sighed. "It's just me, Mom."

"Is everything okay, sweetie?" Her mother gripped the lapels of her terry cloth robe to ward off the cold. "What are you doing out this late?"

"I wanted to see you."

"At this hour?"

"It's never too late to come home, is it?"

"Of course not." Her mother wrapped her in a hug so tight Rachel saw stars. "It's been ages since you've made the trip out here. Come inside before you catch your death of cold." She pulled Rachel into the house and called out for Rachel's father. "Gene, wake up and get out here. Rachel's home."

Rachel's mother linked her arm through hers and led her through the living room to the kitchen.

"You look skinny. Haven't you been eating?"

"Yes, but not as much."

"I can tell. I can practically see your ribs." She poked a finger into Rachel's side for emphasis. "There's some leftover apple pie in the refrigerator. I'll put on a pot of coffee and we'll have a nice chat." She warmed two slices of pie, pressed a healthy scoop of vanilla ice cream on top of each, then placed one saucer in front of Rachel and saved the other for herself.

Rachel's latest conversation with Griffin had left her feeling at odds. Family meant so much to Griffin. How could she not want one of her own? At Avenue C, Griffin had paid her the ultimate compliment by saying she thought she'd make an excellent mother, but the kind words reminded Rachel that Griffin didn't want to be a mother herself.

She eyed the thick slice of apple pie dripping with melting ice cream. How long had it been since she'd had real sugar?

One slice couldn't hurt.

She grabbed a spoon and began to help herself to the pie.

The smell of brewing coffee drew her father to the room. Gene Bauer's sleep-tousled silver hair was sticking straight up on his head like Don King's in his heyday.

"Jane and Colleen are having a baby," Rachel said around a mouthful of ice cream.

Her mother squealed in delight, but her father was noticeably underwhelmed.

"Glad to hear it, but I doubt that's the real reason you dragged yourself all the way out to Long Island." He tightened the sash of his robe across his round belly and bent to give her a kiss on the forehead. "What's her name?"

"Who?"

He sat across from her and reached across the table to give her hand an affectionate pat. "Whoever has you this bright-eyed and bushy-tailed. What's her name?"

Rachel came clean. "Griffin Sutton."

Just saying Griffin's name made her heart flutter. She pushed the pie away. She had eaten only two spoonfuls and she felt like she was about to explode. Her mother pulled the leftovers toward her.

"Is she anything like Isabel?" her father asked, his voice a protective growl.

"No. She's unlike anyone I've ever met."

But how much did she really know about her? Griffin had admitted to being a player. Did that admission brand her as a cheater as well?

"Griffin Sutton," her mother said to herself as she finished the rest of the second slice of apple pie. "Why does that name sound so familiar?" She dropped her spoon on her saucer with a clatter. "Is she the one I see on the *Today* show from time to time? She is, isn't she? You remember her, Gene. She's the cute chef Aggie Anderson was drooling over the last time she dropped by. She was trying to make a spinach salad and Aggie couldn't keep her hands off of her."

"I must have missed that episode," her father deadpanned. "Good catch, Rachel."

"There's no need to congratulate me. We're just friends."

"Tell me about her anyway." Her mother propped her chin on her hand as if she were about to hear some juicy gossip.

Rachel told her parents about her first meeting with Griffin, their night at B&B, and Griffin's plans to take her on a culinary trip around the world. She told them about Jane and Colleen's party and the mind-blowing gift Colleen had given Jane.

Reliving the past few weeks put a smile on her face. A smile that matched the one forming in her heart. When she finished her tale, her parents shared a look. A familiar sight. Not for the first time, she wished she could decode their silent communication.

"Granted, I haven't met her yet," her mother said, "but Griffin sounds like a good egg."

"No pun intended, right?"

"What?"

"She's a chef and you called her a—never mind." Rachel grinned. Her mother could be delightfully clueless sometimes.

Her father took a sip of his coffee and set the mug on the table with a thud, his usual indicator he had come to a decision about something.

"I want to meet her."

"Wait a second." Rachel nearly choked on her coffee. "You want to what?"

"Ooh, that's a good idea, Gene," her mother said. "I can make the tuna casserole you love so much. I may even have one in the freezer."

Rachel felt the evening begin to spiral out of control. In the past, her parents hadn't expressed an interest in someone she was seeing until after the third date. She and Griffin had been out a couple of times, but their trips to B&B and Avenue C had been spontaneous, not premeditated. They hadn't been on an official date yet, and her father already wanted to meet her?

If having her father play Twenty Questions didn't scare Griffin off, the menu certainly might. Her mother's tuna casserole was the kind of dish professional chefs looked upon with disdain. What would Griffin do when she was presented with a plate piled high with tuna, mayonnaise, and egg noodles topped with crumbled potato chips? Would she force it down or push it around her plate until someone mercifully took it away?

Rachel held her head in her hands. "This can't be good."

"If I promise to save the baby pictures until after dessert, would that help?" her mother asked.

"And it gets worse. Mom, why do you insist on showing everyone who walks through the door pictures of me as an infant naked and grinning toothlessly on a bear skin rug?"

"Because they're such cute pictures, dear. You look adorable in them."

Rachel made a mental note to burn the embarrassing photo the first chance she got. Her mother could make all the promises she wanted, but Rachel knew she'd probably have the photo albums ready and waiting before the main course hit the table—if she didn't convert the prints to digital files and create a multimedia presentation that played in the background during the course of the evening. Rachel cringed at the thought of images of her during her awkward adolescent years flashing across the TV screen while she, Griffin, and her parents broke bread.

"So it's a date?" her mother asked hopefully.

"I'll ask her and see what she says. If she says yes, we'll have to do it on a Sunday. That's her only day off."

"Perfect. I'll put you down for next week. That will give me a chance to get my hair done." Her mother patted her graying roots.

Her father stared at his hands. "And I really need to do something about my nails."

Rachel rolled her eyes. "I think I'm in the wrong house."

❖

Griffin placed a slice of roasted turkey and a scoop of apple walnut stuffing onto the thick paper plate held by the last diner in what had been a seemingly endless line.

"Merry Christmas," she said to the bedraggled man wearing three layers of soiled clothes and a pair of mismatched shoes.

"God bless you." He tipped his battered fedora before shuffling off to the nearest table, a small dog at his side.

Griffin had lost track of how many meals she had served. The only thing she could be sure of was she had never felt so tired yet so fulfilled. Or so homesick. When the man began to share part of his meal with his canine companion, she began to cry. She was embarrassed by the display. This wasn't like her. She didn't cry. She didn't show weakness. Of all her siblings, she was the one with the hardest shell. The one least likely to puddle up over a sappy movie or get all googly-eyed over pictures of someone's new pet. Showing her emotions was such a rarity, her brothers teased her about being the alpha male in the family.

She knuckled away her tears, but more began to fall.

Rachel put down the pan she was holding and rushed to her side. "What's wrong?"

"Seeing all these families makes me miss mine even more. My parents, my brothers, my nieces. I can't stop wondering what they're doing right now. Are they opening their gifts? Are they gathered around the table? Are they missing me as much as I miss them?" She didn't realize how badly she needed a hug until Rachel drew her into her arms, her full breasts pressing against her chest.

"Have dinner with me and my parents tonight," Rachel said when she let go.

Griffin dried her eyes with the hem of her apron. "I wouldn't want to impose."

"You wouldn't be imposing. You'd be doing us a favor. My mom always makes way too much food, and the three of us can't possibly eat it all. Besides, my parents would love to meet you. They practically twisted my arm until I promised I'd ask you to come over for dinner sometime. I can already picture you turning my dad into a blushing schoolboy and my mom into a gushing fan. What do you say?"

"When do we eat?" She drew a deep, shaky breath as she tried to regain her composure. "Sorry for the meltdown."

"What did you tell me a couple of days ago? Don't apologize for being human. I'm not one of your critics. You don't have to be perfect to impress me. In fact, I think I prefer you the way you are right now. With gravy on your sleeve, flour on your forehead, and tearstains on your cheeks. You're not just beautiful on the outside, Griffin. You're beautiful inside, too. Today has been magical in so many ways. Thank you for sharing it with me. I'll never forget it. But I do have one question."

"What?"

Rachel bit her lip. "What are your feelings about tuna casserole?"

Griffin laughed. "I think it's the unsung hero of the food world."

Rachel's shoulders sagged in apparent relief. "In that case, my mother's going to love you."

Rachel squeezed her arm to make sure she was okay, then returned to her station. As they worked throughout the afternoon, Griffin felt their developing bond grow stronger. When she began filming *Cream of the Crop*, she would be contractually obligated not to tell anyone what she was up to during the three weeks she was away. Keeping the secret might earn her a chance to compete for the respect she craved, but it would put her connection with Rachel to the test. She hoped their bond would hold up under the strain.

CHAPTER SEVEN

Rachel felt like she was about to throw up. Dinner with her parents had gone better than she had hoped, despite the nosy neighbors who caught wind of Griffin's presence and kept dropping by to gawk at the celebrity in their midst. Taking the extra attention in stride, Griffin had regaled the hordes with stories of her adventures both in and out of the kitchen. By the end of the night, Rachel's parents were the most popular couple on the block and they had given Griffin two enthusiastic thumbs up.

Now it was Rachel's turn to run the gauntlet. Would Griffin's friends welcome her with open arms or give her the cold shoulder?

She wasn't sure what time to make her appearance. The invitation said the party would start at ten, but the real festivities wouldn't begin until midnight. She decided on eleven. Plenty of time to get her bearings and get comfortable before the countdown began.

She loved New Year's Eve. Any holiday that came with the promise of a fresh start was all right by her. She and Isabel used to make an annual pilgrimage to Times Square on December 31, showing up early no matter what the weather to stake out a good spot to set up camp and watch the ball drop. But those days were over. Now it was time to establish a new tradition.

Griffin had said the party would be low-key, but Rachel didn't want to show up looking too casual. She had dressed up her jeans and white Oxford shirt with a velvet blazer. The jacket looked black, but its official color was midnight blue, which, considering the occasion, seemed fitting. She had owned the jacket for years but had worn it only a handful of times. She usually felt like a bit of a dandy when she put it on, but tonight it felt right. Tonight, for the first time in a long time, she felt comfortable in her own skin.

She hadn't checked the scales to see how much weight she had lost because the number didn't matter. Her clothes fit better and she had more energy. When she looked in the mirror, she liked the person she saw staring back at her. That was what mattered.

Everyone at work had commented on the change in her demeanor. She had a bounce in her step. Her swagger was back. She would need it. Jane and Colleen had other plans for New Year's Eve. Griffin would most likely be the only person with whom she was personally acquainted and they'd known each other for a grand total of sixteen days. The prospect made her understandably anxious but also, in a perverse way, excited. How long had it been since she had stood on her own? Since she had been judged on her own merits, not those of the woman at her side.

She climbed the stairs leading from the subway to the street and walked toward Griffin's building. She headed to the elevator after the doorman let her inside. Then she punched the button for the penthouse level and took a deep breath as the doors closed.

It was considered bad form to arrive at a dinner party empty-handed so she had picked up some Bollinger Blanc de Noir on the way. Looking at the bottle in her hands, she began to second-guess her decision. The party wasn't BYOB, so there should be more than enough alcohol. And buying such an expensive vintage could be seen as presumptuous. Or arrogant. She decided to go with presumptuous.

The elevator doors slid open. *I've come too far to back out now.* She stepped out of the elevator and located Griffin's apartment. Channeling Stuart Smalley, the character Al Franken played so memorably on *Saturday Night Live*, she silently ran through a daily affirmation. *I'm good enough. I'm smart enough. And, doggone it, people like me.*

"Here goes nothing."

She rang the bell. A man she didn't recognize opened the door. He had a closely trimmed beard, carefully styled hair, and a wardrobe inspired by *The Great Gatsby* (linen pants, a light blue poplin shirt, and spectator loafers). With a courtly bow, he ushered her inside. "Join the party. The more, the merrier." She stepped across the threshold and he closed the door behind her. "I'm Tucker, Griffin's personal assistant. And you are?"

"Rachel Bauer."

Tucker added her name and e-mail address to the growing list on the tablet computer in his hands.

"Will I get a bill for this in a few days?" she asked only half-seriously.

"No," he said with a charming smile as he tucked the computer's stylus behind his ear. "An electronic thank-you card. Griffin sends one to each attendee each time she has an event."

"And how often is that?"

"Two or three times a year. There's always one on the Fourth of July—hamburgers, hot dogs, and the occasional block of tofu. The other events move around according to Griffin's schedule and the availability of quality products." He indicated the bottle of Bollinger. "Shall I take that for you?"

"I'd like to hang on to it, if you don't mind." She wanted to present it to Griffin herself. She didn't want the credit. Well, maybe she did, but what she really wanted was to see the look on Griffin's face when she read the label. And to be there when she poured the first glass.

Tucker flashed a knowing smirk. "She's around here some-where. When you see her, do me a favor and shove something in her mouth. She usually forgets to eat when she's running around like a crazy person."

That explained her lean and hungry look. Apparently, it wasn't just figurative.

"How long has she been throwing these parties?"

"Since culinary school. I've only been her P.A. since last March, but from what I hear, the parties get bigger every year." More guests walked in and Tucker excused himself to greet the new arrivals.

"Low-key, my ass," Rachel said under her breath.

A DJ spinning a mix of classic songs and the latest club hits was set up by the bar. The music drew Rachel further inside. She followed it like an enchanted child chasing after the Pied Piper of Hamelin.

The crowd was mostly female, though there were a few straight and gay couples in the mix. She didn't recognize anyone. No, that wasn't entirely true. She saw a few familiar faces—people she recognized from screens both large and small—but they weren't exactly her close personal friends so she gave them a wide berth.

She circled the room, then stopped and helped herself to a bottle of Stella Artois out of the ice chest next to the buffet table.

She checked out the spread. There was no deep-dish pepperoni in sight. Instead, all the pizzas were gourmet, each one presented with its own tent card. There was white pizza topped with thick slices of aged mozzarella, spinach pizza drizzled in olive oil and dotted with feta cheese crumbles, barbecue Thai chicken pizza with peanut sauce, and the one she was most curious about—duck à l'orange with slices of grilled sugared Valencia oranges on the side. There was even a breakfast pizza topped with bacon and a fried egg. It was appropriately titled Sunny Side Up. Some of the crusts were paper-thin, others thick and substantial. All looked handmade.

Rachel was tempted to grab a plate and create her own sampler platter, helping herself to a small slice of each variety, but she wanted to find Griffin first—and get rid of one of the bottles in her hand.

There were four penthouses in the building, one facing in each direction. Griffin's faced west, affording her what must have been a spectacular view at sunset. Her apartment was huge. Tasteful decorations made it seem less like a showroom and more like a living space. Black-framed photographs of California landmarks adorned the walls. The Golden Gate Bridge greeted visitors in the foyer. The iconic Hollywood sign rose above the stone fireplace in the living room. Pumped-up bodybuilders on Venice Beach pointed the way to the guest bathroom. A stunning shot of an overhead view of the curvy Pacific Coast Highway dominated the master bedroom.

Rachel examined a photo of Fisherman's Wharf on the wall outside the den/home office. Like the others, it was signed by Madeleine Sutton.

Is she a relative?

Rachel pulled out her phone and quickly Googled Madeleine Sutton. She clicked on the link to the artist's official website and navigated to the biographical information section. Madeleine was not simply a relative; she was Griffin's mother. Her smile lit up the home page, her gently-lined face a stunning example of a life well-lived. Madeleine was an incredible beauty, and a dead ringer for her only daughter.

When she put her phone away, Rachel spotted Griffin coming out of the kitchen. A pizza in each hand, Griffin slowly made her way through the crowd.

"Hot stuff. Behind you," she called out, evidently forgetting she wasn't at work.

She was wearing a Kiss the Cook apron, which would have seemed tongue-in-cheek even if she didn't have a sprig of mistletoe dangling from a silver halo above her head. The accessory made the message on her apron seem like more of a command than a suggestion. Just about everyone she passed followed her unspoken order. Most aimed for her mouth; she offered her cheek instead. The busses made her trip from the kitchen to the dining room last a lot longer than it should.

She placed the new additions—*quattro formaggi* and rustic vegetable—on the buffet table and turned around. She spotted Rachel as she pulled off her oversized potholders. The one on her left hand looked like Kermit the Frog, the one on her right Oscar the Grouch. Had she taken Colleen's suggestion to heart? Was she saving her Christmas gifts for role play? Rachel's breath quickened at the thought.

Griffin glanced in her direction and indicated she'd be with her as soon as she could. An attractive woman laid a hand on Griffin's arm, demanding her attention. The woman's hair was as black as a raven's wing. Her piercing eyes were almost the same shade. Her olive skin hinted at Mediterranean roots. Rachel recognized her immediately. Aggie Anderson.

Griffin's face lit up. She gave Aggie a brief kiss and a warm hug.

Rachel remembered the story her mother had told her on Christmas Eve about Griffin's recent visit to the *Today* show and Aggie's romantic overtures during her presentation. She wondered if Griffin and Aggie were seeing each other. If they were, she had to admit they certainly made a striking couple.

Griffin and Aggie chatted for a few minutes, Aggie flirting shamelessly all the while. She tossed her shining tresses back and forth, licked her bee-stung lips, and touched Griffin's hand, arm, or shoulder every five seconds.

Rachel heard Griffin say, "I'll call you," as she gave Aggie another hug. Aggie leaned in for another kiss. Rachel turned away before their lips met. When she looked up again, Griffin was standing in front of her.

"Puddles, you made it," she said, her smile a mile wide.

Rachel held up her half-empty bottle of Stella. "I heard there was free beer."

"I love this jacket on you." Griffin rubbed her hand over Rachel's sleeve, copping a feel of the lush velvet fabric.

"Just something I threw on." She pointed to the mistletoe hanging over Griffin's head like the Sword of Damocles. "Hedging your bets?"

Griffin adjusted her halo. "I've never been kissed at midnight on New Year's Eve. Not by someone who counts, anyway. Tonight, I hope that's going to change."

"Is the line forming now or later?"

"There isn't going to be a line. I'm saving my kisses for someone special. I just have to make sure she doesn't run out on me before the clock strikes twelve."

Rachel wondered if the "someone special" to which Griffin was referring was Aggie Anderson.

"Don't worry," she said with faux cheer. "I'll trip her before she gets to the door." She presented Griffin with the champagne. "For you."

"You didn't have to do this." Griffin looked at the label and whistled. "You *really* didn't have to do this."

Her face was a portrait of unbridled joy. That was the expression Rachel hadn't wanted to miss. After witnessing Griffin's encounter with Aggie, she knew exactly how the champagne would be put to use: morning-after mimosas.

"This will definitely not be going on the bar tonight. I think I'll save it for a special occasion."

"It's New Year's Eve. The biggest party of the year. What could be more special than tonight?"

"The morning I wake up lying next to you."

Rachel felt herself start to blush, ruining her attempt to appear nonchalant. "What about Aggie? Won't she have something to say about you waking up lying next to me?"

Griffin frowned. "That's not the kind of relationship Aggie and I have."

"But you do have a relationship."

"She invited me to her place for drinks once. Tonight I'm returning the favor."

"Are you dating her?" Rachel felt like an investigative reporter chasing an uncooperative interviewee. She was the late, great Mike Wallace, and Griffin was a double-dealing corporate executive trying to avoid what was coming to her.

"Aggie and I had one night together, but I haven't seen her or anyone else since the night you and I went to B&B."

Her comment took Rachel's breath away.

"Really?"

"Yes, really. Is it so hard for you to believe I want to spend time with you?"

Rachel didn't know whether to believe her eyes or her ears. Her eyes said Griffin was involved with Aggie, while her ears said Griffin was only interested in her.

Griffin grinned and Rachel forgot everything she'd told herself about wanting to be just friends. She tried to find a way to regain her footing. Then she remembered her directive from Tucker.

"Have you eaten? Today, I mean." Griffin's sheepish smile was a dead giveaway. "Poker must not be your game. Let's go." Taking Griffin by the shoulders, she turned her around and led her to the buffet table. "I know you're biased, but what are your favorites?"

"All of them," she said, displaying a bit of well-earned hubris. She was good and she knew it.

The pan of Tropic Thunder—a dessert pizza topped with cream cheese and fresh fruit—was almost empty. Rachel filled the pan with slices from the other pizzas. *There goes my diet. Just my luck. I finally gain some semblance of control over my eating habits and I meet a professional chef.* Griffin bent to grab a couple of beers out of the cooler. Rachel admired the view of her blue-jeaned ass. *A very sexy professional chef.*

Griffin led her to her favorite refuge: the kitchen.

"Pay no attention to the man behind the curtain," she said, asking Rachel in her own inimitable way to ignore the cavalcade of dirty pots and pans scattered all over the butcher block-topped island in the center of the room.

Rachel had expected to find a squad of sous chefs scurrying around, but the empty kitchen proved her wrong. Griffin had managed to pull off the evening on her own. No wonder eating was so low on her list of priorities. It came a distant second to keeping about a dozen other balls in the air. For Griffin's sake, Rachel hoped a cleaning crew would swoop in the next day to take care of the mess. Otherwise, she'd be up to her elbows in dirty dishes for hours.

Rachel took a bite of the duck à l'orange. The pizza tasted so good it made her want to cry. No wonder Griffin's bosses had flown three thousand miles to make her an offer. Rachel would fly twice that distance to proposition her, even if she knew beforehand the answer to her question would be no.

While Griffin opened the beers, Rachel looked around the kitchen. The appliances were stainless steel and professional grade. The high-tech stove looked like it could whip out a four-course meal by itself. The see-through refrigerator was stocked with all sorts of exotic ingredients. Some Rachel couldn't pronounce; others she didn't even recognize. She pointed to a chicken with purple skin. "Is it supposed to be that color?"

"Yes. *Wu gu ji* is a delicacy I'll introduce you to when we get to the Chinese leg of our journey. The skin and bones are black, the meat is grayish-black and incredibly gamy, but it makes wonderful chicken soup."

"If you say so." Rachel took a longer look at the bird. "I'm trying to be open-minded, but the only thing I've ever eaten that color was a bowl of blue corn nachos—and it came with a side of salsa, not a warning label."

"You're funny," Griffin said from her perch on the counter. A half-eaten slice of veggie pizza dangled from the ends of her long fingers.

"You think so? I hadn't noticed."

"I have. And your sense of humor isn't the only thing I've noticed."

"Oh, yeah? What else has caught your eye? I'm not fishing for compliments, mind you, but they're certainly welcomed."

Griffin laughed again. "You look gorgeous tonight. How's that for a compliment?"

"I need to keep you around. You're good for my ego."

"Egos aren't the only things I'm good at stroking."

Rachel felt her ears redden—and her nipples harden. She turned away so Griffin couldn't see how much her words had affected her. She doubted Griffin found drooling attractive. "Where's your spice rack?"

"I don't have one."

"Yeah, right. You couldn't have created the smorgasbord on the buffet table without one."

"I don't have a spice *rack*. It's more like a spice *room*."

She began to climb off the counter, but Rachel held up one hand to keep her in place. "Keep eating. Just tell me where it is and I'll find it myself."

She pointed to a door Rachel had assumed led to the pantry. Instead, it was a walk-in closet filled with bottles, boxes, and jars in all shapes and sizes. Arranged by country of origin, the containers spanned the globe.

"Have you been to all these places?"

"I wish." Griffin reached for a slice of Thai chicken pizza. "I have good relationships with most of the spice merchants in town and, in a pinch, the Internet is a wonderful thing."

Rachel opened one of the jars and inhaled the musky aroma of the dark brown powder that rested inside. The label said the contents were smoked Spanish paprika. It looked like ground cinnamon but smelled like freshly-tilled earth after a summer rain. She replaced the jar on the shelf and reached for a bag of something called li hing mui powder. Crafted in Hawaii, it smelled like a vague combination of citrus and sodium. She took a bigger whiff of the burnt orange-colored crystals. "What's this made of?"

"Salted dried plums. Try some on one of the oranges." Rachel's expression must have let Griffin know how much she doubted her sanity. "Just trust me."

Rachel sprinkled a little bit of the powder onto one of the grilled orange slices and tentatively slid the fruit into her mouth. The combination of flavors was out of this world. Her taste buds stood up and saluted.

"See," Griffin said with a self-satisfied smile. "I told you."

Rachel replaced the mui powder on its shelf and reached for another container. This one she hid behind her back. "Is it true chefs are trained to recognize spices by smell and taste, not just by sight?"

Griffin nodded. "It's one of the many taste tests in culinary school."

"How did you do?"

Taking a page out of Rachel's book, Griffin turned self-deprecating. "The first time I took the test or the second?"

Rachel walked over to her. "Close your eyes," she said, standing between Griffin's spread legs.

Griffin took a sip of beer to cleanse her palate. Her eyelids fluttered shut. "What are you going to do to me?"

"Test you." When Rachel brought her hands up, Griffin opened one eye. "Don't cheat."

"Okay, okay. I'll play it straight."

Rachel couldn't resist teasing her. "Don't do that, either."

Griffin opened her eyes again. "I walked right into that one, didn't I?"

After Griffin closed her eyes a second time, Rachel tied a dish towel around her head and fashioned it into a makeshift blindfold.

Griffin wrapped her legs around Rachel's waist and pulled her closer. Rachel didn't pull away as she felt their relationship begin to make the wide turn from platonic to something undefined but decidedly different.

"You're not turning all *9½ Weeks* on me already, are you?" Griffin asked.

"Maybe," Rachel said as the heat from Griffin's body blended with hers. "Would you like that?"

Griffin reached inside Rachel's jacket and rubbed her hands up and down her sides. "Only if we leave Mickey Rourke at home and both of us get to be Kim Basinger."

"I'll start practicing my Southern accent." Rachel uncapped the jar in her hand and waved it under Griffin's nose.

"Hold on. I wasn't ready."

Griffin's hands stopped moving and Rachel could tell she was frowning underneath her blindfold. Griffin was taking the challenge more seriously than she had anticipated.

She reached into the jar with two fingers and pulled out some of its contents. "Open wide."

Griffin's lips twitched as desire crossed her features. Her legs tightened around Rachel's waist, drawing her even closer.

Rachel placed the mystery ingredient on Griffin's tongue. Griffin worked it around the inside of her mouth, took a couple of tentative crunches, and swallowed it down.

"When Tucker told me to shove something in your mouth," Rachel whispered in her ear, "I don't think this is what he meant."

"Tuck's had worse things in his mouth than a roasted cacao nib." Griffin had passed her test. Her hands, meanwhile, moved toward the final exam. One headed north, the other south. "What time is it?" she asked, nuzzling the side of Rachel's neck.

"Almost midnight." Rachel could hear the countdown beginning in the living room. Griffin's lips brushed her skin, causing the fine hairs on the nape of her neck to stand on end. "If you're serious about kissing someone who counts, you'd better find her in a hurry."

Griffin reached up and removed her blindfold. "I already did." She drew a finger across Rachel's lips. "Ever since I met you, I've been wondering how it would feel to kiss you."

Rachel had been having similar thoughts.

In the living room, the countdown reached one, the guests roared, and the DJ started blasting "Auld Lang Syne."

"Happy New Year, Puddles."

Griffin bridged the short distance between them and pressed her lips to Rachel's. Her lips were impossibly soft, her tongue the best thing Rachel had tasted all night. Griffin kissed the way she cooked. Freely. Passionately. Expertly. Rachel was breathless when she finally broke free.

"Same time next year?" Griffin asked.

"It's a date." Rachel rested her forehead against Griffin's. "Speaking of which, I've decided where I'd like to go for the first of the thirty you promised me."

"Yeah? Where?" Griffin's hands slid down Rachel's back and over the curve of her ass. Rachel's nipples grew even more rigid as she imagined Griffin's hands moving that deliberately over her bare skin.

"How's your French?"

Griffin flashed a cocky grin. "I don't know. You tell me."

She kissed Rachel again and slowly slipped her tongue between Rachel's parted lips. Their tongues slid against each other's in a slow and torturous dance that kept pace with the sinuous rhythm their bodies had unconsciously assumed.

Rachel closed her lips around Griffin's tongue and exerted gentle pressure as she drew it deeper inside. She groaned deep in her throat as she felt her body become infused with warmth.

"It seems to me," she began in a hoarse whisper, "your French is pretty damn good."

Griffin kissed the tip of Rachel's nose. "You should hear my Spanish."

CHAPTER EIGHT

For their first date, Griffin took Rachel to France via Harlem. The venerable borough, home to the Harlem Renaissance in the '20s and '30s, had fallen on hard times over the years but seemed to be on the upswing. New businesses were popping up everywhere in order to accommodate the influx of Yuppies who had taken up residence in the area. Drawn by the hip multicultural vibe, lower rent, and the best soul food north of the Mason-Dixon Line, thousands of New Yorkers had abandoned Manhattan for Harlem. Griffin couldn't blame them. Navigating the streets was like walking with one foot in the past and one in the future. It was the best of both worlds.

Walking arm in arm, she and Rachel window shopped at half a dozen stores and visited several art galleries. She wanted to buy one of everything, but she limited herself to a Big Mama Thornton/ Muddy Waters album she unearthed at a locally-owned record store on Lexington Avenue. Jazz was the perfect background music for the beginning of a romantic evening, but the blues provided her preferred soundtrack for the end of the night—when sweet nothings were replaced by impassioned pleas.

After a productive hour perusing the stacks at Hot Wax, she took Rachel to Bordeaux, a tiny restaurant that seated ten—if that. Located a stone's throw from the historic Apollo Theater, Bordeaux looked more like a home than a place of business. It felt like one, too. Instead of individual tables interspersed throughout the restaurant, one long dining table occupied the center of the room. Patrons shared it as if they were all attending the same dinner party or family reunion.

The owner, Aravane De Montbrai, was a striking beauty of French-Algerian descent. She and Griffin greeted each other effusively, kissing each other's cheeks the Continental way.

"It's good to see you, my friend," Aravane said in French.

"You, too," Griffin responded in kind.

"How long has it been?"

"Five years? Six?" Griffin wracked her brain for the answer. She hadn't seen Aravane since they had spent nine months learning the fine art of French cooking at Le Cordon Bleu in Paris.

"Longer than I care to remember."

Griffin indicated the crowded restaurant. "You're certainly doing well for yourself."

"But not as well as you." Aravane glanced at Rachel. "She's adorable."

"Keep that sexy accent to yourself. I saw her first."

Aravane seated Griffin and Rachel in two recently vacated spaces at the communal table. Next to them were two couples having a spirited conversation about the Giants' chances of winning another Super Bowl. According to the men, the team's fortunes rested on the starting quarterback's shoulders. The women, on the other hand, argued defense was the key. Griffin thought both were right. The quartet could have been perfect strangers at the start of the evening but, given the close quarters, that was no longer the case.

"Would you like to see the menu or will you give me the honor of crafting one for you?" Aravane asked in the delightful French-accented English that had been making women swoon for years. Her appearance was as captivating as her voice. She was tall and olive-skinned with hazel eyes, an aquiline nose, and pert Cupid's bow lips framed by a curly mane of coal black hair.

"We're in your capable hands," Griffin said.

"Then please allow me to start you off with Salade Niçoise with a Dijon vinaigrette dressing, followed by an entrée of *coq au vin* and, to finish, chocolate mousse with white chocolate drizzle."

"Sounds wonderful."

"I think you mean decadent," Rachel said after Aravane took her leave.

"Do me a favor. Stop worrying about how many crunches you're going to have to do to work off the mousse and just enjoy it, okay?"

"I'll try. But, just so you know, the answer is fifty for the mousse and another fifty for the rest of the meal."

"Rach, as far as I'm concerned, you're the most beautiful woman in here. How many times do I have to say it before it sinks in?"

"I'm guessing thirty. Maybe more, depending on my mood."

Shaking her head, Griffin reached for a slice of rustic homemade bread and covered it with a liberal helping of strawberry preserves. "I've never dated anyone who's as into numbers as you are."

"What type of women do you normally date? Besides temperamental chefs, that is."

"I don't have a type. I love women, plain and simple."

"So I've noticed." Rachel glanced toward the kitchen, where Aravane was presumably whipping up their first course. "I Googled you," she said after Griffin followed her line of sight.

"What did you find?"

"Let's just say you enjoy women."

"Don't you?"

"Not as much as you do. I didn't do much more than a cursory image search and I uncovered a treasure trove of pictures of you out on the town with a string of women on your arm."

"Not at the same time, I hope." Griffin took a bite of her appetizer and licked preserves off her fingers. "As my brother the cop would say, I've had motive and opportunity. But that doesn't make me a criminal, does it?"

"No, it makes you *very* popular."

"Is this the point where you run screaming for the hills?"

Rachel flashed a coquettish smile. "Why don't you give me a reason to stay?"

"I could give you several."

"I'll settle for one."

"Okay." Griffin thought for a moment. "None of those other women were you. They either wanted to be seen with me or wanted something from me. You want me. Or, at least, that's what it feels like." She leaned back in her chair as Aravane served the salads. "I'm not going to lie. I've had my share of relationships. Some good, some bad. One long-term, some just for the night. I'm not going to apologize for anything I've done. I didn't do anything that wasn't consensual, and I didn't leave a trail of broken hearts behind me."

"More like a sea of happy faces."

Griffin took a sip of wine to break the rhythm of the conversation. Or was it an interrogation? First the questions about Aggie on New Year's Eve and now the ones today about women who, in some cases, hadn't been in her life in years. She couldn't tell if Rachel was being inquisitive or paranoid. "I hope my past isn't going to be a problem for you. Because my only two concerns right now are my present and my future."

"I'm not brave enough to ask you if you see me in your future so I'll ask about your past instead. Tell me about your first kiss."

Griffin let loose with a throaty laugh. The experience—and the story behind it—was the stuff of family legend.

"I was nine. For my brother Duncan's thirteenth birthday, my parents threw him a surf party on the beach. While the adults grilled burgers and hot dogs, the kids took turns riding the waves. I spent more time on the water than on the sand. In my dreams, I was Kelly Slater, one of the greatest surfers of all time. In reality, I was anything but. Still dreaming, I tried to impress all the girls with my picture-perfect form. I impressed them all right, but in the wrong way. I had a spectacular wipeout and everyone saw it. I could hear their collective groan when my body went one direction and my board the other. The wave drove me so deep under the water I felt like a sailor being buried at sea. I clawed my way to the surface coughing and sputtering and happy as hell to be alive. By the time I dog paddled to the beach, my brothers had had plenty of time to fashion homemade scorecards."

"I'm assuming you didn't earn any perfect tens."

"Far from it. If I remember correctly, my combined score was a minus two. I spent the rest of the afternoon hiding under the pier hanging my head in shame. Eventually, Tara Marshall took pity on me and sought me out. Even though we went to the same school, Tara and I didn't hang out because she was one of the cool kids and I was the nerd who swapped recipes with the lunch ladies in the cafeteria. She brought me a plate of food, told me my wipeout was the most awesome thing she had ever seen, and kissed me right on the mouth. To this day, whenever I hear seagulls screeching overhead or smell the smoke from a grill, it takes me back to that moment. I can feel the sand between my toes and taste Tara's bubble gum lip gloss on my tongue. Too bad she ended up dating Duncan instead of me."

"Where did you go to school, Sweet Valley High?" Rachel asked, referring to the titular institution that served as the locale for a series of '80s-era teen novels. A school populated by beautiful girls and handsome boys who never seemed to have any problems that couldn't be neatly resolved in just under two hundred pages.

"I admit Newport Beach isn't Long Island." Griffin pronounced it Long *Guy*-land like most comedians and, truth be told, most Long Islanders did. The fingers of her left hand drummed the table in time with the mellow music playing in the background. "Can you do better? What's your story?"

"My first kiss came about the way it's supposed to: as the result of a dare."

Griffin set her empty salad plate aside and leaned forward in her chair. "This I've got to hear."

"Mine occurred at a party, too. That's one thing you and I have in common. In my case, a friend of a friend threw a basement party. I'm sure you know what those are."

"A group of kids gathers in someone's basement, listens to music, eats chips and dip, and waits for someone to do something interesting. Kind of like a school dance with less attentive chaperones."

"When the hostess suggested we play Seven Minutes in Heaven, everyone perked up. Especially when she said it was no-holds-barred."

"What does that mean?"

"No do-overs. If you spun the bottle and it stopped in front of someone of the same sex, you wouldn't get to spin again. Most people dropped out when they heard that particular wrinkle, but I wasn't one of them. It's probably the only reason I played."

Griffin leaned back in her seat and uttered a quiet "*merci*" as Aravane placed their entrées on the table. "And who were you hoping to spend time with?" she asked, focusing on Rachel again.

"Joanna Gregson. She was the starting center and best player on the girls' basketball team. I had a huge crush on her. Six foot two, eyes of blue, and the sweetest fallaway jumper you've ever seen."

"What's not to love?"

"Exactly. I was fifteen, so my gaydar was still being fine-tuned back then, but I always felt like she and I had more in common than school spirit. The night of the party, I discovered I was right. The first few spins went according to form. A boy spun the bottle, it stopped in front of a girl, and they spent seven minutes groping each other in the broom closet. A girl spun the bottle, it stopped in front of a boy, and yadda yadda yadda. Then it was Jo's turn. She spun the bottle and it ended up pointing straight at me. When the bottle stopped moving, you could have heard a pin drop. Even the music stopped. Everyone waited to see what would happen. So did I."

"What did you think would happen?"

"I expected her to find an excuse not to go through with it."

"Why?"

"Because she was a jock, everyone assumed she was gay. She never said if she was or she wasn't, but she spent so much time deflecting attention from her sexuality that most of us thought the only thing she could ever love was a basketball. But at the party, she didn't hide. She stood up, held her hand out to me, and said, 'Let's do this.'"

"And you dropped trou right on the spot."

"Almost." Rachel paused to take a bite of Aravane's incredible stewed chicken as Griffin poured two more glasses of burgundy. "The walk to the broom closet was the longest and the shortest of my life. It was all I could do not to race across the room and hold the door open for her. When we got inside, there wasn't much clearance, so Joanna kept banging her head against the low ceiling."

"What were you doing, trying every position in the *Kama Sutra*?"

"I wish. We started off with the usual two minutes of awkward conversation. I told her I was a big fan and I never missed a game. She said she'd spotted me sitting in the stands a time or two. Then, when I started to babble about her stats, she planted one on me. The next thing I knew, I was floating. Literally floating. She picked me up so she wouldn't have to bend over so far and my feet were dangling in mid-air. I wrapped my legs around her waist and hung on for dear life. Those remaining five minutes ended much too soon. I realized after thirty seconds that basketball was only her second-best sport."

"I almost hate to ask this, but what was her first?"

"Tonsil hockey."

Griffin groaned at the bad joke as she finished the rest of the delicious main course. "Like I said, I knew I was going to regret it. So what happened when you came out of the closet? Figuratively speaking."

"Joanna and I were together for three years, but we split up after graduation because we enrolled in different universities. She earned a scholarship to play college ball in the Midwest and I stayed at home to attend Columbia. She liked the area so much she never came back. I get a card from her every Christmas. She and her partner run a successful landscaping business. She seems happy."

Griffin reached across the table and laced her fingers through Rachel's. "What about you? Are you happy?"

Rachel looked down at their clasped hands. "I'm getting there."

Aravane brought out the mousse—just one serving so Griffin and Rachel could share—and two cups of chicory-infused coffee.

Griffin didn't want the coffee. She wanted to sweep the plates off the table, drape Rachel across it, and drink from her until she got her fill. She forced herself to be patient. When she had proposed their culinary journey, she had promised to woo Rachel with her mind, not her body.

"What about your first time?" she asked, trying not to turn herself into a liar before the end of the first leg. "Was it with Joanna, too?"

"Yes, but it didn't go nearly as well as our first kiss. Neither of us knew what we were doing, but we were determined to see our way through. Put it this way: the end was a lot better than the beginning."

"Does practice make perfect?"

"I wouldn't say perfect, but I would say my technique has improved since then."

Griffin dipped her dessert spoon into the mousse and offered it to Rachel. "You'll have to show me what you've learned."

"You first. And I'm not talking about chocolate."

"Neither am I." Griffin smiled as Rachel tasted the mousse. She sampled some for herself. The rich, creamy dessert slid across her tongue.

"Tell me something."

Rachel leaned in for more. Griffin slipped the spoon between her lips.

"Anything."

"Since you were bosom buddies with the cafeteria ladies, you must know what was in the mystery meat my school served every Wednesday."

"I could tell you, but I'd have to kill you. And I don't want to do that because I like having you around."

Chapter Nine

G ood evening, Fernando."
"Good evening, Miss Bauer. How was dinner?"
"The paella was excellent. Thank you for the recommendation."
"I'm glad you liked it." Fernando looked up from a Spanish-language magazine and arched an expressive eyebrow when he noticed Rachel wasn't alone. "Enjoy the rest of your evening." He watched as Rachel and Griffin headed to the elevator.

For their second date, Griffin took Rachel to Spain. Before they had finalized their plans, Rachel had asked Fernando if he knew any restaurants in town that offered authentic Spanish cuisine. He had enthusiastically told her about a neighborhood eatery he and Montserrat considered "a little slice of home." Griffin met her there and they spent a pleasant three hours stuffing themselves with gazpacho, paella, and a tart that featured the unlikely but surprisingly good combination of almonds and lemons.

Upstairs, Rachel unlocked her apartment and ushered Griffin inside. While Griffin checked out the living room, Rachel headed to the kitchen to grab some drinks.

"I like your place," Griffin said.

From the sound of her voice, she was standing near Rachel's collection of antique subway tokens. She had started amassing the tokens when she was five. She had never had the collection appraised, however, figuring the collection held more sentimental than monetary value. She grabbed two bottles of mineral water out of the refrigerator and joined Griffin in the living room. "Check out the view. It's amazing."

Griffin walked over to the oversized window. She peered out at the Empire State Building then lowered her sights to the scenic pier down the street. By day, it was an architectural marvel. At night, it was the perfect spot for a romantic stroll by the water. "I love that little park on the corner. The way the snow covers the lamp posts and the light shines softly through makes this seem more like a Currier and Ives painting than real life."

Rachel joined Griffin by the window. "You should come by when the weather's warmer. Bands give free concerts on the pier every weekend. We could pack a picnic lunch, sit on the grass, and listen to the music. Maybe we can convince the organizers to book a jazz band or two."

"Sounds like a plan to me."

They tapped their plastic bottles in a toast and took a sip of water to seal the deal.

"Let me show you around," Rachel said.

Her place was relatively small—foyer, bedroom, bathroom, and a combination living room/dining room that led to the kitchen—so the grand tour took less than five minutes.

In the living room, the sofa and loveseat were angled toward the entertainment center, where a DVD player, TV, CDs, and assorted DVDs shared space. Behind the loveseat was the desk that served as her home office. She had traded her desk chair for an exercise ball, which gave her a chance to work her body and her brain at the same time. The dining table was small but seated four comfortably. At least it was supposed to. She hadn't invited anyone over to test the salesman's theory. Perhaps that would soon change.

The walls in her bedroom, like the ones in the rest of the apartment, were unadorned. Marble-topped nightstands flanked the queen-sized bed. The lamp on her side of the bed was a flea market find that looked antique but probably wasn't. It looked cool and it worked. What more could she want? Oh, yeah. Someone to occupy the other side of the bed.

"What's this?"

Griffin picked up a four foot by six foot frame leaning against the mahogany dresser. A world map, the paper dotted with tiny pin holes, was affixed to the front of the frame.

"I bought that about four years ago to chart my world travels."

"Where did you go?"

"I never got past the planning stages. Work, either mine or Isabel's, always seemed to get in the way."

"We need to fix that. Do you have a hammer and nails?"

"Somewhere."

"Could you get them for me?"

Rachel located what Griffin needed in the storage closet in the kitchen. After she returned to the bedroom, she held the frame while Griffin took off her shoes and climbed on the bed. Griffin drove the nails into the wall with an ease that made Rachel think she had spent a serious amount of time working for her brother the general contractor.

"Push pins?" Griffin asked after she mounted the frame.

"Right here." Rachel reached into the nightstand and pulled out a box.

"We've been to France and Spain." Griffin stuck red pins in Paris and Madrid. "Morocco's next." She pressed a green pin into Casablanca. "Where do you want to go after that?"

"How about England?" Rachel joined Griffin on the bed. "We haven't been there yet."

"England it is." A green pin speared London. "After that, I'm thinking Germany." A yellow pin went there. "And we'll need at least two weeks for Italy—one for northern cuisine and one for southern." Two more yellow pins pricked the map.

"Then Greece?"

"You can't visit one ancient culture without wanting to see another."

"That's eight."

"Eight down and twenty-two to go."

"What happens when we get to the end?" Rachel asked, wondering if the end of their trip would also mark the end of Griffin's interest in her.

"When we get to the end, we'll start over again."

They charted their way around the world, pinpointing regions both large and small. Rachel looked at the map. From the looks of it, she was going to be in for the culinary adventure of a lifetime. And she wouldn't have to use up any of her Sky Miles to do it.

She opened the Day Planner Jane and Colleen bought her for Christmas. She penciled in Morocco for the following Sunday and England for the Sunday after that. Then she began to fill in the subsequent months.

"Where are we going in June?" Griffin asked.

Rachel consulted the map. "Hawaii, California, Texas, and Louisiana."

Griffin nodded purposefully. "I'll have to make those legs extra special."

Rachel filled in July with Georgia, North Carolina, Illinois, Vermont, and, finally, New York. "Why those in particular?"

Griffin shrugged. "Because I want to."

She took the Day Planner out of Rachel's hands and placed it on the nightstand. Rachel's heart thudded in her chest as Griffin gently lowered her onto the bed.

She had made a resolution of sorts to just be friends with Griffin. The new year had barely begun and she was already in danger of breaking that pledge.

Griffin's past—and even her present—made her leery of planning a future with her. Right now, though, she didn't care about the past or the future. This moment was all that mattered. This moment was everything.

Griffin swung her left leg over Rachel's body and straddled her hips. She placed her hands on either side of Rachel's head. Her dark purple shirt spread open and the top of her black lace bra peeked through. Rachel's eyes were glued to the sight. Griffin languorously unbuttoned another button, affording her an even better view.

Rachel's breath caught when she saw the rise of Griffin's firm breasts. She slid her hands up the back of Griffin's legs. Griffin lowered her hips. Rachel rose to meet her. The pressure felt oh so good, but she needed more. She cupped Griffin's ass in her hands and pulled her closer. She heard Griffin's sharp intake of breath when her mouth found the warm skin of her chest. Griffin's back arched as Rachel's tongue slid across her skin. Her hips flexed against Rachel's kneading hands. Rachel kissed the curve of one breast, then the other. Her lips brushed against the hollow of Griffin's throat.

"I want you," Griffin whispered, her voice as ragged as her breathing.

"Then take me."

Griffin covered Rachel's mouth with her own. Rachel groaned deep in her throat as Griffin's tongue met hers. Griffin gently kneaded her breasts. Her thumbs teased her nipples through the material of her blouse.

Rachel slipped one hand between their bodies, her fingers pulling at the clasp of Griffin's black leather belt. She wanted to slip inside Griffin's smooth folds and feel her muscles contract around her fingers. She wanted to watch her eyes darken, her skin mottle. She wanted to hear her keening cries of pleasure as her body tensed, flexed, and released.

She unbuckled Griffin's belt and began to unfasten her jeans. Then something pulsated against her leg.

"Is that a vibrator in your pocket or are you just happy to see me?"

Griffin's face reddened as she pulled away. "My phone's ringing." She fished her cell phone out of her pocket and looked at the caller ID. "Crap. I've got to take this. It's a reporter for *The New York Times Magazine*. He wants to interview me for an upcoming feature on female chefs." Sitting on the side of the bed, she pressed the phone to her ear and talked for a few minutes. Then she covered the receiver with her hand and turned back to Rachel. "I've got to go," she said apologetically.

"It's okay," Rachel said.

"Are you sure?"

"I'm positive." Rachel buckled Griffin's belt and smoothed her rumpled shirt. "Now go do your interview before I change my mind."

Griffin gave her a quick kiss. "Thanks, Puddles. I'll make it up to you. I promise."

Rachel waved her away with a smile. "I'll see you next week."

Next week meant Morocco. Griffin had promised her belly dancers, couscous, and a DVD of *Casablanca*. Rachel didn't know what she was looking forward to most.

CHAPTER TEN

Griffin normally viewed publicity as a necessary evil, but she was giddy after she finished her latest round. She felt like she was breathing rarefied air. During the course of the two-hour question and answer session, the *Times* reporter had revealed the identities of the four other chefs who would be featured in the article. She admired all four. Two, in fact, were on her short list of culinary heroes. It blew her away to think she may have finally become their equal.

The only downside was Rachel. She felt awful about leaving Rachel so abruptly when they had been about to make love for the first time. Rachel had said she was okay with her leaving, but Griffin had her doubts.

She thought about the cautious looks Rachel gave her every now and then, usually after Aggie's name was mentioned. The looks said she was taking Griffin's interest in her with a grain of salt. It was almost as if she was waiting for Griffin to get bored and decide to move on. Griffin didn't want to kiss and tell, but she found simply having a conversation with Rachel infinitely more enjoyable than the forty-five minutes of frenetic groping she'd spent with Aggie. And when they did more than talk, their chemistry was so powerful Griffin wished she could bottle it and sell it. She'd be a multimillionaire in no time flat.

When she got back to her apartment, she gave Rachel a call so they could pick up where they'd left off.

"Are you in bed?" she asked as she sifted through her CD collection.

"Yes."

"What are you wearing?"

"My birthday suit," Rachel said with an amused chuckle that indicated she was probably joking.

Griffin, on the other hand, was dead serious.

"Happy birthday to me." As she turned on the sound system, she pictured Rachel lying on her side, her curvaceous body moving lazily under the covers. "Are your sheets flannel or silk?"

"I'm an accountant. What do you think?"

"Whatever they are, throw them off."

"It's the middle of winter. What do you want me to do, freeze my ass off?"

"If you close your eyes, you can feel me lying beside you." Griffin closed her own eyes as Melody Gardot's seductive voice wafted through the air. "You can feel me keeping you warm. I'm right behind you, Rachel. My arm is around your waist. My breasts are on your back. My leg is between yours. Can you feel me?"

"What are you doing?" Rachel asked quizzically.

"What I promised to do." Griffin kicked off her shoes and headed to her bedroom. "Wooing you with my mind, not my body. I'm going to make you come without even laying a hand on you." She undressed and crawled into bed. "Are you ready?"

Rachel took a moment to answer. When she finally spoke, her voice was several octaves lower. "Yes."

"Then throw the covers off."

Griffin heard the rustle of sheets through the phone.

"Okay," Rachel said, a hint of excitement creeping into her voice. "Now what?"

Griffin slowly trailed a hand across her stomach. "Now we get to have some fun."

"How much fun?"

"As much as you want." She stopped stimulating herself so she could concentrate on stimulating Rachel. "This is your symphony. I'm simply the conductor. Where are my hands?"

"On my breasts."

"Like they were earlier?"

"Yes."

"Like they are now?"

"Yes."

"I'm cupping your breasts in my hands and rolling your nipples between my fingers." Griffin could tell by Rachel's breathing that she was mimicking the act she had just described. "How does it feel?"

"Incredible."

"Do you want more pressure or less?"

"More."

"Do you want me to pinch your nipples?"

"Yes."

"Do you want me to lick them?"

Rachel gasped and said, "God, yes."

"Your nipples are so hard they could cut glass, Rachel. Can you feel my tongue on them?"

"Yes."

"Can you—"

"Wait," Rachel said in an urgent whisper. "I want to touch you, too."

"Not yet. Let me please you first."

"I want to taste you, Griffin."

Just the thought of feeling Rachel's tongue on her was nearly enough to get Griffin off. "You will. Until then, tell me where you want me."

"Inside me."

"One finger or two?"

"Two."

"Take my hand. Guide me in," Griffin said, wanting Rachel to tell her what she was doing so she could add it to the collection of images in her mind.

"I've got you. Do you feel my fingers curled around your wrist, leading you past my stomach, over my mound, and between my legs?"

"Yes. Can you feel my fingers on your clit?"

"Yes," Rachel hissed.

"Can you feel me stroking you?"

"Oh, yes."

"Can you feel my fingers inside you?"

"Yes. Fuck, Griffin, I'm so close."

"Then come for me."

Griffin listened to Rachel's moans increase in intensity and volume. She imagined her with her head thrown back and her mouth open wide in a silent scream of ecstasy. She imagined Rachel's fingers moving in and out, her hand pistoning faster and faster as she crept closer and closer to the edge.

"Griffin?" Rachel asked, her voice reaching out to her in the darkness.

"I'm still here, Rachel. Come for me."

Griffin heard her cry out as she went over the side. And she was there to catch her when she fell. Then Rachel did the same for her.

Afterward, Rachel was quiet for so long Griffin thought she had fallen asleep. Finally, Rachel gave voice to the desire that was running through her mind as well.

"I want to do that again."

"We will."

"When?"

Griffin smiled, enjoying the give and take. Why couldn't the later stages of a relationship be like the early ones? "How does next Sunday sound?"

"Like it can't come soon enough."

❖

At work the next day, Rachel couldn't stop smiling. Even the deadly dull weekly staff meeting hadn't been able to temper her excitement. When was the last time she had been this happy? Had she ever been this happy? She doubted it. As she waited for her English muffin to brown in the toaster oven, she found herself whistling the song that had been playing in the background when Griffin called her last night. She still couldn't believe what had happened. Even now, it seemed more fantasy than reality.

"You got some last night, didn't you?"

Rachel nearly jumped out of her skin.

"Etta! I'd expect a question like that from Mike, but not from you."

She placed her English muffin on a paper plate, squirted a thin line of honey on each half, then grabbed a bottle of orange juice and headed to her desk.

Stirring cream into her coffee with a swizzle stick, Etta followed Rachel out of the break room. "I've been married long enough to be able to ask anybody anything. Now did you get some or not?"

"Not."

"Trust me," Etta said, continuing to press for details. "I know when someone is getting done right. And you, girlfriend, are keeping the neighbors up at night."

Rachel spun around in her desk chair. "I feel like I'm in *Invasion of the Body Snatchers*. Who are you and what have you done with my friend?"

Etta started to say something else, but the Bluetooth in her ear beeped before she could. She spoke into the receiver then ended the call. "Saved by the bell. Your ten o'clock is here."

Rachel wolfed down her mid-morning snack, washed it down with the orange juice, and prepared to meet with her client. A musician whose performances were held not at Carnegie Hall or Madison Square Garden but on subway platforms throughout the city, he had recently received a notice from the I.R.S. that he was being audited.

Accountants hated audits as much as their clients did. It meant their work was being called into question. Rachel had reviewed the flagged return that morning and she felt confident there were no addition or filing errors. The issue as she saw it was the fact that, though her client earned just north of thirty thousand dollars a year, he lived in a seven-figure apartment on Central Park West. His father paid his rent and most of his bills, though he didn't want those facts advertised or reported.

While Junior was out busking, Senior used the apartment to entertain his mistress(es). Junior lived there rent free in exchange for keeping Dad's trysts a secret from Mom. Dear old Dad was going to have to come clean unless he wanted to spend the next three to five years talking to his son through a Plexiglass window.

As Rachel headed to the conference room, though, her client meeting was the last thing on her mind. She was wondering what Etta would say if she knew how close she had come to the truth. And she was counting the minutes until she saw Griffin on Sunday.

She smiled to herself. Why wait when a phone call was just as good?

CHAPTER ELEVEN

G riffin was ready for their next adventure. Their previous outing had been heartwarming. She had invited Rachel's mother—a hoot if there ever was one—to tag along with her and Rachel as they spent the afternoon of Rachel's birthday filling up on pub grub at Cock of the Walk, the restaurant local British ex-pats swore was just as good as if not better than the pubs back home. After lunch, they had watched Helen Mirren light up Broadway in a matinee performance of *The Tempest*. Rachel's mother had called it a day after that, leaving Griffin and Rachel free to wander the streets of Times Square, the once-gritty area that had been given a Disney-style makeover to become New York's latest family-friendly tourist attraction. Griffin liked some of the improvements, but she missed the good old days when the city had more of an edge.

What would today bring?

She and Rachel got off the train in Yorkville, the Upper East Side burg that had also been tamed into submission.

"At one time," Rachel said, sounding like a tour guide, "this area was a middle- to working-class neighborhood occupied by people with Hungarian, Czech, Slovak, Polish, German, and Irish backgrounds. A few of the longtime residents still live here, but most of the businesses they owned have disappeared. Only a few holdouts remain."

Turning onto Second Avenue, they headed for one of them.

The Heidelberg Restaurant billed itself as Manhattan's favorite beer garden. When she and Rachel walked through the door, Griffin saw smiling waitresses in traditional German outfits carrying trays laden with glass boots filled with beer. Red-and-white checked cloths covered the tables. Most of the patrons' eyes were focused on the soccer match playing on the tiny TV in a corner.

Griffin and Rachel grabbed two empty seats and examined the brunch menu.

"What are you going to order?" Griffin asked, eyeing the farmer's breakfast—home fries, bacon, eggs, and onion. Then again, the potato pancake with smoked salmon, sour cream, and capers looked good, too.

"The camembert with toasted almonds and fresh fruit."

"Is that going to be enough? We're going to be walking all afternoon. You need the calories."

"I'm going to be with you, remember? You know the location of every food truck in New York City. If I get hungry, I'm sure you'll point me in the right direction. You haven't steered me wrong yet," Rachel added with a wink.

"May I bring you something to drink?" the waitress asked.

Griffin ordered two glasses of Liebfraumilch. "It's a sweet dessert wine that will serve as a perfect complement to the fruit and cheese in your entrée," she explained after the waitress took their drink order to the bar and their food order to the kitchen.

Rachel chuckled. "I'm doing wine and cheese pairings now? I've been hanging around you too long. I take that back. I haven't been hanging around you long enough. I wish we could do this more often. I look forward to our Sunday get-togethers, but there are six other days in the week."

Griffin spread her napkin in her lap. She hoped Rachel wasn't about to press her to change their arrangement. Their relationship was like Classic Coke—perfect the way it was. Why tinker with the recipe?

The time they spent apart allowed her to focus on work and whetted her appetite for their Sunday adventures. If they saw each other more frequently, she feared their relationship might lose some of its spark. After all, it had happened to her before.

If Rachel pressed her to spend more time together, Griffin might bend, but she wouldn't break. Not on this issue. Absence made the heart grow fonder. In her case, proximity made it run cold.

She and Rachel were more than friends but not quite lovers. She was in no rush to change the definition of their relationship. But would spending more time with Rachel really be so bad? Rachel was asking to see her more than once a week. It wasn't like she was planning on moving in. Was she?

"I'll see how my schedule looks. Maybe I can take some time off."

Rachel beamed. "That would be great. Memorial Day's coming up soon. We could use the long weekend to go to the beach."

"Awesome. It's been way too long since I've felt sand between my toes."

"Memorial Day will be here before you know it. If we're serious about going somewhere, we need to make reservations now. Where would you like to go?"

Griffin actually found herself looking forward to the trip. She had to leave for *Cream of the Crop* on June 1. A mini-break beforehand might be just the thing she needed to get her head on straight for the competition.

"I don't care where we go as long as there's a large body of water nearby. Surprise me."

"Okay," Rachel said with a broad smile. "I will."

After they finished their meal, Griffin paid the bill and they headed outside. She checked the settings on her digital camera while Rachel unfolded the map. Red lines indicated several paths they could follow.

"Which way?" Rachel asked.

"You decide."

Rachel selected a route that led them from Second Avenue to Central Park. Griffin captured dozens of intriguing images along the way. They wandered through Strawberry Fields, into and out of Belvedere Castle. They stopped next to several iced-over ponds to capture hockey players crashing into each other, figure skaters twirling as fast as spinning tops.

Griffin didn't think any of her photos came close to rivaling her mother's in terms of artistry or composition, but she couldn't wait to load them into her computer and take a closer look. To relive the day.

"This was great," Rachel said as they rode the subway to her apartment.

Griffin tightened her grip on a worn leather strap as the crowded train car rattled over the tracks. She'd let Rachel have the last remaining seat. "You started out sounding like a tour guide and ended up acting like a tourist."

"I felt like one. I saw some things today I haven't seen in years and others I've never seen before. I feel like I should thank you for introducing me to the city I've called home for fifteen years."

"Thank me later. I have a few more cities to introduce you to before we're done."

CHAPTER TWELVE

The following Sunday, Rachel linked her arm through Griffin's as they walked to Battery Park. The twenty-five acre area on the southern tip of Manhattan normally teemed with tourists. The cold weather was keeping most of them at bay, though a few diehards braved the wintry conditions to line up to buy tickets for the ferry to the Statue of Liberty and Ellis Island. Thankfully, their tickets had been pre-purchased.

They boarded the boat and went inside to escape the bitter wind. After they bought cups of hot tea from a food vendor, they searched for seats with an unobstructed view. The view was spectacular, but the ride was rough thanks to the choppy water. Rachel couldn't wait to get to dry land. When the ferry docked at Ellis Island, she and Griffin left the tour guides behind and carved out their own path.

"Before we continue forward, I thought this would be an opportune time to reflect on the past," Griffin said as they stood next to the Wall of Honor.

Rachel looked at the monument bearing the names of more than seven thousand people who had left their former lives behind to immigrate to America.

"I did some research," Griffin said. "Did you know our great-grandmothers came to America on the same ship? They were both processed at Ellis Island on July 4, 1908. Your great-grandmother Agnieska settled in New York while my great-grandma Saoirse continued across the country to California. Call me romantic, but

I like to think they shared a laugh or two before they went their separate ways."

Rachel found Saoirse O'Malley's name first, followed by her own ancestor's. She imagined the two women protecting themselves from the elements with lace parasols as they walked arm in arm on the deck of a vast ship much the same way she and Griffin were walking today.

The woman her mother referred to as Grandma Agnes died long before Rachel was born, but she had seen photographs of her in family albums—sometimes smiling, usually serious, her thick brown hair piled on top of her head in the voluminous bun considered fashionable in the late nineteenth and early twentieth centuries. She was one of the group of women history referred to as Iron Jawed Angels, activists who fought for women's right to vote and sought to be seen as equals both at home and in the workplace.

Rachel ran her fingers over the black letters of Grandma Agnes's name. "Thank you for everything you did to make life better for women everywhere. Thank you for your courage and your indomitable spirit. I can't even begin to imagine the hardships you faced as a woman alone in a foreign country."

She turned to Griffin.

"Until I met you, I felt like a woman alone, too, though not by choice. When my last relationship ended, I thought my last real shot at happiness ended with it. Then I met you. I didn't know what to make of you at first. I didn't want to take a chance on you—I didn't want to trust you, but I'm glad I did."

She examined Griffin's eyes to see if her words held as much meaning for Griffin as they did for her. Griffin's eyes searched hers just as thoroughly.

"You said you wanted to get to know me," Rachel said. "To peel my defenses away one layer at a time until you found what lay beneath. In the process, you've revealed yourself to me as well. I like what I see—an intelligent, creative woman with boundless enthusiasm and a heart as big as the great outdoors."

Griffin's hand in hers felt not like the lifeline she'd thought she needed but a bridge. She no longer felt like she was floundering. She felt like she was moving on. With Griffin.

"I love spending time with you," she said. "I love being with you. I don't want this journey we're on to ever end."

"Do you have plans for dinner tonight?"

"No."

"You do now." Griffin steered her toward the docked ferry. "Give me a few hours to get everything set up, then come to my apartment. Call me when you get to the lobby."

"Why?"

"I'd tell you, but it would ruin the surprise."

Griffin wrapped her arms around Rachel's shoulders. Rachel leaned against her, enjoying the feel of her body. Solid. Strong. Dependable.

"A good surprise or a bad surprise?"

Griffin chuckled. "I'll let you decide."

❖

When she reached the lobby of Griffin's apartment building, Rachel pulled out her cell phone and called upstairs as directed.

"I'm here."

"Come right up. Dinner's ready."

She rode the elevator to the top floor and stepped out as soon as the doors opened wide enough to allow her passage. When she passed Tucker in the hallway, he tossed her a key to Griffin's apartment.

"You can let yourself in."

"Aren't you staying?"

"I wasn't invited," he said with a strange little smile. The kind of smile that said he knew a secret she didn't.

What was he up to? Or, more likely, what was his boss up to? She'd worry about that later. First things first.

"Can I talk to you for a second?"

"Sure. What's up?"

"Griffin and I want to take a trip for Memorial Day. She doesn't want to know any of the details, so that means I have to do all the planning myself. I want the trip to be unforgettable. I could use your help. You know Griffin's schedule better than I do."

"I know her schedule better than *she* does."

"Exactly. I already have something in mind. It might be expensive, but if it works out, it would be worth every penny. Do you think I could run my idea by you and perhaps get your help making reservations?"

"Not a problem." He reached into his messenger bag and pulled out a business card. "Call me tomorrow. I'll be happy to help in any way I can. In the meantime, enjoy your meal."

She slipped the key into the lock and opened the door. Diana Krall was crooning seductively on the sound system, but Griffin wasn't around to enjoy it. Rachel headed to the kitchen but still no Griffin. Where was she?

Rachel returned to the living room.

"Griffin, it's me." She didn't receive a response, but a note on the coffee table caught her eye.

Waiting for you in the bedroom, the note read. *Hope you brought your appetite.*

She followed a trail of orchids to the bedroom, pausing only once to take a sip of the chilled plum wine Griffin had poured for her.

A string of paper lanterns circled the bed, bathing the room in a yellowish-orange glow. For dinner, Griffin had laid out a variety of sushi rolls on the most beautiful buffet table Rachel had ever seen: her body.

Pieces of Philadelphia roll atop a "plate" of woven bamboo leaves were precariously perched on her breasts. An orderly line of cucumber rolls marched down her rippled stomach, pointing the way to the California roll that formed a semicircle on her pubis. Or was that semicircle really a smile?

"I thought we could visit Japan a few weeks early." Griffin's voice sounded like it did the night they had phone sex. The way it always sounded when she was filled with desire. Desire for her. "Hungry?"

Unable to speak, Rachel nodded mutely.

"Then why don't you get out of those clothes and slip into something more comfortable?" She indicated the silk kimono draped across the foot of the bed.

Rachel downed the rest of the wine like she was drinking a shot of whiskey and hurriedly exchanged her Dockers and long-sleeved polo shirt for the kimono. Goose bumps formed when the luxurious material slid across her skin. Or was her condition the result of the sumptuous feast that lay before her?

Griffin extended her arm, offering Rachel a pair of ornately carved jade chopsticks. "Enjoy."

Rachel took the chopsticks and slowly lowered herself onto the bed, being careful not to send any of the sushi rolls skittering across the sheets. She captured a piece of Philadelphia roll with the chopsticks, then tossed the plate aside and lowered the sushi until a firm nipple imbedded itself in the cream cheese.

Griffin hissed when the cold cream cheese touched her skin. Rachel curled her tongue around Griffin's nipple and licked it clean. Then she popped the roll into her mouth and slowly chewed, making Griffin wait as long as possible before she repeated the process with the other piece.

"So much for the appetizer."

She dragged the opposite ends of the chopsticks across Griffin's skin, gently sliding down the valley between her breasts until she reached the cucumber roll. She took the first piece for her and gave Griffin the second. She was going to need fortification to withstand all the things Rachel had in mind for her.

After she finished the last piece of cucumber roll, Rachel bent to retrieve the slice of palate-cleansing pickled ginger draped across Griffin's stomach. With her tongue, she slowly circled Griffin's navel, then gently probed its depths.

Griffin gasped, her fingers raking through Rachel's hair. "God, Rachel, do you have any idea what you do to me?" she asked in an urgent whisper.

Rachel reached down and rubbed her free hand between Griffin's slick folds, coating her fingers in the evidence of her arousal. "The same thing you do to me?"

On the sound system, Diana Krall's smooth jazz piano gave way to a driving blues guitar. A woman's rich, earthy voice joined the instrument in a sensuous game of call-and-response, evoking images in Rachel's mind of sweaty bodies grinding against each other on the darkened dance floor of a long-ago Delta nightclub. She felt the sinuous rhythm wrap around her. Guide her. Propel her forward.

Griffin's back arched as Rachel rubbed her thumb across her swollen clit. She bit her lip to keep from crying out. "Eat faster," she urged her through gritted teeth.

At a loss for a snappy comeback, Rachel did as she was told, inhaling the three pieces of California roll in what felt like record time.

"Come here."

Griffin untied the sash, spread the kimono open, and pulled Rachel to her. Rachel covered Griffin's body with hers. The kimono covered them both, the cool silk smoothly gliding across their overheated skin.

Griffin ground against Rachel's thigh. Rachel could tell by Griffin's insistent thrusts she was already dangerously close to the edge. The thought caused a flash flood between her legs.

"What do you want?" she asked as she painted Griffin's body with kisses. "How do you want me to take you?"

"I want to taste you while you make me come."

Her words—and the sexy rasp in her voice—made Rachel even wetter.

Rachel shrugged off the robe and changed positions, burying her face in Griffin's warm, wet center while Griffin lifted her head to drink from her.

Beyond words, beyond manners, beyond everything but desire, Rachel licked and sucked until her face was covered with nectar.

Griffin came first, her body shuddering so violently she nearly bucked Rachel off her. Her ecstatic moans vibrated against Rachel's clit, sending her hurtling to her own earth-shattering orgasm.

Rachel rolled off and collapsed on the bed, her chest heaving, her body coated in a fine sheen of sweat.

Griffin lay next to her and wrapped her long limbs around her. "I think I like Japan," she whispered. "Can we go there every week?"

"Yes, please."

Griffin rolled Rachel onto her back. "My turn."

She slid her palms over Rachel's nipples, garnering their immediate attention. Rachel groaned when Griffin's lips replaced her hands. She groaned even louder when Griffin took her nipple into her mouth, grazing the sensitive tissue with her teeth. She laved Rachel's breasts with her tongue then pulled away.

"What's wrong?"

"Nothing. I just want to look at you."

Her eyes roamed across Rachel's body. Up her legs, past her curvy hips, over her slightly rounded belly. They lingered on Rachel's breasts before coming to rest on her face.

"You're beautiful," she whispered.

This time, Rachel didn't argue with her. She hooked her arms around Griffin's neck and drew her to her. Their breasts touched then flattened as their bodies pressed against each other.

Rachel drew Griffin's lower lip into her mouth and gently sucked. Griffin gasped as Rachel worshiped her mouth with her tongue.

Griffin's hand slipped between their bodies and slid down Rachel's stomach. Her searching fingers found Rachel's clit. Rachel bucked against her hand. Then her hips began to move in slow circles, matching the movement of Griffin's fingers as they teased her to greater and greater heights. Griffin massaged her clit until Rachel begged for release. "Now. Please take me now."

She slipped two fingers inside. Rachel's howls of pleasure were music to her ears.

"Stop," Rachel rasped after Griffin took her over the edge the third time. Or was it the fourth?

Griffin grinned. "Had enough?"

"Not even close." Rachel kissed her long and hard. "I'm just getting started."

"If I'm going to have enough energy for the next round, I must have food."

Griffin gave her a quick kiss, then changed her mind and returned for a lingering one. She slid her leg between Rachel's as her fingers sank into the small of Rachel's back. She felt Rachel opening up to her, beckoning her body to meld with hers. Again. She groaned in displeasure when Rachel broke the kiss.

"If you don't get out of here," Rachel said, giving her a slap on the ass, "the only thing you're going to eat is me."

Griffin licked her lips. "Sounds good to me." She kissed Rachel on the tip of her nose. "Be right back."

She loosely wrapped the kimono around her and padded to the kitchen. She returned a few minutes later and carefully placed a loaded food tray on the bed. The bottle of Bollinger Rachel had bought for New Year's Eve rested in the center of the tray. Next to it were two champagne flutes, a bowl of fresh fruit, and a plate filled with several pieces of toasted wheat bread topped with salted slices of avocado. She placed a strawberry in the bottom of each flute and slowly filled the glasses with champagne.

"To us." She gently touched her glass to Rachel's.

"To us."

Griffin closed her eyes as the champagne slid down her throat. It was the best thing she had ever tasted. Second best. She could smell Rachel on her fingers. Taste her on her tongue. *Talk about nectar of the gods.*

"Was it worth the wait?" Rachel asked after Griffin lowered her glass.

"The champagne or making love with you?" She laughed when her question made Rachel blush. "I'd have to say both were definitely worth the weeks of anticipation."

She took Rachel's empty glass and set the equally empty food tray on the floor. Then she laid Rachel down on the tangled sheets.

"Ready for the next round?"

Rachel opened her legs as Griffin positioned herself in between. "I thought you'd never ask."

CHAPTER THIRTEEN

I knew you were getting some." Etta pulled Rachel's collar aside to get a better look at the hickey on the side of her neck. "And I don't even have to ask if it's good. I can tell by the look on your face that it is. You go, girl."

Jane echoed Etta's sentiments after she and Rachel finished their yoga class. Rachel hadn't mastered the practice, but she had progressed enough that she no longer needed one-on-one attention. And the increased flexibility certainly came in handy.

"You don't have to thank me," Jane said, "but keep in mind I was the one who brought you crazy kids together."

"I'll be sure to put an extra lump of coal in your Christmas stocking this year. How's Colleen?"

Jane grimaced as if Rachel had touched a raw nerve.

"She's cranky and hormonal. The least little thing happens and she bites my head off. If I bite back, she bursts into tears. I end up feeling like the bad guy either way. If the next six months are anything like the first three, I'm going to have a nervous breakdown."

"It will all be worth it in the end. Have you picked out names yet?"

"If we have a boy, we're going to name him Steven. Steven Lambert-Mangano."

"And if you have a girl?"

"McKenzie. McKenzie Ryan." Jane lapsed into uncharacteristic giggles. "I'm in love with her already and I haven't even met her yet. Right now she—or he—is just a tiny speck on an ultrasound."

Rachel ruffled Jane's spiky hair, which was still wet from the shower. "You and Colleen are going to make such great moms. And your taste in godmothers is excellent."

Jane squeezed styling gel into her palm and worked it into her hair. "Do you think I should dye these?" She indicate the patches of gray on her temples. "Colleen thinks they make me look wiser. I think they make me look older. What do you think?"

"Stay away from the shoe polish. You look great."

"I know," Jane said with a wink. "I just wanted to hear you say it." She quickly ran a comb through her hair and pronounced herself ready to leave. "You should come over this weekend. You and your new girlfriend."

"She's not my girlfriend."

"Then what is she?"

Rachel didn't rightly know. A girlfriend was someone with whom you shared a trip to the movies or the occasional candlelit dinner. A girlfriend was temporary, not permanent. She wanted Griffin to be permanent. What Griffin wanted, however, was still up for debate.

"She's my tour guide."

They had traveled through Italy, Greece, Egypt, and Russia before spending three weeks visiting the various provinces of China. On their most recent date, Griffin had formally introduced her to black chicken. The experience was not one she cared to repeat. Griffin had warned her about the meat's wild flavor, but she wasn't prepared for the intensity of the gaminess. Eating it was like munching on roadkill.

Note to self: if someone refers to a dish as a delicacy, avoid it like the plague.

As March prepared to give way to April, Thailand loomed. Rachel hoped the trip would offer a return to more recognizable fare. Namely pad thai and chicken satay.

"You didn't answer my question about getting together this weekend. After your date, of course. I know nothing's allowed to get in the way of your world tour. What's on tap this week?"

"This Sunday, we're going to grab lunch in SoHo and spend the afternoon going to open houses." When Jane arched an eyebrow, Rachel anticipated her question. "Before you ask, no, we're not considering moving in together. I told her one of my favorite childhood memories was going to open houses with my parents and seeing how the other half lived. On Sunday, we're going to re-create the experience by touring some of the multimillion dollar apartments in Manhattan everyone dreams of having but only the very rich can afford."

"Don't agents make sure people pre-qualify for those apartments so they can keep lookie-loos like you and me away from the free *hors d'oeuvres?*"

"Yes."

"I've seen your investment portfolio. Unless you're sitting on a secret stash I don't know about, you sure as hell don't qualify. And if Griffin's raking in that much money, I might have to change my line of work."

"After you learn to cook."

"Minor obstacle. If you still have time for the little people, drop by when you're done. You can rub Colleen's baby bump."

Jane's excitement was contagious. Like her, Rachel was already in love with the little whippersnapper, too. If she was lucky, maybe she'd give little McKenzie or Steven a playmate one day.

❖

The apartments they toured varied widely in terms of design and presentation. There was the three-story industrial chic apartment on Fifth Avenue with the heated indoor pool and glass-walled sunroom. The overdone studio in SoHo that sported so much chintz it looked like it belonged to a seventeenth century French courtesan instead of a thoroughly modern psychologist and his socialite wife. And finally, the two-story loft in Tribeca with gorgeous exposed brick interior walls and a gallery-worthy art collection.

Griffin admired an original Georgia O'Keeffe. The work, one of the artist's infamous flower paintings, oozed sensuality. "I don't think the paintings come with the apartment, do you?"

"I doubt it," Rachel said, "but you could ask."

Griffin turned away from the painting and surveyed the loft. "Don't you love this place?"

"Yes, I do, but I hate the price tag. Seven million dollars is too rich for my blood. I can't imagine having a monthly rent payment that's nearly as much as my annual salary."

"You and me both."

Rachel's phone rang. Griffin thought she saw Tucker's number on the caller ID. "Ooh, I've been waiting for this call all day. Would you excuse me for a second?"

Rachel found a quiet corner to conduct her conversation. Griffin left her to it. If Rachel had enlisted Tucker's help, their trip to the beach was taking on a life of its own. Besides, the interruption gave her a chance to make another circuit of the loft. Unless the owners hired her to cater a meal, she didn't expect to see the place in person again. She wanted to enjoy her stay as long as she could. She headed downstairs to take another look at the gorgeous art.

Dozens of agents and prospective buyers wandered through the impressive space, some redecorating as they went.

"Our china cabinet would look fabulous against that wall," one couple said.

"Love the brick walls, but these hardwood floors have to go," another added.

The vintage red oak flooring was one of Griffin's favorite features. It would be a shame to see it go. *I guess there's no accounting for taste.*

"This is a lovely apartment, don't you agree?" someone asked.

Griffin turned to face a woman with green eyes and flowing chestnut hair. She was wearing black pants and a form-fitting black sweater. Her accessories—Gucci loafers, Prada belt, and Fendi glasses—would have earned Tucker's seal of approval.

"It's an amazing space."

"Are you thinking of making an offer?"

Griffin grabbed a complimentary glass of white wine off a passing waiter's tray. "Unfortunately, it's a bit out of my price range."

"Mine, too, but my partner loves it. I might have to resort to eating bag lunches for the foreseeable future, but I have to give her what she wants."

"Is she here?"

"She's in the little girls' room." The woman dropped her voice to a conspiratorial whisper. "She's eight months along, so the bathroom is practically her home away from home."

"Understood." Griffin raised her glass. "Congratulations, by the way."

"Thank you." The woman tapped a well-manicured nail against her lips. "You look awfully familiar. Have we met?"

"Perhaps you've eaten in my restaurant. I'm the head chef at Match."

The woman gasped. "You're Griffin Sutton? *The* Griffin Sutton? I can't believe it. My partner and I have read all the articles about you, but we're on your restaurant's notorious waiting list. Ah, there she is now." A woman who was obviously expecting slowly made her way toward them. "Honey, this is Griffin Sutton."

The second woman's eyes widened in disbelief. "Christine Schultz," she said as she pumped Griffin's hand. "It's an honor to meet you. I'm glad Isa and I ran into you here because it'll be months before we have the pleasure of experiencing your food."

"I'll talk to the bookers and see what I can do." Griffin turned to the first woman. "I'm afraid I didn't get your name."

"It's Isabel. Isabel Fischer." She shook Griffin's hand before protectively resting hers in the small of Christine's back.

Griffin wondered how many Isabel Fischers there were in New York. Dozens? Hundreds? She only needed two. That would guarantee this Isabel Fischer wasn't the one whose mistakes she had been warned not to repeat.

"This might seem like an unusual question, but do you know—"

"Rachel?" Isabel's voice rose in disbelief.

Griffin turned to follow Isabel's line of sight. Rachel stood at the top of the stairs. Her face was as white as the knuckles of the hands with which she gripped the stainless steel railings. Her wide eyes were focused on Christine's stomach.

Rachel couldn't believe what she was seeing. Isabel and Christine. Here. Together. Deliriously happy. And with a baby on the way.

How could this be? Isabel had been adamantly opposed to starting a family. She had said over and over again she didn't want kids. Like so many other things Isabel had told her, that was a lie. Isabel obviously wanted children. Just not with her.

Rachel flinched when an old wound she thought had finally begun to heal ripped open. Her knees nearly buckled after the pain set in.

"Rachel." Isabel stepped toward her. "We need to talk."

Rachel wanted to run. She wanted to curl up on her couch and stay there for the next month. But she couldn't run from this. Not again.

"I know just the place."

CHAPTER FOURTEEN

The instant she walked into one of her old haunts, Rachel was assaulted by the smell of cold grease and hot coffee. Or was it the other way around? She'd had it both ways. Neither was especially memorable. Determined not to take any chances this time, she planned on ordering tea.

Isabel headed straight for their old table. The booth in the back by the window. It was cozy, comfortable, and all theirs. At least it used to be for a few hours every Sunday morning while they read the paper and stuffed themselves with thick slices of bacon and fluffy Belgian waffles drowning in butter and maple syrup while the other diners nursed hangovers from the night before or had a quick bite to eat before they made their way to church.

The diner was a short walk from their old apartment. The one Isabel and Christine currently shared. Rachel and Isabel had passed the building on their way to the restaurant. When she had spotted it, Rachel hadn't felt any of the expected nostalgia. Instead, she felt curiously empty.

Isabel slid into her side of the booth and perched her glasses on the top of her head. She hadn't changed a bit in the many months since Rachel had seen her. In her black sweater, black pants, black boots, and cutting-edge designer eyewear, she was all New York chic.

The waiter took their drink orders. After he returned to the table, Rachel silently sipped her Earl Grey. The cab ride from Tribeca had been decidedly icy. Rachel had sat on one side of the backseat, Isabel on the other. A vast divide had yawned between them. Griffin and Christine had each headed home, allowing Rachel and Isabel all the time they needed to resolve the unanswered questions that lingered between them.

"Aren't you going to say something?" Isabel asked. "I know today must have come as a terrible shock to you."

"A shock? I feel like I've been blindsided."

"Chris has always wanted kids," Isabel added in a whisper.

"So have I. You were the one who didn't. At least, that's what you told me."

Isabel winced. "So I did." She stared into the depths of her coffee mug. "Why did I expect you to make this easy for me?"

Rachel's temper flared. "You mean like you did? With no warning and barely an explanation, you sat me down and told me you were walking out on an eight-year relationship. If you think that was easy for me, please allow me to correct your mistake. Don't beat around the bush, Isabel. Just tell me why. Why wasn't I enough for you? What did I do wrong?"

"You didn't trust me."

"With good reason, don't you think?"

"What went wrong in our relationship wasn't Christine's fault so let's leave her out of this. Even before I met her, you were constantly accusing me of being interested in other women. I got tired of dealing with your insecurity."

"Are you saying it's my fault you cheated on me? I didn't push you into Christine's arms. I didn't twist your arm and force you to sleep with her. You did it on your own and, by your own admission, you did it willingly."

Isabel slowly blew out a breath. "I didn't come here to assign blame, but I'll gladly take it if you want me to. Yes, I was wrong for what I did. I should have ended one relationship before I began another, but it doesn't change the fact that you and I weren't happy and hadn't been for a while."

"I offered to sign us up for couples therapy. You refused."

"Because seeing a professional wouldn't have done any good. We were broken and there wasn't anything a therapist could do or say to make it better. I did what you couldn't. I ended something that wasn't working. Yes, I went about it the wrong way, but it was the right thing to do."

Isabel's voice was gentle, but listening to her speak was like being subjected to the Chinese Water Torture. Each word brought increasing pain. But with the pain came clarity.

"We tried to make it work, but we weren't right for each other," she said more to herself than Isabel. "I have to stop holding on to what I think we could have been and accept what we were: two people who loved each other but weren't meant to be."

"Yes," Isabel said with the fervor of a Baptist preacher. "Put me in the past and embrace your future. It's time."

She reached across the table and squeezed Rachel's hand. Rachel returned the pressure. She had directed so much negative energy toward Isabel for the past year she had almost forgotten how to stop. But it was time she tried. She had to. For both their sakes.

"So you're having a baby."

Isabel flashed a grateful smile. "Actually, Christine's the one who's doing all the hard work." Her voice softened. "I know how much you wanted to be a mother, but having a baby wouldn't have solved our problems. It would have made them worse. I wasn't ready to be a parent when I was with you. I was too focused on my career. My only goal was reaching the corner office and staying there as long as I could. Once I got there, I realized the view wasn't any better than the one I already had. Now my priorities have changed."

"Why didn't you tell me any of this before?"

"It's a lot easier to analyze an issue after you remove emotion from the equation. Back then, the emotions were too raw to handle. We should have counted to ten instead of continuing to stand toe-to-toe. Each time you asked for something as simple as more time with me or as complex as having a child, I felt like a failure for not being able to give you what you wanted. All I wanted to do was retaliate instead of trying to figure out why I couldn't give you those things. I think I do a much better job of that now."

"I'm glad I managed to teach you something in eight years," Rachel said with a smile.

She had once planned on spending the rest of her life with Isabel, then she had hoped their paths would never cross. After a year of acrimony, they had finally managed to broker an uneasy truce.

"We were friends once," Isabel said. "I hope we can be again."

Rachel hoped the same. "You can start by inviting me to your baby shower."

CHAPTER FIFTEEN

May drove out the last of the winter weather. As the temperatures climbed, so did Griffin's stress level. She had to report to the set of *Cream of the Crop* in two weeks. The closer the date crept, the edgier she got. She rubbed her shoulders to ease the tension that had seeped into them. Her early-morning jog had done nothing to relieve her increasing discomfort. Last night, she had bitten Erica's head off for no reason. She owed her an apology. Her entire staff, for that matter. She had been a raging bitch for weeks—impatient, short-tempered, and overly critical. She reminded herself of the insecure amateur she used to be, not the self-assured professional she thought she had become.

Not knowing her competition was unnerving. What if the producers threw a five-star chef into the mix to shake things up? Did she think she could go head-to-head with Wolfgang Puck, Mary Sue Milliken, Thomas Keller, or Susan Feniger? In her dreams, maybe.

She was also nervous about how she would be portrayed on the show. Which type was she supposed to be, the hero, the heel, or the comic relief? She didn't feel like any of them.

Vacation couldn't come fast enough. She needed time away. Rachel did, too. Her workload had finally decreased now that the tax filing deadline had passed, but she spent so much time planning their trip to the beach it had almost become a second job. She was treating it more like a honeymoon than a simple road trip.

"It's way too soon for anyone to be getting down on bended knee."

Rachel was far more invested in their relationship than she was. She cared about Rachel, but she didn't have time to become fully vested in anyone or anything except her career.

After their vacation ended, her commitment to *Cream of the Crop* would begin. She still hadn't thought of a way to explain her upcoming absence. She thought she could concoct a plausible lie to explain her whereabouts, but she wished she didn't have to. Contract or not, why couldn't she tell Rachel the truth? If she wanted to earn Rachel's trust, she couldn't do it by lying to her. But what choice did she have?

She glanced at the clock, then pulled out the ingredients she needed for today's lunch date. Seasoned flank stank was simmering in the slow cooker. She busied herself chopping plantains and boiling black beans so she wouldn't have to think about the conversation she was putting off.

❖

Sitting in her home office, Rachel made a notation in her Day Planner as she waited for Griffin to arrive with lunch. She was trying not to look too far ahead. If she did, her work week would drag on endlessly, or something would go horribly wrong and she and Griffin would have to cancel their trip. But try as she might, she was already counting down the days.

She couldn't wait to see Griffin's face when she saw her family for the first time in months. She had already bought the plane tickets to Newport Beach. Now she needed Tucker to work his magic and find a rental property that wouldn't cost an arm and a leg. He had been looking for weeks with no luck. If he didn't find one soon, she and Griffin might have to stay in a hotel. At this point, Rachel was willing to settle for anything just so they'd have a place to lay their heads.

The inbox on her computer chimed, letting her know she had a new e-mail. She glanced at the screen. The message was from Tucker.

We're a go, the message read. *I rented a beach house for a song. It's located near The Wedge, a famous surfing spot at the end of Balboa Peninsula. The location might not mean much to you or me, but trust me when I say Griffin will love you for selecting it. A copy of the reservation is attached. The place is roomy enough to comfortably accommodate the twenty-five people expected for dinner next weekend. Twenty-six if you count me. And I WILL be there to pick up the Gucci loafers you owe me. Black. Size eleven.*

Meeting Griffin's family one at a time, let alone all at once, can be overwhelming so I've attached a cheat sheet to help you put faces to names. You'll also find fun facts about each of her nieces so you'll have something specific to say to each one. If you want to pass the girlfriend test they will undoubtedly subject you to, you need to do your homework.

Even though the logistics were a nightmare, this was a great idea, and I'm glad to do my part to help your plan come together. If you need anything else, please don't hesitate to give me a call or shoot me an e-mail. I won't even charge you next time. See you in sunny California. I'll be the one with the new pair of shoes.

She downloaded the five-page attachment and waited for the file to open. She looked at a photo of Griffin's parents first. She had already seen Griffin's mother, so she quickly moved on to her father.

Dr. William Sutton, tanned and handsome with a face that inspired trust, looked like a cross between Gary Cooper and Robert Redford. Griffin's brothers were all tall, blond, and male model gorgeous. Her nieces were beautiful, already heartbreakers or soon to turn into them. Their skin tones varied from gold to brown.

Duncan's wife was African-American and both their daughters had piercing gray-green eyes and gorgeous café au lait skin. Kieran—or was it Pearson?—was married to a woman from India; their three girls were a beautiful bronze. Logan and his partner were parents to a four-year-old girl they had adopted during a trip to China. And Pearson—or was it Ryan?—and his two girls seemed to have spent so much time in the sun they were baked a permanent brown.

She took a closer look at the photos of Griffin's brothers and their families, conveniently labeled with everyone's names. Underneath each picture was a list of the girls' hobbies and interests. The list was, predictably, wide-ranging. With the final exam on Saturday, she had less than a week to prepare. Failure was not an option.

When the doorbell rang, she stashed the photos in her desk and got up to answer the door. Griffin stood in the hallway rubbing her shoulders as if the weight of the world rested on them.

"You've been doing that a lot lately. Is there something on your mind?"

Griffin leaned over and picked up the picnic basket resting next to her foot. "Nothing four days of down time won't solve."

"Next weekend, you'll have all the time you want."

"But after that will be a different story."

"What do you mean?"

Griffin paused. "When we return from vacation, I'll be out of touch for a while. In fact, we'll be seeing even less of each other than we are now."

"I didn't think that was possible considering we see each other only one day a week as it is."

"I can't get out of it. It's a work thing."

"I guessed as much."

More and more, Griffin reminded her of Isabel. The *old* Isabel. The one who had been so focused on climbing the corporate ladder she didn't have time for anything else. Griffin's long work hours limited their time together. Her responsibilities to the restaurant, her employers, and her staff always came first.

Rachel felt disheartened. She wanted to be in a relationship with someone she could depend on. Someone who was present in every way. It became clearer a little more each day Griffin might not be that person. Like Isabel, Griffin's priorities could change one day. But what if they didn't? Did she want to spend months or maybe even years coming in second to someone else's career? Once was enough.

Griffin seemed to sense her uncertainty.

"We're not going to solve anything today, this week, or next. Let's have lunch, take some time off, and have a good time. In a few weeks, we'll sit down and talk and try to figure things out."

"All right," Rachel said.

Even though Griffin hadn't made a commitment to their future, at least she seemed open to the idea. Rachel's mood brightened. Though it may be incremental, they finally seemed to be making progress.

Outside, she enjoyed the feel of the sun on her skin as she and Griffin walked hand-in-hand to the small park down the street from her apartment. They found an empty spot and spread a large flannel blanket on the grass.

Griffin placed a picnic basket on a corner of the blanket. She cocked an ear toward the pier, where a five-piece band was playing a mixture of cover songs and original material.

"It's not Central Park, but it'll do in a pinch," Rachel said. She opened the wine while Griffin served lunch.

After a trip to Mexico, when Griffin's handmade tostadas and albondigas soup left Rachel shouting, "*Olé*," they had arrived in Cuba. The picnic basket was packed with shredded flank steak, black beans, yellow rice, and plantains. The meal looked heavy but was practically vegetarian in comparison to their protein-laden trip to Brazil when they had visited a churrascaria. The waiters had circled the dining area carrying huge skewers laden with steak, sausage, fish, or chicken and kept (re)filling their plates until they were forced to throw in the towel and say, "*No más*."

Rachel flipped through the pages of her organizer. "Next week marks our return to the States. Then it's two months of regional fare I actually recognize. But if you're not going to be here, I guess I'll be eating it by myself."

"You won't even know I'm gone."

"I doubt that."

She stared at the bright red circle around July 29. The day would mark their last official date. The end of the journey on which they had embarked in January. Fighting a wave of nostalgia, she closed the organizer and set it aside.

After they finished eating, Griffin lay on her back and pulled Rachel on top of her. "Tell me about our vacation."

"I thought you didn't want to know any of the details."

"It's a woman's prerogative to change her mind, and I've changed mine. I want to know what you've been working on so feverishly these past few weeks. Where are we going?"

"You'll find out when we get to the airport."

"The airport? We aren't driving?"

"Are you kidding? Traffic will be terrible. I'm staying as far away from the freeway as I can."

"So our destination is a plane flight instead of a car ride away. How will I know what to pack?"

Rachel laughed. "We're going to the beach. No matter which one we end up on, I think warm weather attire would be most appropriate."

"Will I need a passport?"

"Better to have it and not need it than need it and not have it."

Griffin snapped her fingers. "I know where we're going."

Rachel froze. Had Tucker spilled the beans? "Yeah, where?"

"Atlantic City for a little fun in the sun, a little gambling, and a lot of salt water taffy on the boardwalk."

Rachel began to breathe again. "That sounds like a wonderful way to spend a weekend, but it isn't how we'll be spending ours."

Griffin's smile grew broader. "I'm not going to stop trying until I figure this out."

"Good luck." Rachel rolled off Griffin, grabbed the picnic basket, and began to walk away.

"Where are you going?"

"Back to my apartment. It isn't the beach, but it's definitely clothing optional."

"Mind if I tag along?"

Rachel looked over her shoulder. "I was counting on it."

Griffin scrambled to her feet, hurriedly folded the blanket, and jogged to catch up with her. She slipped an arm around Rachel's waist. "What if I forgot my sunscreen?"

"Don't worry," Rachel said, already imagining how they would spend the rest of the afternoon. "You won't need it."

❖

"This is good practice for when the baby starts pre-school." Colleen organized her handmade flash cards. The cards were more elaborate than Rachel expected for a task as simple as theirs. Then again, Colleen had time on her hands.

She had developed preeclampsia, the dangerous condition in which an expectant mother's blood pressure soared and her extremities swelled from fluid retention. To protect her and the baby, Colleen's doctors had put her on bed rest for the duration of her pregnancy. She was going stir crazy being stuck in her apartment all day so she volunteered to help Rachel "study." With only one day left before her flight to California, Rachel was running out of opportunities to bone up.

"Okay," Colleen said, sounding like the enthusiastic host of a children's TV show. "Let's start with this one."

As Colleen held up the first picture, Rachel took a deep breath and tried to remember all the information she had crammed into her head the past three days.

"That's Kieran the pediatrician, his wife Deepika the engineer, and their daughters Amber, Layla, and Maya. Kieran's the oldest brother. He and Deepika met when Kieran did six months of volunteer work in Mumbai after his final year of medical school. They've been married for twenty-one years. Amber is a freshman majoring in internal medicine at Johns Hopkins. Layla is an aspiring actress. She's the president of her high school drama club and, last year, she won the role of Mimi in a local production of *Rent*. Maya, the youngest of the three girls, is a serious Janis Joplin aficionado."

"She's my favorite." Jane turned away from the Yankees-Red Sox game long enough to offer her two cents.

"You would say that." Jane was such a Joplin fan she once strained her vocal cords trying to duplicate the famous rocker's trademark raspy delivery. *The quietest week of my life.*

"Okay, next one." Colleen put Kieran's flash card on the bottom of the pile and pulled out another.

"That's Pearson the bicycle cop. He's the middle brother. He's married to Kelly, a former Miss California. They've been together for twenty years and married for sixteen. Their daughter, Tracy, prefers motorcycle helmets to tiaras."

"I've changed my mind," Jane said. "*She's* my favorite."

"I don't think you have a say. You're doing great, Rachel." Colleen flipped the cards again.

"That's Ryan the general contractor. He's the second oldest. He's been married for eighteen years to Shannon, who's a stay-at-home mom. Their daughter Shayanne is a few weeks away from starting her first summer job."

"Which is?"

Rachel's mind went blank. "Let me think."

"It's not too late for cue cards," Jane said.

"You're not helping."

"I'll give you a clue," Colleen said. "Mind the…"

"Gap! Yes, she's going to be a clerk at the Gap this summer. Her sister Brandi is a standout on her high school track team. Her specialty is the fifteen hundred meters, and she already has three of the fastest times in state history. Her parents are thinking scholarship, but she's aiming higher: Olympic gold."

"Nice save."

"Thanks, but I can't afford to have a slip up like that this weekend. I'm not going to have you around to give me helpful hints."

"That's what Griffin's for. Just make sure you're standing next to her at all times."

"She's going to be pulled in so many directions she won't have time to babysit me. Besides, this is something I want to do on my own."

She indicated she was ready for the next set of photos. She had only two brothers left. By process of elimination, she had a fifty-fifty chance of getting it right. Colleen held up the next picture.

"That's Logan the real estate agent. He's the youngest brother. He and his partner Daniel, a documentary filmmaker, have been together for seven years. Their daughter Diamond is four and the baby of the family. She got her unusual name because she's 'the shining jewel in her fathers' eyes.'"

"Cue the hearts and flowers," Jane said with light sarcasm.

"Two more months and you'll be just as bad if not worse." Her heart skipped a beat when Colleen flinched and rubbed her stomach. "Okay?" she whispered, trying not to alarm Jane.

"I'm fine. He's really active tonight. If the Jets need a field goal kicker, I think I've found their man." Colleen lifted her shirt and Rachel could clearly see the outline of a tiny heel poking against the side of her stomach. She lowered her shirt and held up the last photo. "One more left."

"That would be Duncan the graphic designer. He's married to the former Tara Marshall. Tara, who gave Griffin her first kiss way back when, is an architect who owns her own firm. Duncan and Tara have two daughters. Nicole is an avid reader whose goal is to read two books per week during summer vacation."

"She sounds like someone I know," Jane said. "What was your record?"

"I read a hundred books the summer before I started tenth grade."

"Then you discovered girls and everything went to hell in a hand basket."

"Whatever."

Clearing her throat to get Rachel's attention, Colleen tapped her finger against the third face in the picture she was holding.

"That's Lindsay. She's Griffin's eight-year-old doppelganger. She's into surfing and she wants to be a—drum roll, please—chef when she grows up."

"If the next thing out of your mouth is Lindsay's a left-handed lesbian," Jane said, "I'll need to see the results of the kid's DNA test."

Colleen put the flash cards away. "I think you've got this."

"I had a good teacher."

When the Yankees hit into an inning-ending double play, Jane stood and stretched her back. "Come on, Rach. Let me show you the baby's room. We've made some changes since the last time you were here."

Even though Jane had kept her abreast of every brush stroke and design update, Rachel dutifully followed her down the hall. Jane obviously wanted to discuss something other than non-toxic paint, antique cribs, and interactive mobiles.

Jane picked up a stuffed animal and hugged it to her chest. "I'm scared," she said in a voice so low Rachel had to strain to hear her. "If something goes wrong, I could lose one or both of them."

Rachel put her hands on Jane's shoulders as she started to cry. "Nothing's going to go wrong. Colleen's doing everything the doctors have told her to do. She's doing great." She ducked her head to try to force Jane to look her in the eye. "Unless there's something you're not telling me."

Jane shot her a guilty glance.

Fear made Rachel's heart gallop in her chest. She tightened her grip on Jane's shoulders. "What is it?"

"Colleen started spotting last week. Just one day, but it was the longest day of our lives. Her doctors say she and the baby are fine, but I'm not going to be able to relax until the baby's born. Until I'm holding both of them in my arms."

"Have you shared your fears with Colleen?"

Jane shook her head forlornly. "She's under enough stress. I don't want to add to the burden she's already carrying. Her ob-gyn says she has to remain as calm as possible or she could have a placental abruption. She could bleed to death and the baby could die from lack of oxygen."

Rachel wrapped her arms around her and held on tight. She thought of Colleen and the quiet strength she exuded that served as an inspiration for all who met her. If something were to happen to her, Jane wasn't the only one who would feel the loss. She tilted Jane's chin upward until her eyes met hers.

"Everything's going to be fine. In two months, you're going to have everything you've ever wanted: a wife, a son, and a kick-ass godmother at your beck and call."

Jane laughed through her tears. "That was a pretty good pep talk. I'll try to remember it when it's my turn to give it to you. You'll get everything you want one day, too. I know it."

"I hope you're right." Wiping her eyes, Rachel tried to pull herself together. "We'd better get back before your better half starts thinking we're carrying on a torrid affair."

Jane took on the breathy tones of a *Dynasty*-era primetime soap diva. "I've always been hot for you. I don't care who knows it."

Rachel assumed the ramrod straight posture of an iron-jawed hero. "Be strong. We must resist temptation."

She gave Jane's shoulder another squeeze before they returned to the living room. She stayed a few minutes longer before calling it a night. She called Griffin on her cell phone as she headed to the subway station. The restaurant was probably a madhouse, but she needed to hear Griffin's voice.

"I'm a little busy, Rachel," Griffin said, her voice straining to rise above the cacophony of background noise. "Can I call you later?"

"Can I have a hug first?"

"What's wrong?"

Rachel quickly filled her in on Colleen's precarious medical condition.

"Give me a few minutes to wrap things up. I'll be there as soon as I can."

"No, don't do that. This is a waiting game. There's nothing any of us can do except cross our fingers and hope for the best. Now how about that hug?"

"Close your eyes. Rest your head on my shoulder. My arms are wrapped around you. My hands are stroking your back. Can you feel me holding you?"

"Yes." Rachel could feel Griffin's strong arms encircle her and pull her close. She felt Griffin's hair brush against her neck. She could almost smell her cologne.

"Better?"

"Much, thank you. Go cook something before you forget how."

"You got it. Are you sure you're okay?"

"I'm fine."

She wished she could say the same about Colleen without feeling like she was tempting fate by doing so.

"You don't sound fine. I'll come by your place after I finish up here."

"You'll be exhausted after your shift and our flight leaves at the crack of dawn. You don't have to hold my hand."

"I plan on holding much more than your hand. I'll see you in an hour. No, make it two. I need to stop by my apartment first and pick up my bags so we can leave from your place in the morning."

"You want to spend the night with me?"

This was new. Griffin was fanatical about sleeping in her own bed. No matter how late the hour, she always returned home at the end of the night. Rachel felt their relationship make another incremental turn. She would have preferred an exponential one, but she'd take what she could get.

"Do you have any objections to me sleeping over?"

"I can't think of any off the top of my head."

And she couldn't think of anything better than waking up in Griffin's arms.

❖

Rachel clutched at the harness around Griffin's hips, imploring her to quicken the pace of her strokes. Griffin refused to comply. Moments like this would soon become only a pleasant memory. She wanted to enjoy every second.

She braced her hands on the bed, her arms trembling from the effort of keeping her body aloft—from holding herself back. She wanted to come as badly as Rachel did. She licked her lips in anticipation. Her hips moved in and out. She gradually increased her rhythm. Faster. Faster. Then faster still. With each thrust, she drove deeper and deeper.

"Please." Rachel clutched at her shoulders, her back, her hips. "Please, Griffin."

She gave in to the yearning she heard in Rachel's voice, the pleading in her eyes. She gave in to her own body's demand for release. She lowered her head, grazed her teeth across one of Rachel's nipples, took it into her mouth, and flicked it with her tongue.

Rachel growled her assent. Her back arched as if it were a bowstring being tugged by an expert archer. Then the string snapped. "Yes. Oh, yes."

Griffin pressed tightly against her and closed her eyes as the long-delayed orgasm pinballed around her body. She shuddered when Rachel ran a finger down her back.

Rachel laughed, the throaty post-coital chuckle Griffin loved almost as much as the act itself. "My turn." She rolled Griffin on her back and unbuckled the harness strapped around her waist. Then she reached for another toy from the treasure chest tucked under her bed.

"You truly are insatiable, aren't you?"

Rachel licked the shallow pool of sweat that had formed in the hollow of Griffin's throat. "Only when it comes to you. This is one of the last times we're going to be together like this for weeks. I want to give you something to remember me by."

Griffin smoothed Rachel's tousled hair and held it away from her face. "You already have."

CHAPTER SIXTEEN

G riffin was running out of time. If she wanted to guess where they were going, she needed to do it now. She wracked her brain for possible destinations. "Bermuda."

"No."

"Jamaica."

"No."

"Miami."

"No. Do you give up yet?"

"No, because you're enjoying this too much." Griffin inched forward as the harried airline employee motioned for the next baggage-wielding traveler to exit the maze and approach the ticket counter. "Judging by the length of this line, I've got another fifteen minutes of guesses left."

"But I don't have another fifteen minutes of patience."

Rachel handed her a copy of their itinerary. Griffin scanned the entries until she found their final destination. Newport Beach.

"I wanted to see one of the famous Sutton family clambakes for myself," Rachel said. "Do you think you can help me out?"

Griffin couldn't speak around the lump in her throat.

"From what I hear, we're going to need enough food to feed an army. Clams, mussels, lobsters, potatoes, sausage, onions, and corn on the cob. Plus salad, dessert, and multiple bottles of wine. Tucker said he'd stock the pantry before we land, but you might want to—"

Griffin kissed her to stop the flow of words. "Thank you. This is without a doubt the sweetest thing anyone has ever done for me."

"You're welcome."

"Next!" The ticket agent's shout nearly drowned out Rachel's whispered reply.

"Let's get up there before he calls someone else."

❖

"We're here."

After the six-hour flight to California and the short drive from John Wayne Airport to Newport Beach, Griffin turned the rental car onto a quiet street and parked in a private drive. "Come on." She grabbed Rachel's hand and dragged her toward the beach.

"Don't you want to unload the car first?"

"Unpacking can wait. I want to show you something."

They walked toward the rock jetty on the west side of Newport Harbor.

"This is The Wedge."

Griffin pointed at the water. Towering waves—some nearly twenty feet high—rolled toward the shore.

"It looks dangerous."

"Only if you don't know what you're doing. The waves here break in one to two feet of water. Fall off at the wrong time and you could break an arm, a leg, or worse." Griffin rubbed her hands together. "I can't wait to get my board."

Rachel shuddered as a powerful wave crashed against the rocks. The sound was like nothing she had ever heard. "I'll stick to the shore, thank you." They slowly walked back to the beach house. "When do I get to meet your family?"

Griffin's smile faded. "I was hoping they would be waiting for us at the airport." "I've sent a couple of text messages, but no one has responded. Let me try my mom one more time." She pressed speed dial and held her phone to her ear. "Voice mail again." She shrugged. "She's probably on a photo shoot somewhere. We'll catch up to them sooner or later."

Sooner than you think.

Griffin popped the trunk on the rented convertible and retrieved the luggage. Trembling with anticipation, Rachel followed her up the front steps.

"How much did you pay for this place?" Griffin asked.

"Not as much as you think."

"Arc you sure? This placc is practically a landmark."

Rachel recognized the house. Two stories tall with ultra-modern furniture and a twenty-seat home theater, it had been featured in everything from *Architectural Digest* to *Coastal Living*. She felt like she was about to check into an exclusive high-end hotel.

Griffin turned the key in the lock and deposited her suitcase in the foyer. "Let me help you with that," she said, reaching for Rachel's bag.

"I can manage."

"Let me—"

"Griffin, turn around." Over Griffin's shoulder, Rachel could see her family waiting to run into her arms.

"Turn around? What—" She spun as if an armed robber was sneaking up behind her.

The ensuing roar was so loud Rachel's eardrums vibrated. "Surprise!"

Remaining rooted in place, Griffin looked back at her as if she was requesting permission.

"Go ahead."

Griffin ran across the room and was immediately swept up by a sea of bodies. Her mother. Her father. Her brothers. Her sisters-in-law. Her nieces. Everyone took a turn giving her a hug. Some went back for seconds.

Tucker wandered over and gave Rachel a hip check. "And the award for best girlfriend ever goes to…"

"Thanks, Tuck. I couldn't have done it without you."

"Don't worry. I won't let you forget it."

Griffin crossed the room, her parents in tow. William Sutton was holding a worn Tickle Me Elmo doll that must have belonged to one of his many grandchildren. Madeleine Griffin Sutton was carrying her omnipresent camera.

"Mom, Dad," Griffin said, her voice shaking with emotion, "this is Rachel."

"Dr. and Mrs. Sutton, it's a pleasure to meet you."

Rachel held out her hand, but Madeleine pulled her into her arms instead. "I can see why Griffin has been raving about you," she said, drawing back. "Thank you for bringing our daughter home."

"You're welcome."

"That goes double for me," Griffin's father said, giving her a hug of his own.

"Thank you, sir."

Everyone Griffin introduced Rachel to repeated her parents' sentiments. Rachel felt like crying. She couldn't remember the last time she had been made to feel so welcome.

About half an hour after their arrival, Ryan held up a carton of beer from a regional brewing company. "What do you say, sis? Want to split a sixer of Angel City with your brothers like you used to or do I need to find some of the fancy imported stuff?"

Griffin punched him in the arm. "Give me a break, bro. I haven't changed that much."

"Then what are we waiting for?"

She looked at Rachel as if she didn't want to leave her alone.

"Go ahead."

"Are you sure?"

"I'll be fine."

Griffin was barely out the door before four of her nieces surrounded Rachel and began peppering her with questions.

Layla, the wannabe actress, wanted to know all about Broadway, Times Square, and New York's thriving theater scene. Her cousins' questions were much more personal.

"Is it true you and Aunt Griffin met on a blind date?" Amber asked, her arms folded across her chest. Tracy and Shayanne mirrored her stance. They looked like Charlie's Angels minus the feathered hair. "How's that working out for you?"

"So far, so good."

"Are you serious about her or are you just looking to have some fun?" Shayanne asked.

"I'm too old for fun." Rachel nervously cleared her throat when the girls frowned at her attempt at humor. "I don't know where this is going to lead, but I'm enjoying the journey. And I would never, ever intentionally do anything to hurt your aunt."

The girls conferred for a few moments before Tracy, the verbally economic member of the trio, passed judgment. "I'll buy that."

"Not so fast," Amber said. "You said the same thing about Veronica, and you were wrong about her."

"I wasn't the only one. You liked her, too."

"Before I realized what a hot mess she was."

"Dudes, Veronica is yesterday's news," Shayanne said. "Can we get back to today's headlines?"

"One last thing and we can move on." Amber, the apparent ringleader, turned back to Rachel. "We want to know what your intentions are. Getting us together like this is a cool move and you get major brownie points for it, but did you do it because you thought it would make Aunt Griffin happy or because you thought it would make us like you?"

"Both?"

Tracy held up her hand for a high five. "Good answer."

❖

Duncan downed the rest of his pale ale and clapped Griffin on the back. "If you're as fond of airplane food as you used to be, you must be starving. Why don't you get cleaned up so we can head to lunch? I think Tara made reservations at Tapas."

Tapas Restaurant and Nightclub served up some of the best Spanish cuisine and salsa dancing on the West Coast.

"I love that place," Griffin said.

"We know," her brothers said as one.

Pearson patted his stomach. "The portions are too small for me. If you need me, I'll be at the Benihana down the street."

"Do it and die."

Pearson laughed and wrapped one of his burly arms around her neck. "Just kidding, sis." He easily flipped her over his shoulder.

She held her empty beer bottle in a death grip. She wanted to save the container for the picture of Charlie Parker on the label—and the sentimental value she had already attached to it. "Let's get you back to your girlfriend before she thinks you've abandoned her."

She didn't bother to correct him. Rachel wasn't her girlfriend, so to speak, but whatever she was felt pretty good.

Pearson deposited her on the deck just as Amber, Tracy, Layla, and Shayanne walked through the French doors that separated the deck from the living room.

"If you start giving airplane rides next," Tracy said, "I'm first, Dad."

"Get in line." Griffin ruffled Tracy's stylishly messy hair. The flyaway locks made her look like she had just rolled out of bed, but Griffin was willing to bet she had spent hours in front of a mirror getting it to look that way. "How's Andrea?"

Tracy beamed at the mention of her girlfriend. "Good. Beyond good. She's amazing."

"Are you bringing her to lunch?"

"No. Mom said it was just family today. No girlfriends or boyfriends allowed."

"Tomorrow then. Bring her to the clambake."

"For real?"

"The more, the merrier."

Tracy immediately pulled out her cell phone.

"Speaking of girlfriends." Amber jerked her thumb toward the living room, where Rachel and Deepika were sharing a laugh. "That one's a keeper."

"Yeah," Layla said. "Don't screw it up."

"I'll try not to. You're going surfing with Lindsay and me in the morning, aren't you?"

"Duh. Someone's got to show you how it's done."

"Ah, the prodigal daughter returns," Deepika said when Griffin joined her and Rachel in the living room. "I hope Amber wasn't too hard on either of you."

"She didn't string us up by our thumbs, if that's what you're wondering," Rachel said.

"She's probably saving that for tomorrow," Deepika said with an indulgent smile. "See you at the restaurant. It was nice meeting you, Rachel."

"You, too."

After Deepika left, Rachel shook her head as if she had been put through the wringer.

"That bad?"

"Your nieces are something else."

"Please tell me they didn't give you the treatment."

"I feel like I've been water boarded."

"Remind me to kill them later."

"No, don't do that. I thought what they did was sweet."

"Torturing you was sweet?"

"No, but caring about you is. I can tell how much they love you. And I'm so glad I get to share this weekend with all of you. If I didn't know before, I certainly know now: you're something special."

She gave Rachel a gentle kiss. "So are you."

❖

"Regular or unleaded?" Daniel asked the next day, offering Rachel a cup of coffee.

While their other halves jogged on the beach or rode the waves, Daniel and the other spouses spent the morning giving themselves some retail therapy. They showed up at the beach house laden with shopping bags and sipping whipped cream-topped Frappuccinos.

Rachel grabbed a skinny latte and a low-fat raspberry muffin from the bag of treats. The group wandered out to the beach to watch Griffin and her brothers quibble over the proper depth to dig the fire pit for the afternoon's clambake.

Griffin's neoprene surfing suit was unzipped to the waist, the arms flopping against her legs as she shoveled sand. Her lean muscles flexed in the sun. Her brothers rushed to lend a hand. Sand flew in all directions.

"Do they do everything together?"

"You get used to it," Daniel, Tara, Shannon, Deepika, and Kelly said in unison.

Joining in the group's easy laughter, Rachel felt like she had found five sisters she never knew she had. Her days of being an only child were over.

Supervised by their grandfather, Griffin's younger nieces gathered seaweed at the shoreline, depositing their finds in a large plastic storage container filled with sea water. The older ones were in charge of finding enough round stones to line the bottom of the fire pit. Tracy and her girlfriend Andrea competed to see who could carry the most weight. Heated in a wood fire until they were glowing hot, the stones would radiate heat. Wet seaweed would be placed on top of the rocks, a layer of food alternating with a layer of seaweed until the supply of both was exhausted. The potato sacks that Tucker was soaking in the ocean would trap the heat from the stones, forming the steam that, over the course of several hours, would cook the food.

Daniel and Madeleine documented everything with their cameras, capturing memories that would last long past the end of the meal.

"Shouldn't we be doing something?" Rachel asked.

"In due time," Shannon said. "Feeding this rowdy bunch is a ton of work. Getting the portion sizes right, remembering who likes what. Until Griffin rings the dinner bell, let's enjoy the quiet before the storm."

"Seeing everyone laughing, smiling, and enjoying each other's company will make the hard work worth it in the end," Kelly said. "We should do this more often."

"Do what?" Deepika asked. She kept a watchful eye on the water, where Griffin, Layla, and Lindsay were paddling out on their surfboards.

"Get together to celebrate something other than a wedding, a funeral, or some other special occasion. We're always saying we're going to, but except for Christmas, we never do."

"You plan it and we'll be there," Shannon said.

"So will we," Tara said.

Daniel winked at Rachel as he took a bite of his bear claw. "See what you started?"

A loud whoop drew Rachel's attention back to the beach. With her family cheering her on, Griffin chased a huge wave as it barreled toward shore. When she caught up to it, she popped to her feet and pinwheeled her arms as she tried to find her balance.

"Go, Aunt Griffin!" Brandi yelled.

Rachel covered her mouth with her hand. She remembered the story Griffin had told her about her spectacular wipeout when she was nine. She also remembered the cautionary tale she had told her when they arrived the day before. *The waves here break in one to two feet of water. Fall off at the wrong time and you could break an arm, a leg, or worse.* If Griffin wiped out now, the results might be disastrous instead of amusing.

Griffin rode the wave all the way in. When her board slid across the wet sand, she hopped off and thrust her arms in the air. Maya and Nicole ran over to give her high fives. Then she turned and pointed at Rachel like a rock star zeroing in on an ardent fan mid-concert.

"I've never seen her look this happy," Kelly said. "You must be doing something right."

Rachel planned to keep doing it as long as she could.

❖

Hours later, the sun had set, night had fallen, and the temperature had cooled considerably. The kids were passed out from sensory overload, the adults were huddled in blankets next to a roaring bonfire. Logan and Kelly provided the entertainment. Logan played acoustic guitar while Kelly sang.

Griffin looked up at the canopy of stars. The same ones she used to make wishes on while she lay spread-eagle in her parents' backyard. She moved closer to the woman in her arms. Rachel. The woman who had made one of her fondest wishes come true.

"Okay?" she asked, wrapping the blanket tighter around them.

Rachel turned and kissed her cheek. "I'm perfect."

"Yes, you are."

"I fielded a call from a fellow realtor today," Logan said, idly strumming his guitar after Kelly finished singing. "Grandpa's old place is up for sale again."

Griffin did a double take. "The comedy club went out of business?"

"I drove by this afternoon to confirm. There's a For Sale sign in the window."

Daniel tossed another log on the fire. "You two are always talking about buying the place. Here's your chance."

"It's quite an investment. I don't know if we can swing it. We do have to put Diamond through college one day, you know."

"Yeah, in fourteen years."

"Those years will fly by before we know it. Yesterday, she was learning to crawl. In a few months, she's going to start kindergarten."

"I feel your pain," Kieran said. "If Amber hadn't earned a free ride to Johns Hopkins, Deepika and I might have to sell a couple of kidneys to scrape up the money to send Layla to USC."

"I know buying the club would require some serious penny-pinching, but if we all do our part, it wouldn't hurt quite as much," Griffin said. "Logan could handle the sale. Ryan could do the renovations. Duncan could create the marketing materials. Pearson could be in charge of security. I could audition the chef and the wait staff. Kelly and the girls could point us toward some good local musicians. Shannon could run the house. And Rachel could do the books. For free, of course."

Rachel held up a warning hand. "That part's negotiable."

Griffin pressed her lips to Rachel's ear. "I'll pay you in other ways."

"It's a deal."

Griffin made eye contact with each person huddled around the fire. "We don't have to make a decision tonight, but let's give this idea some serious thought. Grandpa's legacy has been in the hands of strangers for far too long. Isn't it time we brought it back where it belongs?"

Pearson stood up. "I don't know about these blockheads, but you've convinced me. Count me in."

He hoisted his bottle of beer. Griffin and her other brothers followed suit. They toasted their joint venture as their parents looked on with pride.

Logan sat down and began playing a celebratory tune on his guitar. Griffin and Rachel remained standing.

"Is this the beach where you had your first kiss?" Rachel whispered.

"The infamous pier is right down there."

"Show me."

Logan stopped playing when they began to walk away. "Two at once. Is this a comment on my performance?"

"If you have performance issues, bro, you need to talk it over with Daniel, not with me."

Griffin led Rachel down the beach to the lighted pier that glowed in the distance.

"This is it," she said when they arrived. She leaned against a pillar. Her feet sank into the sand as water lapped at her ankles. "What do you think?"

"It's incredible. Just like you. Tara gave you your first kiss. I want to be the one who gives you your last one."

Rachel pressed her lips against Griffin's. Griffin pulled her closer, deepening the kiss. Rachel tasted like strawberries and mint, the main components of the mojitos they'd shared after dinner. She wanted to take her to bed and part her with her tongue. To slide the tip with deliberate slowness across her clit. She wanted to feel her grow hard. To hear her come. She groaned when Rachel pulled away but held her by her waist to make sure she didn't go far. Everyone in her family had cautioned her not to let Rachel get away. Perhaps she should heed their warning.

"Tell me what you want."

"I want some time alone with you," Rachel whispered in the dark. "I want to be with you with no one else around."

"That can be arranged. What else? Tell me what you want so I can give it you."

"I want someone I can trust. I want someone I can start a family with. I want someone who loves me as much as I love her. And I want that someone to be you. Can you give me that?"

CHAPTER SEVENTEEN

Griffin pulled her suitcase behind her as she strode down the hall. Her luggage's plastic wheels clacked against the hardwood floor. A camera crew trailed her as she approached the apartment that would be her home away from home for the better part of the next month. She turned the knob and opened the door.

"Cut," the floor director said before she could step inside. He, the cameraman, and assorted technicians brushed past her and walked through the door, leaving her standing on the threshold. "Wait there and enter on my signal. We want to get a reaction shot of you coming in."

She flinched when the door slammed in her face. She had spent the last twenty minutes shooting the same scene from three different angles. She was dying to see who the rest of the contestants were, but she had yet to reach the inside of the apartment.

Apparently, reality TV isn't very real after all.

"Action."

She opened the door and finally stepped inside. Five men were gathered in the apartment. One tossed her a beer.

"Six down, two to go," he said.

She caught the beer and popped the top. "It's five o'clock somewhere."

The men wandered over and introduced themselves one by one.

"Trevor Wright. You can call me Mr. Wright, but I'll settle for Mr. Right Now."

Griffin pegged him instantly. With his gelled hair and too-tight pants, he was the resident lothario. The pretty boy. If his cooking skills were as weak as his lines, he'd be gone by the end of the first episode.

"James Cavanaugh. Nice to meet you. Don't feel bad when I take you out."

He was easy to figure out, too. He was the cocky one the viewers—and the other chefs—would love to hate.

"Brady Rosen."

Soft-spoken, prematurely balding with thick glasses and an apparent fondness for sweater vests. He was the cute, cuddly nebbish.

A man whose muscles had muscles came forward next.

"Damian Myers."

He was the only one she recognized. A former professional baseball player, he was the ex-athlete who was finding it difficult adjusting to life out of the spotlight.

And, finally, the one who had tossed her the beer.

"Salvatore Iocovozzi. Call me Sal."

Damian was the jock. Sal was the shirtless guy swilling beer in the stands. The burly Everyman who singlehandedly disproved the theory that only snobby intellectuals could find their way around a kitchen.

Griffin flashed back to her childhood. "This feels familiar. Five guys and I'm the only girl."

"I like those numbers," Trevor said with a leer. "Any combination that includes the two of us getting it on is fine by me."

So much for not judging a book by its cover.

The guys had claimed two of the three dorm-style bedrooms. Griffin deposited her bags in the third, the one with two standard beds instead of three twins.

Beer in hand, she returned to the living room. "How long have you guys been waiting?"

Sal opened another cold brew. "Long enough to start a second round. This hurry-up-and-wait shit's for the birds." He turned to the camera hovering over his left shoulder. "You're going to edit that out, right?"

"Don't address the camera." The floor director looked nonplussed. "Pretend it's not here."

"Yeah, right," Sal grumbled. "I'll try to remember that when you're filming me taking a dump every morning."

Griffin laughed so hard she nearly spewed beer all over the couch. *I've just inherited five more brothers. Maybe this experience won't be so bad after all.*

A few minutes later, a seventh chef entered their midst.

Another guy. I'm detecting a pattern.

He introduced himself as Jorge Gonzalez. The owner of his own catering company, he was the self-starter. The one who proved you didn't have to be professionally-trained to be successful in the food service industry. He seemed nice enough, but she was hoping a few more female chefs had made the cut so she'd have someone to commiserate with when the guys' testosterone levels got too high.

Based on the way the bedrooms were set up, she assumed at least one more woman was in the cast, but where was she? And more importantly, *who* was she?

She didn't have to wait long to find out.

When Veronica Warner walked through the door, Griffin felt the pieces click into place. She no longer wondered what role she had been chosen to play. She knew. She was the foil.

"Well, well, well," Veronica said, folding her tattooed arms across her chest. "It looks like the angel and the bad girl are together again. Let the catfights begin."

❖

After the chefs spent a couple hours socializing—and ignoring the cameraman recording the bonding session—they were driven to the studio where most of the cooking scenes would be filmed. They posed for group and individual photos. Then they were herded to the set. It was time for the first Pressure Cooker challenge, the contest that would determine who would be exempt from the next day's elimination challenge.

The hosts were Elinor Davies, the Auckland native who was once Miss Universe, and Stewart Sands, the force behind a string of wildly-successful restaurants specializing in New American cuisine.

"Good afternoon, chefs," Elinor said as the contestants lined up behind their randomly-selected stations.

Griffin ignored the six-foot Maori beauty's stunning exterior and focused on the words she was saying instead of the way her luscious lips formed them.

"Welcome to the seventh season of *Cream of the Crop*. You have been brought here to compete for two hundred fifty thousand dollars in cash, a feature in *Fresh Take* magazine, a showcase at the Fresh Take Fiesta in Austin, Texas, a suite of professional grade kitchen appliances, and the right to be called the cream of the crop."

"This season will provide a stern test of your creativity as well as your mental endurance," Stewart said. His passion for his profession filled the TV screen each week, making the portly restaurateur an unlikely sex symbol. "Before we get to the team challenges, let's begin with an individual one. Today's challenge is a test of your speed and accuracy. It will take place in three rounds. In the first round, your mission is to dice two cups of onions. The six who do it fastest will move on. In the second round, the four who dress two chickens the fastest will advance. In the final round, the two competitors who shuck ten oysters in the shortest amount of time will compete for immunity during tomorrow's elimination challenge."

Elinor took over for Stewart. "Your chance to see who can rise a cut above starts now."

Griffin grabbed three onions, cut off the ends, and began to chop the tear-inducing vegetable into pieces small enough to be considered diced. No chunks allowed. She prided herself on her knife skills. Advancing to the final round of today's challenge shouldn't pose a problem. *They don't call me Edward Scissorhands for nothing.*

She scooped the last of her onions off the cutting board and dropped them into the measuring cup next to it. She checked the measurement. Two cups exactly. "Chef." She raised her hands, indicating she was done.

Stewart checked the size of the pieces to make sure none were too large. "Congratulations, chef. You're moving on."

Griffin clenched her fist. *Step one.*

James finished second, followed by Veronica, Sal, Brady, and Jorge. Trevor and Damian were eliminated.

In the next round, James finished dressing his second chicken a split second before Griffin did. Veronica and Sal moved on while Brady and Jorge fell by the wayside.

Griffin flexed her fingers and waited for the third round to begin. Her first job was working at a seafood restaurant in her native Newport Beach. She could shuck oysters in her sleep.

I've got this. Everyone else is competing for second.

James finished second, leaving Veronica muttering curses as she cleaned her station.

"And now for immunity," Elinor said. "Griffin, James, you have thirty minutes to create an entrée using some or all of the ingredients you've been working with today."

Griffin felt the pressure mount. If she won today, she would set herself up as one of the favorites—and paint a large bull's-eye on her back. Which of the hundreds of recipes in her head should she choose? Should she play it safe or take a risk?

"Ready?" Stewart said. "Go."

Griffin sprinted to the pantry and gathered the items she needed to prepare a creamy seafood risotto. Dicing the onions in the first round had saved her some time, but she had to hustle to prep the rest of the ingredients. Risotto was tricky. If the rice was undercooked, the flavors refused to marry and the dish wasn't worth eating. Most risotto recipes took a minimum of thirty minutes to prepare and the clock was already ticking.

She tossed the onions into some heated oil and waited for them to soften. Then she added seafood stock and fresh garlic and increased the temperature so the mixture could come to a rapid boil. She needed to get the rice on as soon as possible.

She looked over at James's station as she julienned her oysters. His dish—chicken in oyster sauce—was already coming together. Hers was barely underway.

James finished plating his dish with plenty of time to spare. Keeping a close eye on the timer, Griffin waited until the last possible second. She spooned the risotto into the judges' bowls just before the display on the LED readout changed to zero.

James stared at her as if he knew he had her beat. "Nice try," he said under his breath.

"Let's see what the judges have to say." Some might find his trash talking intimidating, but she wasn't one of them.

The judges didn't give anything away as they sampled each dish. They conferred with the producers, then returned to announce their decision.

"James," Stewart said, "you get bonus points for using all of the selected ingredients, but your chicken was slightly undercooked. Griffin, you took a risk by deciding to make risotto, and by opting not to include chicken."

"Griffin," Elinor said after a dramatic pause, "your gamble paid off. You are the winner of today's Pressure Cooker. You have immunity this week."

Griffin was happy to come away with the win, but she wasn't satisfied. Not yet. A bigger prize lay ahead.

All the chefs offered their congratulations, though some seemed more sincere than others. Back at the apartment, when the cameras were off and everyone could finally relax, Veronica sought to make amends for their troubled past.

"Risotto, huh? That was a ballsy move. Nice going." She stood in the doorway of the bedroom she and Griffin were sharing, a glass of wine in each hand. Her short dark hair was wet from the shower. She wore a pair of low-riding gray sweatpants and an olive tank top. The drab colors were in stark contrast to the colorful tattoos that adorned her arms from her shoulders to her wrists. Pin-up girls posing provocatively with kitchen utensils were etched into her skin.

Griffin accepted the proffered glass of wine. "Is this supposed to be a peace offering?"

Veronica sat cross-legged on her bed. "That's up to you. We're going to be sharing space for the next eighteen days. We should put our big girl panties on and let bygones be bygones."

"Agreed." Griffin didn't want to say too much. Veronica was infamous for twisting her words into shapes they weren't meant to take. "What did you mean when you said we were 'the angel and the bad girl'?"

"You've got the manners of a Girl Scout and the merit badges to prove it. I'm the one who blows snot rockets and scratches herself in public. You're the one women take home to meet their parents. I'm the one who fucks them senseless and tosses them a few bucks for cab fare. You're perfect and I am your diametric opposite." Veronica snorted. "But we both know better than to buy that line of bullshit, don't we? You've bagged as many babes as I have, if not more."

Griffin tried to defend herself against Veronica's verbal attack. "I'm seeing someone."

"Just one? What happened? You used to keep one in the batter's box and one on deck."

"That happened once."

"I know. I was the one on deck, remember?" Veronica ran a hand over one of her gym-toned arms. "Let's face it. You're not a happily ever after kind of woman, Sutton. It's not the way you're built. Why else would you be the only member of your incredibly fertile family who isn't married or civil unioned or domestic partnered or whatever the hell you want to call it? I give you and Little Mary Sunshine six months max before you start craving something new."

Griffin could tell Veronica was trying to bait her into a confrontation, but she refused to play along. "The cameras aren't on, Ronnie. Stop trying to play head games and tell me what you want."

Veronica ran her hands through her hair. The letters F-O-O-D were stenciled across the fingers of her right hand, W-I-N-E on the left. "If I don't walk away with the top prize, I'd rather you did instead of one of those blowhards in the other room. No woman has ever won this show. The only way to guarantee that happens this season is for both of us to make it to the final round. Once we get there, it's every woman for herself. Then we can finally settle the issue of who's the better chef. Look me in the eye and tell me that doesn't appeal to you."

"If I did, I'd be lying."

Veronica raised her glass. "Then let's hear it for the final two."

Why do I feel like I'm about to make a deal with the devil?

Griffin toasted their unlikely alliance. "To the final two."

❖

"You got off to a slow start, Veronica," Stewart said, "but you've certainly made up for it. Congratulations."

"Thank you, chef. I've always said it's not how you start." She tossed a withering glance in Griffin's direction. "It's how you finish."

While Elinor rattled off the details of the two-week, all-expense paid trip to France Veronica had just earned by claiming her third straight victory, Griffin dropped her head and wondered what had gone wrong.

She had started off like a house on fire, winning the first Pressure Cooker challenge and coming in second to James in the elimination challenge. Since then, she had fallen to the middle of the pack, in no danger of being voted off, but no threat to the top contenders. Veronica had flown past her to stand next to James as the co-favorite to win the competition. Three elimination challenges remained; the third would determine the finalists—the two chefs who would compete for the grand prize. If she didn't get her act together, she, like Trevor, Damian, and Jorge, would watch the final episode instead of competing in it.

I need to right the ship in a hurry. But what am I doing in this position in the first place?

She sighed as she peered out the tinted windows of the courtesy van that ferried her, Veronica, Sal, James, and Brady across town. Filming the show was like being in a sensory deprivation chamber. She kept time by the number of challenges she had participated in and the number that remained. Six down and six to go, not including the final. With no real point of reference, she barely knew what day it was, let alone what week.

Was Erica in her second week of filling in for her or her third? How was she holding up under the pressure? What was Rachel doing? Had she been to Texas yet or was she still recovering from both her literal and figurative trips to California?

"You're thinking too much," Veronica said as they piled out of the van. "I can smell your brain frying from here. What's on your mind?"

How much should she share with Veronica? Everything? Nothing? They were friends before they were lovers, but they hadn't been either for a very long time.

"Too many things I can't control."

"Can I help?"

"Yeah. Stop being so good at what you do."

"Sorry. Can't help you there," Veronica said with a rakish grin. "No one said it would be easy, Sutton, but I know you'll figure it out."

"That sounded a lot like a compliment. Careful. Someone might hear you."

Griffin couldn't reconcile the villain role Veronica played when the cameras were rolling with the mentoring role she played when they weren't. Which one was the real deal?

Upstairs, she sat at the small writing desk. Veronica unbuttoned her chef's coat and began to undress despite the presence of the camera crew. Unlike her exhibitionist roommate, Griffin hadn't learned to ignore the omnipresent cameras. She was always aware of being watched.

"Relax," the floor director urged her during their one-on-one meetings after each challenge. How was she supposed to do that with a video camera in her face every second of every day and no one to vent to who wouldn't try to use her perceived weakness to their advantage?

She pulled out her chef's notebook, the journal she used to jot down ideas for recipes or meal presentations. She began to sketch an idea she had for a very special meal. Perhaps the most important meal of her life. The one she planned to serve the first day she got her life back.

"The boys and I are going to climb in the hot tub." Veronica peered over Griffin's shoulder. "Do you want to join us or are you going to spend the next hour doodling in your sketch pad?" Veronica took offense when Griffin covered the drawing with her hand. "What's the matter? You still don't trust me?"

When they were in culinary school, Veronica had violated chef law by claiming their collaborative dish as her own. Did she have the balls to steal an idea outright?

"I'm not the same person I was when we were in our twenties, Griffin. Besides, I thought we agreed to let bygones be bygones."

"We did." With a pang of guilt, Griffin uncovered the drawing.

"Then put on your swimsuit and protect me from Brady."

"Brady's a teddy bear."

Veronica rested her hands on her narrow hips. "The teddy bear gets a boner every time he comes near me. Don't make me deal with Little Brady by myself."

"All right. All right." Griffin reluctantly closed her notebook and pushed her chair away from the desk. "I didn't bring a swimsuit so you'll have to lend me one of yours."

"Not a prob."

Veronica tossed her a skimpy string bikini. Griffin held the swimsuit against her body. "Two pieces of floss would provide more coverage than this."

"I hope you've been working out. The camera adds ten pounds, you know." Veronica flopped on her bed and folded her hands behind her head. "Now hurry up before Sal drinks all the beer."

Griffin went to the bathroom to change clothes. When she came back, Veronica was right where she had left her. So was her notebook. Maybe she really had changed. Or not. Veronica's hungry eyes ravished her body.

"Screw the party out there." Veronica crawled off the bed and pinned her against the wall. "Let's start one in here."

She pressed her mouth to Griffin's in a kiss so fierce it was almost primal. Her insistent tongue tried to pry open Griffin's tightly-clamped lips.

Griffin used to be titillated by Veronica's brash personality and competitive nature. Now both turned her off. She longed for what she didn't have: Rachel. She hadn't expected to miss her so much.

Every night she went to sleep with visions of their dream vacation to Newport Beach dancing in her head. And every morning she woke to the nightmare that was Veronica. She preferred the dream.

As the cameraman zoomed in for a close-up, she put her palms in the center of Veronica's chest and pushed her away. Veronica landed on the bed with a melodramatic flop. Griffin rolled her eyes at Veronica's blatant theatrics. "You said you needed a chaperone while you were in the hot tub. Are we going to do this or not?"

Veronica shook her head in disapproval. "Domestic bliss has made you boring."

"You're breaking my heart." Griffin dragged her off the bed. "Come on. Let's go."

❖

Today's challenge was the biggest yet. The winner would receive a trip for two to Tuscany, fifty thousand dollars, and a guaranteed spot in the finals. Even if she didn't win the trip or the money—neither of which was anything to sneeze at—Griffin had a chance to make her mark. To go out on a high. Today's challenge was tailor-made for her. She, Veronica, and James would be serving dim sum for a hundred people. Their dishes would be judged based on technique, creativity, presentation, and, most importantly, authenticity.

She and her fellow chefs had been up until midnight prepping their dishes. In two hours, she would begin serving. Her inspiration was the meal she had shared with Mr. Li and his wife Peng in December—and the conversation she'd had with him at his store the following day.

"*Dim sum is about being together,*" he had said. "*That makes tea more important than the food. Tea, unlike a meal, cannot be rushed.*"

When service began, she would fill the diners' steamer baskets with a variety of dishes, but tea would be the centerpiece of the meal.

After today's winner was decided, the show would take a short break before the finalists went head-to-head. Griffin needed the respite. She was mentally and physically exhausted. But she could see the light at the end of the tunnel. Win or lose, she was going home tomorrow. She was going to see Rachel. If she went home with a trip to Italy and a guaranteed spot in the final in her pocket, that would make up for all the time she and Rachel had lost while she was away.

Almost.

She rubbed her palms together as the van and the accompanying support vehicles barreled toward Chinatown.

One more day.

The van parked in front of the restaurant that would host today's challenge. Griffin climbed out and supervised the off-loading of her dishes.

In the kitchen, Veronica checked the levels on her canister of liquid nitrogen. She was a devotee of molecular gastronomy, the cutting-edge technique that combined cooking with science. Practitioners experimented with everything from cooking temperatures to presentation as they sought to create dining experiences that were one of a kind.

In previous challenges, Veronica and her bottle of cryogenic fluid had wowed the judges by putting ultramodern twists on traditional favorites.

"What are you planning on nuking today?" Griffin asked.

"Dim sum's always served with tea, but tea's so boring. I'm going to jazz it up a bit and make some green tea ice cream."

"I give you points for creativity, but I don't think the diners will find your approach very authentic."

"Who cares what the diners think? I'm trying to impress the judges."

"This isn't a popularity contest. The diners should come first, not last, don't you think?"

"The diners aren't going to hand me a big fat check when this competition's over. The judges are."

"Amen, sister," James said.

Veronica's and James's reactions to her statement made Griffin question her strategy. She watched Veronica pull out the thick work gloves and sturdy safety glasses she needed to handle the liquid nitrogen. On the other side of the room, James was braising cabbage to stuff inside pot stickers. Should she ditch her approach in favor of something flashy and attention grabbing?

No. At the end of the day, what matters isn't how the food looks or how it's prepared. What matters is how it tastes. My food tastes good. I don't need a big fat check to prove it.

Veronica primed the canister.

"Good luck," Griffin said.

James sharpened his knives. "You're the one who's going to need luck. I take that back. To beat me, you're going to need a miracle."

She rolled her eyes. "I'll start praying now."

His trash talking smacked of desperation. And defeat. Veronica had won four out of the last six elimination challenges. Was James conceding today's challenge to her, too?

Not if I have anything to say about it.

She had broken Veronica's win streak two rounds prior when her Latin-influenced shrimp cocktail had bested Veronica's tuna ceviche. She had followed that up the next round with the best braised short ribs she had ever served. Could she make it three wins in a row?

She had been initially reluctant to audition for the show, but she was glad she did. Competing against the best of the best was like placing her skills against a whetstone. Each felt sharper as a result. She thought the experience had turned her into a better chef. If she could get through today, maybe she'd get a chance to show it. To prove to Veronica and the rest of her critics that she wasn't, as they claimed, a no-talent hack graced with good looks and an even better PR manager.

She laid out the steam baskets and filled each with shrimp dumplings, steamed buns, rice noodle rolls, and thousand-layer cake. She completed each presentation with a Phoenix talon, the labor-intensive fried chicken foot that was a Chinese delicacy.

Saving the tea for last, she put water on to boil. Pu-erh tea leaves underwent years of fermentation, producing a strong, earthy taste that didn't require much brewing. She lined up a series of small ceramic teapots and placed some of the tea leaves in the bottom of each pot. She poured the hot water on the leaves and signaled for the wait staff to take the pots to the tables. Then she checked on her dishes.

She would have preferred going last instead of first so her food was on the forefront of the judges' minds, not a distant memory. Instead, Veronica would have the honor. Like she needed another advantage. Griffin quashed the negative thoughts.

I've beaten her before and I can beat her again.

Sweat rolled off her face as the timer continued its inevitable march to zero, but she told herself not to rush. She didn't want to make a silly mistake that would undermine all the hard work she had put in. She finished plating with precious seconds left on the clock.

"Yes!" She tossed a dish towel on the counter like a football player spiking the ball in the end zone after a touchdown.

Veronica wandered over to her station. "May I?" She picked up a shrimp dumpling and took a bite. Her forehead creased as she considered the dish. "Nice job, chef," she said at last. Before Griffin could completely take in the compliment, Veronica asked a question she didn't know how to answer. "But is it good enough to beat me?"

"We'll see." Griffin grabbed the judges' baskets and followed the servers into the dining area.

After James and Veronica sweated out their final preparations, the three faced the judges' panel.

"Griffin, your dish left me wanting," Elinor said.

Griffin tried to remain outwardly calm. Inside, she was on the verge of a full-scale panic attack. She mentally replayed her actions, searching in vain for a single false step. *What did I do wrong?*

Elinor's serious mien dissolved into a smile. "Left me wanting more, that is."

"From the perfectly brewed tea to the light yet substantial entrees and that dynamite thousand-layer cake for dessert, it was the perfect progression of flavors," Stewart said. "Great job."

"Thank you, chef."

Stewart's comments to James weren't nearly as complimentary. "Pot stickers are on the menu for most Chinese restaurants, but they aren't considered traditional Cantonese dim sum. Part of the criteria for today was authenticity. If you were intent on serving a dish considered by traditionalists to be inauthentic, you needed to knock it out of the park. You didn't."

"I was underwhelmed," Elinor said. "Your dishes weren't bad. For me, they were only okay. In this competition, okay isn't good enough."

"I stand behind my dish one hundred percent. Ask anyone and they'll tell you—"

"Actually, the diners agreed with us." Elinor read some of the comment cards the diners had been asked to complete. "This one says, 'I've had better airplane food.' And this one: 'Each item in the basket tasted like something that came out of a can.'"

"Then they, like you, are absolutely clueless." Out of the corner of her eye, Griffin could see James trembling with barely controlled fury.

Stewart defended Elinor. "James, Elinor and I are here to offer you constructive criticism."

"Then tell me something constructive."

"Try this: go back to culinary school. In a few years, your skills *might* catch up to your ego."

Seemingly unruffled by the testy exchange, Elinor moved on. "Veronica, the way you use liquid nitrogen continues to amaze me. Making green tea ice cream was ingenious."

Veronica swelled with pride.

"But it's beginning to feel like a parlor trick you've performed before. And performed better. Did you taste the ice cream?"

"Yes," Veronica said warily.

"What did you think?"

"The flavors were right where I wanted them to be."

"I beg to differ," Stewart said. "You used powdered matcha tea. Matcha has intense yet delicate flavors. You overwhelmed the delicacy by using too much vanilla to undercut the intensity. You didn't make green tea ice cream. You made vanilla ice cream that was green in color. Simply put, your ice cream left us cold. The showcase of your meal was so off it was hard to concentrate on the good things that followed. And that's a shame."

"I don't think we need any time to deliberate," Elinor said. Stewart nodded in confirmation. "Griffin, you are the winner of this challenge. Veronica, you advance to the final round. James, I'm sorry, but you are not the cream of the crop."

The information was almost too much for Griffin to process at once. She had done it. She had made it to the end. And she, not Veronica, had the momentum heading into the finals.

As James stormed off the set, Veronica celebrated as if the final outcome had already been decided.

"Did you want to face me in the finals because you thought I'd be harder to beat or easier?" Griffin asked.

"Like I told you the first night, I want a woman to win this thing. So do you."

"Looks like we got our wish."

Stewart came over to offer his congratulations. "Ladies, we'll see you in August."

The live finale was scheduled to take place on August 12, which meant the first episode would air in less than two weeks. Griffin was amazed by the quick turnaround but thankful, too. She was tired of the subterfuge. The sooner she could let everyone in on her secret, the better.

Veronica grinned. "After we knock out this last round of interviews and smile pretty for the camera, why don't I buy you a beer to celebrate?"

She gave Griffin a look that was all too familiar. She trotted out the come-hither glance each time she wanted to channel the emotional energy of an argument into the physical exertion of mad, passionate, mindless sex. Instead of making Griffin's pulse race as it once had, Veronica's sultry look had no effect.

"Rain check on that drink. There's someone I have to see."

CHAPTER EIGHTEEN

Rachel made a reservation for three at a hole-in-the-wall restaurant on East 57th Street that served the best Vietnamese food in the city. She was meeting Jane and Colleen after work. Colleen or the baby—or both—was in the mood for pho, the beef noodle soup that had been a staple of Vietnamese cuisine for over a hundred years.

She took the train from the office to the restaurant. Even though she was a few minutes early, the greeter showed her to her table. Her cell phone rang shortly after she settled into her seat. She reached for the phone, expecting Jane or Colleen to be calling to say they were running late but were on their way. A number she hadn't seen in ages was printed on the display. Griffin's number.

She answered the phone wondering how she should feel. When Griffin had said they weren't going to see each other for a while, she hadn't expected complete radio silence. Rachel didn't doubt Griffin was busy with work, but she didn't know any chefs who worked twenty-four seven. She hadn't seen or heard from Griffin in nearly three weeks. What where they supposed to do now, pick up where they left off, or start fresh?

"Where are you?" Griffin asked without preamble.

"I could ask you the same thing. Actually, what I should be asking is where you've been."

"I told you I'd be out of touch for a while," Griffin said defensively.

"I didn't think 'a while' would feel so long. Why couldn't you call or send me a text?"

"It's…hard to explain."

"Try."

"I will."

"When?"

"Soon," Griffin said with an air of finality. She sighed. "Look. I don't want to fight with you. I've missed you and I want to see you."

"I've missed you, too."

"Then tell me where you are."

"I'm meeting Jane and Colleen for dinner at Saigon. Would you like to join us or are you working tonight, too?"

"No, I'm as free as a bird. Order me some spring rolls, some mint chicken rice, and a bottle of Three Three Three. I'll be there in twenty minutes."

She arrived ten minutes after Jane and Colleen. Rachel wanted to be mad at her for checking out for three weeks and sidestepping her questions about her whereabouts when she finally turned up again, but she was so glad to see her, her anger vanished the instant Griffin pulled her into her arms.

Jane dipped a grilled jumbo shrimp into a bowl of peanut sauce. "Where the hell have you been?"

"Work." Griffin pulled out the extra chair Rachel had requested after they ended their call. "I've been working."

"Nonstop without a break?" Jane asked. "I'd call the Department of Labor if I were you. I think you've got a case."

Griffin breathed a sigh of relief when the waitress interrupted Jane's line of questioning by bringing out bowls of crispy noodles and spicy mustard. If she had known Jane was going to play the protective best friend and grill her on why she hadn't been around lately, she might have refused Rachel's invitation to dinner in favor of a more private reunion. Then she could have defused any questions with a kiss or a well-timed caress. Not to mention they could have gotten an early start on making up for lost time.

While the waitress quizzed Colleen about the baby—a boy, according to the ultrasound—Griffin dipped her hand under the table and placed it on Rachel's thigh. Rachel trembled at her touch.

Griffin leaned over and kissed her cheek. Then she placed her lips close to Rachel's ear and whispered, "I'm not going to be able to make it through dinner. I want you now."

"We haven't been served our entrées. We can't leave now."

"We don't have to leave. We can stay right here." She gave Rachel's leg a gentle squeeze.

"You wouldn't dare."

Rachel's ears reddened. Griffin longed to trace their curves with her tongue.

"Wouldn't I?"

After the entrées arrived, Griffin lifted a forkful of mint chicken rice to her mouth. Under the table, she kneaded Rachel's leg and lightly caressed her inner thigh. Biting back a moan, Rachel tried to squeeze her legs shut before Griffin could press her advantage, but Griffin was too quick for her. She slipped her hand between Rachel's legs and cupped her in her palm. Rachel looked at her as if she didn't know whether to kiss her or strangle her. Griffin tried not to smile.

"Jane and I have been talking about which one of us is going to be the good cop and who's going to be the bad one," Colleen said.

Jane raised her hand. "Bad cop."

"Who was the disciplinarian in your family, Griffin, your mom or your dad?" Colleen asked.

"My mom. Dad talked a good game, but he's such a big kid he was usually right there with us when we did something stupid, fun, life-threatening, or all of the above. Mom was the one who made sure we—and he—never did the stupid, fun, life-threatening thing again."

Griffin's fingers slid against Rachel's jeans, applying the right amount of pressure in all the right places.

"Are you serious?" Rachel asked. Griffin could feel her fighting to keep her hips from following the sensuous rhythm her fingers were setting.

As far as Colleen and Jane were concerned, Rachel was referring to what Griffin said about her father, but Griffin knew better.

"Very," she said, picking up the pace.

"What does your dad do?" Jane asked.

"He's retired now, but he was a pediatrician for forty years. My brother Kieran was his associate for six years before he took over the practice four years ago."

"And your mom?"

Griffin pinched Rachel's clit through her jeans. Rachel couldn't stop the whimper that rose from her throat. Colleen's and Jane's heads swiveled in her direction. "Her mother's a photographer. And a very talented one at that." Her voice shook just the slightest bit, but neither Jane nor Colleen seemed to notice.

Griffin picked up the conversational slack.

"She loves to say her family is her vocation and photography is her avocation. My brothers and I were her favorite subjects when we were growing up, whether we wanted to be or not. When she finally emptied the nest, she threw herself into her art full-bore. She prefers landscape shots, but her portraits are amazing, too."

"Did having a brother who's gay make it easier or more difficult for you to come out?" Colleen asked.

"I actually came out before Logan did so you'll have to ask him that question. But my brothers didn't give him grief about his announcement, if that's what you're wondering. They were as supportive of him as they were of me. They still are."

Griffin's hand flexed and released. Flexed and released. Rachel's hands were shaking so badly she couldn't eat. Her fork clattered against her plate as it slipped from her fingers.

"Would you like me to finish?" Even though Griffin was pointing to the rest of Rachel's dumplings, she wasn't asking her if she wanted her to clean her plate.

"Yes, please. I'm about to burst."

"You've only had a couple of bites. Are you feeling okay, Rach?" Colleen asked, already exhibiting maternal concern.

"I'm fine."

"Are you sure?" Colleen placed a hand on Rachel's forehead. "You're awful warm."

"I'm f—I'm fine," Rachel insisted as her self-control began to slip.

Griffin's own adrenaline was pumping so hard she could hear it roaring in her ears. She turned to face Rachel. She didn't want to miss a second of what was about to happen.

Keeping her face calm and her breathing steady, Rachel rode the wave as it built, crested, and finally fell. In Griffin's opinion, a woman was never more beautiful than when she was coming. Rachel reaffirmed her position. Her eyes were lit from within, the brown orbs transformed into twin pools of glowing amber.

"Damn, that was good." Griffin tossed her napkin on Rachel's empty plate and fixed her with a knowing smile. "Who wants seconds?"

Rachel unspooled a languid smile. "Don't you ever get enough?"

"Not even close." Griffin needed to taste her. To feel her legs wrapped around her waist. To ride her until she came. This time with much more fanfare. "I'm done with the appetizer. I'm ready for the main course. Aren't you?"

Rachel raised a hand to get the waitress's attention. "Check, please."

❖

In Rachel's apartment, Griffin peeled off her T-shirt and dropped it on the living room floor. Then she unhooked her bra and slowly slid it down her arms. She stood next to the window and beckoned for Rachel to join her.

"What are you doing?" Rachel hurriedly closed the blinds.

"The first year I moved to New York, I had sex in a hospitality suite in Arthur Ashe Stadium in full view of the spectators during a night match at the U.S. Open. If the action on court hadn't been so exciting, my date and I might have made the highlight shows instead of the players."

"Sexy, but not something I want to add to my bucket list."

Rachel pulled Griffin away from the window and slowly circled her. Griffin tracked her movements with her eyes.

"You're going to punish me for what I did to you in the restaurant, aren't you?"

Rachel continued to circle her. "Yes, I am."

"I can't wait."

Rachel stopped behind her. She trailed a finger across Griffin's strong shoulders. She wanted to slide her tongue along the nape of Griffin's neck, down her back. She wanted to turn her around, pull her shorts and underwear down to her ankles, kneel in front of her, and take her into her mouth.

All in due time, she reminded herself. She had waited three weeks. She could wait ten more minutes.

She brushed Griffin's hair aside. Her hair smelled like mangoes, her skin like vanilla. "I've missed you."

"I've missed you, too." Griffin shuddered when Rachel's lips found the sensitive place behind her ear. "I like being in control, but I love when the woman I'm with takes the upper hand."

"Like this?"

Rachel wrapped her arms around Griffin's waist and unbuttoned her khaki shorts. She pulled the zipper down and tugged the shorts over Griffin's hips. She grazed her fingertips over the tops of Griffin's thighs. Arching her back, Griffin leaned against her. Her hips pressed against Rachel's front. Her hands snaked into Rachel's hair. Rachel gripped her sides, holding her in place.

"I want you," Griffin said.

Rachel slipped her hand inside Griffin's silk panties. Her fingers came away wet. "I can tell."

Griffin rubbed her back against Rachel's breasts. Rachel's nipples formed into hard points. She turned Griffin to face her. Griffin's eyes were clouded with desire.

"Tell me something I never would have suspected about you."

"Now?"

"Yes, now. We've turned my life into an open book, but a great deal of yours is like a teenage girl's diary. The lock's still on it and you have the only key." She slowly slid her hands over Griffin's rippled stomach. "I opened myself to you. Open yourself to me. Tell me something I don't know."

Griffin's full lips parted. "Being a chef wasn't my initial choice of profession."

Rachel lightly ran her fingertips down Griffin's arms. The fine blond hairs immediately stood on end. "What was your first choice?"

"When I was a kid, I always thought I'd go to medical school and become a doctor like my dad."

"Why didn't you?"

"Cooking's sexier."

"So I've noticed." Rachel teased Griffin's nipples with her thumbs, eliciting a low moan. She pushed Griffin's underwear over her hips and cupped Griffin's ass in her hands. "Ready?" She flicked her eyes toward the bedroom.

Griffin grinned. "I thought you'd never ask."

She took a step toward the CD player, but Rachel pulled her back. "Not tonight. Tonight, the only song I want to hear is yours. Come sing for me."

In the bedroom, Griffin ran through the scales. What she lacked in skill, she made up for in volume. Rachel had never seen a better performance.

CHAPTER NINETEEN

Rachel slid her hand across the bed, searching for the warmth of Griffin's body. She opened her eyes when her search uncovered only rumpled sheets.

"Griffin?"

No answer.

She sat up in bed. Her apartment was ominously quiet. Griffin was gone. Again.

This is becoming par for the course.

Their reunion had been agonizingly brief. After they made love, Griffin had seemed distracted at best and, to be honest, disinterested. She had spent the rest of the night returning e-mails and texts rather than telling Rachel where she'd been or, more importantly, where she thought their relationship might be headed.

The answer was obvious. They were headed nowhere fast. Griffin's promises that they would soon have more time together seemed to be just that. Promises. Rachel didn't want promises. She wanted guarantees. She needed a commitment. Something Griffin was apparently unwilling—or unable—to give.

Life with her was like an endless game of hide-and-seek. She disappeared for weeks on end, showed up for a few hours, then took off again. Rachel didn't have time for games.

Maybe it was time to change the rules.

She rolled out of bed with a weary sigh. She was exhausted and she hadn't gone to work yet.

While the coffee maker brewed a pot of decaf, she opened her apartment door to retrieve the newspaper that lay in the hallway. She greeted a sleepy neighbor performing the same chore, then returned to the kitchen and poured a cup of coffee.

While she waited for the steaming brew to cool to a manageable temperature, she read the headlines on the front page. More of the same old, same old. She skipped to the entertainment section. Her jaw dropped when she saw Griffin on the front page of the section. She took a long swallow of coffee to make sure she wasn't dreaming. When she turned back to the article, the content hadn't changed. The cast list for *Cream of the Crop* had been released and Griffin's name was on it.

Rachel opened the full-page spread. The group photo above the fold showed the entire cast—Griffin, one other woman, and six men. Each contestant's individual photo and a short bio were printed below the fold. Rachel scanned the list of names and read the profiles attached to each.

Griffin Sutton. Veronica Warner. James Cavanaugh. Salvatore Iocovozzi. Jorge Gonzalez. Trevor Wright. Brady Rosen. Damian Myers.

Damian Myers? The same Damian Myers who used to play center field for the Mets? According to his bio, he had made the leap from hitting home runs to flipping gourmet burgers.

"Wow."

Rachel took another hit of coffee. Her father had been a Mets fan since he was a kid. She didn't know which she had been forced to watch more often, her mother's home movies or her father's replay of Game 6 of the 1986 World Series when the Mets had bounced back from being down to their last out to force a decisive seventh game. If Griffin knew Damian Myers, her father would be begging her for his autograph.

Rachel read the accompanying article. According to the story, the preliminary episodes of *Cream of the Crop* had recently finished filming. The finalists had already been determined, but their identities would remain top secret until the penultimate episode aired on August 5.

Rachel shook her head. This was where Griffin had been for the past three weeks. This was the reason she hadn't been able to say what she had been up to. Not because she didn't want to. Because she wasn't allowed to.

Griffin had been so secretive since their trip to Newport Beach, Rachel had started to think she was seeing someone else. She felt silly for doubting her—and relieved her fears had proven to be baseless. But something still nagged at her.

She was happy about the opportunity Griffin had been given by being chosen to take part in the competition, but she was worried about the effect it would have on their relationship, which had been showing signs of strain before their vacation and had been in a holding pattern ever since.

If Griffin performed well on the show or ended up winning, the result would be life-changing. Everyone would know her name. Everyone would want a piece of her. The demands on her already limited time would increase even more. Would she have any time left for her? She barely had any as it was, and she was only a local celebrity not a national one, a distinction that was most assuredly about to change.

She and Griffin needed to talk. Sooner rather than later.

When her phone rang, her heart wanted it to be Griffin on the other end of the line, but her head said it wasn't. As was often the case, her heart came out on the losing end.

"Have you read this morning's paper?" her mother asked, bubbling with excitement.

"I'm looking at it right now."

"Griffin seems so down-to-earth in person I keep forgetting she's famous. I can't believe I get to rub elbows with an actual TV star."

"I'm happy for you, Mom."

As usual, her mother failed to detect the sarcasm in her voice.

"No, honey. I'm happy for *you*. Your father was right, you know. She's quite a catch."

Rachel smiled, accepting defeat. "She certainly is. Too bad she won't allow herself to be caught."

She scanned the sea of smiling faces in the group photo and read the caption underneath. Her breath caught when she finally realized why one of the other cast members' names seemed almost as familiar to her as Damian Myers's.

She stared at the individual portrait of the other woman in the cast. A gorgeous, inked-up brunette who looked more like a motorcycle mama than a seasoned chef. Veronica Warner.

Rachel pressed her suddenly sweaty palms on the countertop. Griffin's former lover was in the cast. Had Griffin known that prior to her audition? Was Veronica the reason she had auditioned in the first place? If so, had Griffin hoped to get back at her or to get back together?

Dozens of questions swirled around Rachel's brain. The way Griffin described it, the end of her relationship with Veronica had been acrimonious at best. In the group photo, they didn't look like bitter enemies. They didn't look like former lovers. They looked like current ones.

Veronica stood with her arms wrapped around Griffin's shoulders as if she were staking a claim to her. Griffin wasn't exactly shying away. Her fingers were curled around Veronica's wrist as if to prolong the embrace.

"I've got to go, Mom. I need to call the TV star."

"Tell her Gene and I will be rooting for her."

"Don't worry. I plan on giving her an earful."

❖

Griffin picked up the newspaper. The official cast photo the producers had chosen was the one she had liked the least. Veronica had grabbed her just before the photographer snapped the picture.

"Come on, Sutton," Veronica had said. "At least act like you like me."

As soon as the photo was taken, Griffin had broken Veronica's hold and changed her position in the lineup. She had moved closer to Sal and Damian, two men who reminded her of her brothers. The photos she had taken clowning around with them were the ones she would have preferred to be used, but she didn't have a say.

She stared at her frozen smile.

"I look like a deer in headlights."

"I beg to differ." Tucker put the three phones in his hands on hold. "You look like you've been ridden hard and put away wet. You need to call Rachel and do some damage control before she sees that."

"I would if I had the time. She's probably getting ready for work, and I have a meeting with Kathleen and Ava in an hour. I can't keep them waiting."

"Is it time for the annual State of the Union address already?"

"Unfortunately, yes."

Once a year, Griffin and Match's owners met to discuss the restaurant. Kathleen and Ava shared the numbers their accountant had crunched, and she gave a detailed presentation that touched on everything from requests for equipment upgrades to process improvements to suggested menu changes to the kitchen staff's strengths and weaknesses. She had sneaked out of Rachel's apartment at five thirty so she could come home and rehearse what she wanted to say during her scheduled sit-down with her bosses.

She tossed the paper aside. She wished the *Cream of the Crop* feature had appeared in Sunday's edition, which would have given her more time to prepare for the media onslaught. Her land line had been ringing off the hook all morning, and her cell was blowing up so much she was sick of hearing the ringtone.

Tucker was managing to stay on top of the many requests for bookings, but she had never seen him look so harried.

"I've got *E! News* on my phone, *Live with Kelly* on the house phone, and *Good Day New York* on your cell," he said. "Which ones do you want me to turn down and which ones would you like me to accept?"

"You decide. But make it fast, okay? We need to be out the door in ten minutes, tops."

"*Live with Kelly* it is. That will provide you with local and national exposure and reach the widest audience. Appearing on the rest would be overkill. You have to promote the show, but you don't want to risk overexposing yourself and make potential viewers sick of you before you're seen cracking your first egg."

She picked up the outfit he had laid out for her and headed to the bathroom to finish getting dressed. "Why do I feel like I'm about to be on the hook for another pair of shoes?"

"Because you are."

He made one booking and turned down the other two. Before they could finally enjoy some peace and quiet, the phones started ringing again.

"Incoming!" Tucker said. As she tucked her shirt into her pants, she saw him check the caller IDs on the land line and her cell phone. "I've got Logan on your cell and Rachel on the land line. Which do you want?"

She glanced at her watch as her pulse began to race. "It's five a.m. on the West Coast. If Logan's calling me at the crack of dawn, something must have happened to someone in our family. Give him to me." She reached for her cell phone, leaving Tucker with the land line. "Tell Rachel I'll call her later. And hurry up."

"I know. I know. You don't want to be late."

"Believe me. Kathleen and Ava are not the kind of people I want to keep waiting. Not if I expect to remain gainfully employed." She pressed her cell phone to her ear and strode toward the living room. "Logan, what's going on?"

"Turn off the alarm bells. Nothing's wrong."

"Then what is it?"

"I spoke to the bank. Grandpa's place is pretty much ours if we want it."

"That's great news. So why the early wake-up call?"

"The guys and I have been talking. If this venture is meant to be a family affair, why should we hire an outsider as head chef? Why can't you do it?"

"The short answer is I'm under contract. My deal renews on an annual basis, but it won't be up for renewal again until next March."

"You've got time. Ryan's great at what he does, but you know how long renovations take. If we want to restore the place to its original look, it will take even longer. Tracking down vintage furniture and fixtures will take forever. Whether we go vintage or modern, the doors won't be open until next year. I don't want to pressure you, sis. If Match is your dream job, tell me and I'll shut up. But if it isn't, I know one that might be."

"I've always wanted to work in New York. You know that. I feel like I'm beginning to make my mark, but I'm not where I want to be. Not yet."

"If you don't want to leave, I understand. I'm sure you'll find someone for our place who's almost as good as you are. Just remember one thing: you can always come home if you want to. We'll be here to welcome you with open arms."

"Thanks, bro. You've certainly given me a lot to think about."

"That was the plan. Love you, sis."

She could hear the smile in his voice.

"Ditto."

"Would it kill you to say, 'I love you,' every once in a while? Take my advice, Iron Chef. You've proven how tough you can be. Don't be afraid to show you can be tender, too. Try it once. For me. Say, 'I love you, Logan.'"

"If I could reach through the phone, I'd strangle you right now."

"Say it." His voice was gentle. He sounded like he was trying to coax a reluctant Diamond into eating her Brussels sprouts.

Great. Now I'm being treated like a four-year-old.

"Say it."

She growled in frustration. "I love you, Logan."

He chuckled. "I knew you had it in you. Have a good day, sis."

Griffin stared out her living room window after she ended the call. She had moved to the East Coast hoping to conquer New York. Now the city literally lay at her feet. Why didn't it feel like enough? Because she wasn't done. She had more work to do. The question was, where?

Part of her wanted to take her brothers' suggestion and become the linchpin of the family business. The other part wanted to continue pursuing her dream. She couldn't follow two paths at once.

"I'm ready if you are," Tucker said.

Griffin turned and headed for the door. "Did you tell Rachel I'd call her later?"

Tucker grabbed his messenger bag off the couch and slung the reinforced strap over his shoulder. "Yeah, but she didn't sound too happy about it."

In the hallway, Griffin jabbed the Down button on the elevator. The doors slid open. She and Tucker stepped into the waiting car.

"Rachel's probably pissed at me for leaving with my shoes in my hand like a cheating husband sneaking into the house after spending the night with his mistress." Griffin pinched the bridge of her nose between her thumb and index finger as the elevator began to descend. "When I called her last night, I almost blew it as soon as she asked me where I've been. I wanted to share everything I'd experienced while we were apart. I wanted to recount every challenge, tell her about each prize up for grabs, and list all the interesting people I met, but I couldn't do it. Any of it. I'm shutting her out when all she wants is for me to let her in."

"You don't have a choice. I read the contract, remember? I've seen the restrictions you're under. Otherwise, I'd be begging you to dish out behind-the-scenes gossip like you were Kathy Griffin on a Bravo special. I knew where you were because I had to handle your business affairs while you were away. Kathleen and Ava knew because the idea was partially theirs in the first place. But no one else knew. Not even your parents. Surely, Rachel understands why you had to keep this from her."

Griffin sighed when the elevator finally reached the ground floor. "If she doesn't, I'll make it up to her when I have the time."

"When's that going to be? You're juggling too many commitments as it is. In addition to Match, you're committed to *Cream of the Crop* for the next two months and the LA property for at least the next year."

"Don't remind me. It's ironic someone often accused of having a lack of commitment suddenly has an overabundance of them, don't you think?"

The elevator doors opened. Griffin and Tucker walked across the lobby. Griffin nodded to the doorman, who tipped his cap and opened the back door of a taxi idling by the curb.

"Did Rachel say what she wanted?" Griffin asked after she climbed inside.

"Yes," Tucker said, "but it seemed kind of odd. She wanted to know where you see yourself in five years."

Griffin watched the sights of the city stream past the window. "I don't know where I'm going to be in five months, let alone five years."

"Yeah, that's what I said."

"And?"

"She didn't sound too happy about that, either."

❖

Rachel stared at the telephone receiver after Tucker ended the call. Tucker's answer to her question was unwanted but not unexpected. Griffin lived for the moment, which was okay if you were in your twenties. Rachel was closer to forty than she was to twenty. Griffin was only a year behind her, yet the gap between them seemed to grow wider every day.

In Newport Beach, there had been no space between them. Rachel had felt closer to Griffin than she ever had. She had seen her as the kid she once was and the woman she had become. She had seen her through the eyes of her family. What a beautiful sight that had been. But California was a world away, and Griffin now seemed just as distant.

She looked in her organizer. Sunday promised a trip to Louisiana via the Bourbon Street Bar and Grille. Griffin might be surprised to discover there would be more on the menu than red beans and rice, crawfish étouffée, beignets, and a couple of Sazeracs to wash everything down.

"Because Sunday is the day we decide if we're finally going to come together or keep drifting apart."

❖

Griffin had skipped breakfast, so her stomach began to growl halfway through her meeting. The conference took much longer than it normally did as Kathleen and Ava tried to drag details out of her about *Cream of the Crop*. Details she couldn't give.

"At least tell us if you made it to the final round," Ava said. "I want to know if we should buy commercial time on the final episode."

Griffin tried to concoct a carefully-worded response.

"I have to appear on the finale whether I'm cooking on the set or sitting in the audience. I'll have face time no matter what, but if you want to make sure the restaurant's name gets mentioned, you'd better contact the publicity department."

"Well played," Ava said with a laugh.

"The restaurant's about to open, so let's wrap things up." Kathleen picked an invisible piece of lint off her Armani suit. "Just between us, how's Erica doing?"

"She has always been a kick-ass chef, but her one drawback was her lack of self-belief. Over the past few months, though, she has grown by leaps and bounds. Her confidence in the kitchen has soared."

"And that's due to?"

"Increased responsibility. Filling in for me these past few weeks has done wonders for her. I would say I should go away more often, but if I did, I might find myself out of a job."

Ava toyed with the strand of pearls around her neck. "As long as our names are on the lease, you'll always have a job here."

"That's good to hear. Thank you."

"Do you think Erica is head chef material?"

"Without a doubt."

"When do you think she'll be ready to take the next step in her career?"

"She's almost there. Six months, maybe nine and she'll be ready."

Kathleen gazed at Ava. "I told you Erica was a hot commodity," she said with an air of triumph.

Ava rested a jeweled hand on Kathleen's forearm. "You were right. Now we need to pay her or risk losing her to someone else."

"Do you trust my instincts?"

"Always. We've found the Next Big Thing. What we need to do now is come up with some numbers we can live with and get her under contract."

Ava tucked a lock of Kathleen's hair behind her ear. Griffin felt like she was intruding on a private moment.

"How have you managed to live and work together for so long without driving each other crazy?"

Ava smiled as if she had fielded the question many times before. "After years of trial and error, we've found the perfect balance. We leave our work lives at work and our home lives at home."

"Of course, it helps to have the right partner in both places." Kathleen's eyes glowed with obvious affection for the woman who had been her partner for longer than Griffin had been alive. "And you should never, ever go into business with family."

"I was afraid you'd say that. But it does bring me to the other matter I'd like to discuss with you today. I've told you about the supper club my grandfather used to own in Los Angeles."

Kathleen nodded. "La La Land. The building has a storied history and is located on a prime stretch of real estate. I'm surprised the new owners haven't been able to turn a profit."

"Well, now it's my turn to try. My family and I have the chance to buy the building and we're going to take it."

"You're going to run your own restaurant?" Kathleen asked.

"I'd be one of the owners, not the principal buyer."

"Like I said, you're going to run your own restaurant."

"You're not planning on leaving us, are you?" Ava fingered her pearl necklace as if it were a string of rosary beads.

"The doors won't open until next year at the earliest. I plan to invest in the restaurant, find a suitable head chef, and offer input as needed but not be a part of the day-to-day operations. If those plans change, I want to know if I'd have your support during the transition."

Kathleen leaned back in her chair. She was silent for several long moments. "We'd hate to lose you, obviously, but you had such a good eye with talent where Erica is concerned that we can afford to grant your wish without worrying about a substantial drop-off in quality. Thanks to you, we have an embarrassment of riches."

"We realize the importance of family," Ava said, putting a more personal spin on the situation. "If you decide you'd rather be closer to yours, Kathleen and I wouldn't stand in your way."

"I appreciate that. Thank you."

"I do have one piece of advice," Kathleen said. "If you do leave, make sure you win that goddamned show before you do." She clapped Griffin on the back. "Now let's eat before you try to convince me you didn't make the final."

Griffin loved the pre-opening meal, when everyone from the busboys to the owners sat at the same table to sample the day's specials. The gatherings helped build team spirit and kept morale high.

She took in the familiar faces surrounding the table. If she left this group behind, she'd be returning to one family but walking away from another.

"See you tonight, chef?" Erica asked after the dessert plates were cleared.

Griffin typically skipped the lunch service in order to focus on dinner, when the crowds were larger and more demanding and restaurant critics were more apt to stop by. Erica was in charge of the lighter afternoon crowds when tourists and office workers filled the tables.

"Actually, I think I'm going to work the afternoon shift today."

"Really?"

"Yes, and I'd also like to switch things up tonight." Whether she returned to California or remained in New York, she needed to insure Erica had the necessary training and experience when the time came for her to take the reins at Match or the restaurant of her choice. "Tonight, you take the lead. I'll be your second."

Erica's eyes widened in panic. Griffin tried to provide reassurance for her young second-in-command.

"I've heard nothing but raves about your performance while I was away. You've impressed everyone else. I want to see what all the fuss is about. The kitchen's yours, chef."

Erica stared at her as if she were waiting for her to say she was playing a belated April Fool's joke. "Um, okay," she said when she realized Griffin was being perfectly serious. "You'll be in charge of the line cooks, prep cooks, and dishwashers. It'll be your job to make sure the food gets out on time and there are enough clean plates to put it on. You'll also be the expediter. Take the orders from the floor and relay them to the kitchen."

She continued with the rest of her instructions, making sure everyone in the kitchen knew his or her assigned roles.

"Yes, chef," each staff member said when she was done.

The day was long and hectic but went smoothly. At the end of the night, Griffin and Erica commiserated over snifters of brandy.

Griffin raised her glass. "Nice work, chef."

Erica beamed, her chest puffing with pride at the compliment. "This was the best day of my career."

"Mine, too. Watching you work today was amazing. You were patient with your staff, confident in yourself, and solid in your decision-making. Three things a head chef needs to be."

"You're just saying that to humor me."

"No, I'm not. Great work tonight." Griffin held out her hand for a fist bump. She took another sip of brandy after Erica met her hand with her own. "Whatever happened with you and Theresa Testi?"

"Which one?"

"The one who needed a private cooking lesson in our kitchen."

"Oh, you mean Caroline. We've been seeing each other for a few months now. I might have given her a cooking lesson, but she's definitely taught me a thing or two outside the kitchen, that's for sure." Erica sipped her drink and slowly lowered the glass to the table. "With so many women out there, I didn't think I could limit myself to one."

"What happened to change that? Oh, let me guess. Caroline."

"She had a great deal to do with it, yes, but I had to make the change. I had to stop listening to the voice in my head that said it wanted more. I sabotaged every relationship I had that showed promise because I didn't think I could sustain it. I had my wobbles with this relationship, too, until I realized Caroline is who I want.

She's the one I want to be with. I have everything I want and I have it with one person. What else could I ask for?" Erica sighed in contentment. "I'm in a good place right now. I have a job I love and a woman who loves me despite my many faults."

Erica's levelheadedness continued to blow her away. She was incredibly talented and wise beyond her years. Could she really be only twenty-four? The thought made Griffin feel old—but honored to have been able to serve as her mentor.

"I don't have anything else to teach you, grasshopper. You're ready. All you need is for me to get out of your way."

CHAPTER TWENTY

Rachel's doorbell rang a little after midnight, waking her from a fitful sleep. She yawned and rubbed her gritty eyes as she padded to the door. She squinted to peer through the peephole. Seeing Griffin's face cleared the cobwebs. Griffin usually looked euphoric after work, adrenaline coursing through her veins as she relived the events of the evening. Tonight, though, she looked exhausted.

"I know it's late, but I had to see you," Griffin said after Rachel opened the door. She kept her voice low, most likely out of respect for the neighbors and the lateness of the hour. "I've had a long day and I need to feel your skin against mine."

When Griffin reached for her, Rachel held out a hand to keep her at bay.

"No." Rachel's body screamed in protest, crying out for the pleasure Griffin's touch never failed to deliver.

Griffin seemed almost shocked by Rachel's refusal. "Why not?"

"Because if you come inside, we'll end up in bed and we can't sleep together again until we figure things out."

"What's there to figure out?" Griffin's weary smile seemed to eradicate her fatigue. "I already know where the noses go. And everything else for that matter. I need you."

"And I need to know where I stand with you." Rachel felt exposed having such a personal conversation in the hall. She pulled Griffin into the foyer and closed the door.

"Is this because of the show?"

"Yes and no."

"I figured as much. When I signed up for the show, we barely knew each other."

"And when you left to film it? What were we then?"

"I wanted to tell you about it, but I wasn't allowed to." Griffin's response seemed designed to absolve her of blame but didn't answer the question at hand.

"I know. I've seen enough reality TV to know how these things work. Contestants go off for some predetermined period of time and make up some lame excuse for the people they've left behind."

"If you know that, then what's the problem?"

"Who am I to you? Am I a placeholder—someone you're having a few laughs with until the real thing comes along—or do I mean something to you?"

Griffin opened her mouth to respond, but nothing came out.

"I want to be more than comfort food you turn to when you've had a bad day," Rachel said. "I could use another metaphor, but it would involve you leaving money on the nightstand at the end of the night."

Griffin looked hurt. "Is that what you think you are to me?"

"I don't know what I am to you. Every time I broach the subject, you steer the conversation in a different direction or you tell me we'll talk about it later. I don't want to talk about it later. I want to talk about it now. I'll go first."

She backed Griffin against the wall and pressed her hands against it, penning her in. Griffin stood with her hands on her hips like a misbehaving teenager about to be given an unwanted lecture from an authority figure.

"I love having sex with you, but sex shouldn't be the only thing keeping us together. I want this." Her right hand settled into the apex of Griffin's thighs. Griffin pressed against her palm. "But I want this, too." She slid her hand up Griffin's body until it came to rest over her heart. "I can't ask for it. You have to give it to me."

Griffin put her hands on Rachel's waist and pulled her closer. "I've been seeing you and only you for months. What else do I have to do to prove I'm interested in you?"

"Make me feel like we're the only ones in this relationship."

"Aggie was a one-night stand that ended almost before it began."

"And Veronica?"

"Is a part of my past I don't care to revisit. There isn't anyone else and hasn't been for a while."

"You barely have time for one woman, let alone two. There isn't some*one* else in your life. There's some*thing*. There are three components in this relationship: me, you, and your career. Your career always comes first."

Griffin released her hold and resumed her previous stance. "What do you want me to do, quit my job? Change professions?"

"Of course not. Cooking is your life. Asking you to do anything else would be like asking you to stop breathing."

Rachel released her from her makeshift holding cell. Griffin bolted for freedom. She paced around the room like a caged tiger looking for an escape route. "I want to feel like I matter more to you than I do. I want to spend more time with you."

"I understand that, but I don't have any time to give. Even if I gave Erica more of my hours at the restaurant, I still have to be available to publicize the show on the Web, in print, and on the air. I'm under so much pressure right now it feels like my head's about to explode. Everyone wants something from me. The producers want me to maintain the confidentiality of the show, which won't be easy considering everyone I know will be constantly grilling me about the results. I have to maintain the quality at Match even though I have less time to keep track of everything. My brothers want me to move back to Newport Beach because they don't want anyone other than family to take on a role as important as head chef. And now there's you."

Rachel tried to slow her racing heart. Why did the first fight always feel like the last?

"You knew what my career was like when we met," Griffin said. "Why is it a problem for you now?"

"Wait. Slow down." Rachel held Griffin by her shoulders. She could feel the nervous energy flowing off her in waves. "I'm not asking you to propose marriage, but I'm falling in love with you, Griffin, and I need to know if I mean something to you."

"I think that's kind of obvious, don't you?"

Griffin swiped at her face, flicking away tears. Rachel had never seen her more in need of comfort. She pulled Griffin into her arms.

"Shh. It's okay."

Griffin's arms circled her and latched on tight.

"You're the most stable thing in my life right now," Griffin said. "I don't want to lose you."

"You haven't lost me, but we have lost our way. We began a journey five months ago. We were going great for a while, but we seem to have taken an unplanned detour." She held Griffin at arm's length. "Let's get back on course."

"How?"

Rachel took her hand and led her to the bedroom.

"You can start by being here when I wake up in the morning."

CHAPTER TWENTY-ONE

On Friday, July 20, Rachel skipped her traditional lunchtime trip to the gym and headed to the hospital instead. Colleen's obstetrician had decided to forego a natural delivery in favor of a C-section. At 8:07 a.m., Steven Lambert-Mangano was born. Jane had sent her a text two minutes later. The photos started coming shortly after and hadn't stopped.

When she walked into the hospital lobby, Griffin was waiting for her.

"I didn't think I'd see you here."

"You didn't think I'd miss out on you holding your godson for the first time, did you?"

Rachel smiled. Since Griffin turned up on her doorstep a few weeks ago, she had been like a different person. Doting, attentive, and always there whenever Rachel needed her. They didn't feel like lunch mates now. They felt like a couple.

Griffin had a stuffed doll that looked like the Swedish Chef from *The Muppets Show* fame tucked under her arm. Rachel, in contrast, was empty-handed.

"I was in such a hurry when I left the office I forgot to pick up a gift," Rachel said as they raced each other up the stairs.

"It's okay. We can tell them it's from both of us."

They joined the crowd of well-wishers in Colleen's room. Colleen's and Jane's parents and siblings as well as their friends and co-workers were taking turns holding the new addition to their extended family. Rachel joined the long line. Griffin congratulated Jane, took a peek at the baby, and pulled up a chair next to Colleen's bed.

"Don't you want to hold him?" Rachel asked when she finally got her hands on the red-haired bundle of joy. Perhaps holding Steven would change Griffin's mind about having one of her own. Looking at his cherubic face could melt the hardest heart.

"No, I'm good. The baby always attracts the most attention in these scenarios. Mom here is the real rock star."

Colleen laughed. "That's funny coming from the actual celebrity in our midst. Jane and I watch you on *Cream of the Crop* every week. We're rooting for you, but Veronica's going to be tough to beat. She and James seem really full of themselves, though. Please tell me neither one of them has a chance to win the whole thing."

"You'll have to keep watching to see if they make it that far."

Rachel gave Griffin a supportive smile. Griffin had been bombarded with questions similar to Colleen's for nearly a month. *Cream of the Crop* had been airing for three weeks. Griffin seemed to be handling the extra attention well, but Rachel knew how much of a toll the show was taking on her. When she wasn't making personal appearances to sign autographs, pose for pictures, or press the flesh, she was doing Web chats after each episode or blogging for *USA Today.*

They had watched the first episode at Match because Kathleen and Ava insisted on having a viewing party, but they had watched the subsequent episodes alone. Griffin squirmed each time she saw herself on screen. Rachel rooted her on during each challenge, even though the contests were completed weeks ago.

Rachel loved the behind-the-scenes details Griffin provided as each episode aired. It was like watching a movie with the director and actors providing commentary. She had often wondered what Griffin was up to during the three weeks she was away. Now, week by week, she was discovering what had once been secret.

She handed the baby to Colleen. "He's adorable, Coll."

Colleen looked beatific as she gazed at her sleeping son. "Maybe next year it will be your turn."

"Maybe." Rachel felt a pang of sadness. Griffin, as much as she loved her nieces, was content being an aunt and had no desire to change the moniker to Mom. "But if it never happens, it'll be okay as long as I get to spoil this little guy rotten."

"You can start," Jane said, "by offering to pay for his college education."

"Thanks, but no. I'll settle for buying him every toy in FAO Schwarz."

"That could be just as expensive."

"But a lot more fun."

CHAPTER TWENTY-TWO

On Sunday, Rachel and Griffin were supposed to have a breakfast of chicken apple sausage and blueberry pancakes as they visited Vermont, but they decided to backtrack and make up the legs they had missed while Griffin was away. They slept in and journeyed to Georgia at brunch by dining on shrimp and grits followed by a decadent dessert of bread pudding topped with praline ice cream. They spent the rest of the afternoon working off the calories.

That night, they settled in front of the TV to watch the fourth episode of *Cream of the Crop*. Griffin guaranteed the elimination challenge in tonight's episode would be a tough one. She wasn't wrong. Each of the remaining contestants was tasked with creating a dish that was like a *trompe l'oeil* painting—one that fooled the eye as well as the palate.

"I can't believe Veronica made watermelon pass for ahi tuna," Rachel said as Griffin refilled their wine glasses. "How did she manage that feat?"

Griffin leaned back on the couch and wrapped her arm around Rachel's shoulder. "That's what molecular gastronomy's all about. Changing not only how food looks but how it tastes as well. Traditionalists say it's a parlor trick more about style and technique than heart and it doesn't serve as a true barometer of someone's ability to craft a meal."

"What do you say?" Rachel laced her fingers around Griffin's.

"The results can be fascinating when properly executed, but I'd much rather consume a meal than a science experiment. And I'd much rather spend more quality time with you than watch Veronica notch yet another victory."

"She won the trip to France? Damn. I was hoping you had bagged that one so we could take a real culinary trip."

"There's always next week."

Griffin grabbed for the remote, but Rachel slid it out of reach. "If we don't watch the episode to the bitter end, I won't be able to hold up my end of the conversation around the water cooler tomorrow."

"I hope you've been working out," Veronica said onscreen. "The camera adds ten pounds, you know." She flopped on her bed and folded her hands behind her head. "Now hurry up before Sal drinks all the beer."

On TV, Griffin went to the bathroom to change into a borrowed swimsuit. As soon as the door clicked shut, Veronica pushed herself off her bed and tiptoed across the room. With one ear cocked toward the bathroom, she opened Griffin's notebook and flipped through the pages, stopping long enough to commit several of the entries to memory. Then she carefully placed the book as she'd found it and resumed her former position on the bed.

Griffin pounded her fist on the arm of the chair. "I knew it. I knew I couldn't trust her. She'd do anything to get a competitive advantage."

Rachel placed a calming hand on her thigh. "Did she use any of your recipes on the show?"

"No, she was too smart for that. If she had used one of my recipes, I would have known right away what she had done. I wouldn't have had to wait until the episode aired to find out. Now I won't be able to…"

She trailed off.

Rachel smiled. "I knew you made it to the final round."

Griffin remained noncommittal. "You said it. I didn't."

"I won't say a word. I promise."

Rachel turned back to the show. On the screen, the chefs were splitting a case of beer while they sat in a bubbling hot tub. Everyone laughed uproariously after Sal told a sidesplitting joke. Veronica put her left arm around Griffin's neck. Her right hand slipped beneath the surface of the bubbling water. Veronica whispered something in Griffin's ear and jerked her head in a gesture that seemed to say, "Follow me."

Veronica climbed out the hot tub. Griffin followed suit.

Griffin reached for the remote again. "Uh, I think we've seen enough."

"No," Rachel said firmly. "We haven't."

"Screw the party out there," Veronica said on the TV screen. She was lying on her bed in the room she shared with Griffin. She crawled off the bed and pinned Griffin against the wall. "Let's start one in here."

Rachel gasped when Griffin's and Veronica's mouths met in a passionate kiss.

"Wait, Rachel," Griffin said. "I can explain."

Rachel held up a hand to silence her. Then she placed the same hand over her mouth. Her fingers trembled against her lips.

On TV, Griffin pushed Veronica away. Veronica landed on the bed, laughing in delight as she bounced on the firm mattress. Griffin took a step toward her. "You're breaking my heart. Are we going to do this or not?"

Then the screen faded to black as Veronica said in voiceover, "It looks like the angel and the bad girl are together again."

"I don't believe you," Rachel said when she finally regained her ability to speak.

Griffin looked stricken. Rachel assumed her face bore a matching expression. She had felt this level of betrayal only one other time in her life. She had hoped she would never feel it again.

"What you saw?" Griffin said. "That isn't how it was. That's not what happened."

Rachel shrugged off Griffin's hand on her arm. "Are you actually going to try to convince me that I didn't just see you and Veronica playing tonsil hockey after she felt you up in the hot tub?

I have six million viewers I can call to the witness stand to back me up."

"For what it's worth, the kiss happened before we got in the hot tub, not after. And she kissed me. I did not kiss her. As for the rest of it, I know what it looks like, but nothing happened."

"Then why didn't you tell me about the kiss?"

"Because the kiss didn't mean anything. Veronica made a pass at me and I turned her down. End of story. Rachel, I promise you—"

"Griffin, your promises don't mean anything to me. I wish I could say the same about you."

"Rachel, don't." Griffin walked toward her, spewing apologies as she held out her arms in supplication. "Before I met you, domestic bliss wasn't on my agenda. Now the only thing I want to do is make you happy. I didn't get to that point overnight, but I'm here now and there's nowhere else I want to be."

Rachel backed away from her. "Too little, too late."

"Rachel—"

"Just go, Griffin. It's over." Rachel wrapped her arms around her middle to keep from falling apart. "Please. Leave."

"Rachel—"

"Go!"

Griffin left without another word. As soon as the door closed on her latest search for a love that would last a lifetime, Rachel collapsed on the floor in tears. This time, she didn't think she'd be able to get up.

❖

Griffin pulled out her cell phone and punched in Tucker's number. "Drop whatever you're doing. I've got a project for you that supersedes everything else."

"Let me guess. Is it about tonight's episode?"

"I need you to get your hands on the original footage."

"I don't know if the producers will hand it over without a court order."

"Get my legal team involved if you have to. I want that footage and I want it yesterday."

"You got it, boss. I know someone who knows someone who knows someone who works at the production company. Let me work my phone tree before you call the guys in the suits."

"Tucker, if you pull this off, I will buy you a pair of shoes for every day of the year. Do you understand?"

"Not necessary, boss. There's no charge for this one. I'll call you as soon as I hear something."

"Thanks, Tuck."

Disconsolate, Griffin walked the streets for hours. How, in a city of millions, could she feel so alone?

Chapter Twenty-three

Rachel wanted to call in sick for the foreseeable future, but she settled for one day. Pep talks from Jane, Colleen, and her mother got her out of bed each morning. She stumbled through the ensuing days but somehow managed to make it through them. Griffin called several times a day for two weeks, but Rachel let the calls go to voice mail. The messages were always the same. Griffin pleading for Rachel to trust her. To believe her version of events when Rachel's own eyes had seen something entirely different.

History had repeated itself. Just like Isabel, Griffin had betrayed her in the worst way imaginable. Rachel had allowed herself to trust again. She had allowed someone into her heart again. What had it gotten her? Hurt. Again.

As she worked through lunch, she tried to concentrate on her client's tax return instead of her own problems. The client had been granted an extension, which meant she had until October to submit the filing. She sorted through the additional information she had requested to see if she had everything she needed to complete the form without having to wait another three months. Her desk phone rang just as she located the receipts she had been waiting on since April.

"Rachel Bauer."

"Ms. Bauer, this is John at the security desk. I have a package for you from a Ms. Trixie Cerrito. Would you like to pick up the package yourself or would you prefer to have someone from the mail room deliver it to you?"

For a long moment, Rachel couldn't speak. She could barely breathe. Trixie Cerrito was Griffin's porn name. Griffin was here. Or had been. And she had left something she wanted her to have.

Rachel had spent the last two weeks trying to excise Griffin Sutton from her heart. Why hadn't the procedure worked? The mention of Griffin's name still made her heart beat faster. She still longed to hear Griffin call her Puddles. To have her hold her in her arms one more time.

"Ms. Bauer?"

"Sorry. I'm on my way."

She locked her computer and took the elevator downstairs. When he saw her coming, John placed a manila envelope on the counter. Rachel broke the seal with her finger. A folded piece of stationery, an unlabeled DVD in a clear plastic case, and three tickets to the live finale of *Cream of the Crop* rested inside the envelope.

Rachel waited until she reached the sanctuary of the elevator before she unfolded the slip of paper. The letter inscribed on it was brief. Not much longer than a note. The note was written in Griffin's familiar slanted script.

Puddles,

I don't make a habit of lying to people I care about, and I care about you, though I don't have the words to adequately express the depth of my feelings for you. Please watch the enclosed DVD and compare the original, unedited footage to what you saw spliced and diced on TV. I'll be waiting for your call. Not to say, "I told you so," but to try to tell you everything I stubbornly left unsaid.

If I don't hear from you, I hope to see you in the audience during the finale of Cream of the Crop. *Whether I win or lose, I can't imagine doing either without you there.*

Trixie

When the elevator doors opened, Rachel sprinted through the maze of cubicles. Griffin had taken a risk by revealing she had progressed to the final round. She had taken an even bigger one by opening her heart. Rachel wanted to trust her. She wanted to believe in her. Did she have the proof in her hand that showed she could?

"Slow down, Bauer," Mike Andrews said after she nearly bowled him over. "Where's the fire?"

Rachel unlocked her computer and placed the DVD in the appropriate drive. She spread her shoulders to block the screen and plugged in her headphones to prevent the playback from being overheard.

The footage was raw, devoid of the underlying score and dubbed-in voiceovers that had been in evidence on the broadcast. A timer in the corner let Rachel know the sequence was unbroken.

On the computer screen, Veronica looked over Griffin's shoulder while Griffin sketched in her chef's notebook. After making a smartass comment about the sketch, Veronica asked Griffin to serve as chaperone while she took a dip in the hot tub with the rest of the contestants. Griffin dragged her feet until Veronica finally managed to convince her.

Rachel itched to hit the fast forward button, but she let the scene play out in real time.

While Griffin changed clothes in the bathroom, Veronica rifled through her notebook.

So far, nothing has changed.

Then Veronica resumed her position on the bed and Griffin came out of the bathroom. On TV, the footage had skipped from the bedroom to the hot tub. Rachel leaned closer to her computer screen as Veronica backed Griffin against the wall and kissed her. Griffin pushed Veronica away.

"You said you needed a chaperone while you were in the hot tub," Griffin said. "Are we going to do this or not?"

Veronica tried to goad her into changing her mind. "Domestic bliss has made you boring."

"You're breaking my heart." Griffin walked toward the bed and dragged her out of the room. "Come on. Let's go."

The cameraman trailed Griffin and Veronica outside to the hot tub, where they remained for less than fifteen minutes before Sal told the joke that had been shown on air. Veronica's left arm wrapped around Griffin's neck. Her right hand disappeared beneath the roiling water. Then she leaned over and whispered in Griffin's ear.

"Boner alert. We've played nice long enough. Let's get out of here."

Griffin nodded. "Right behind you," she whispered.

Veronica climbed out of the hot tub. Griffin followed her. Rachel watched them head to the communal kitchen, where they made grilled ham-and-cheese sandwiches and played catch-up for twenty minutes before going to sleep in separate beds.

This version of the episode was considerably less exciting than the edited one but a great deal more satisfying.

Rachel stared at the computer screen long after the footage ended. Griffin had been telling the truth all along, but she had refused to listen. She had been quick to believe the lie and hesitant to accept the truth.

She owed Griffin an apology. And so much more.

She reached for the phone but thought better of picking it up. Even if she apologized for the past, it wouldn't change the future. As in her and Griffin's respective visions of it couldn't be more different. She planned meticulously for everything. When she wasn't working, Griffin flew by the seat of her pants. She liked stability. Griffin's life was anything but stable.

She and Griffin couldn't be more opposite, but why did it feel so right when they were together?

After Isabel left, Rachel had been afraid to love again. Afraid to trust again. Afraid of so many things. If she wanted Griffin in her life, she needed to face her fears.

Griffin had proven herself worthy of trust. Could Rachel find the courage to bestow it?

❖

Griffin butchered a side of beef. She sliced her carving knife into the meat, breaking it down into its various cuts. Brisket, short ribs, flank steak, round steak, top loin, sirloin, chuck eye, rib roast.

Besides helping her practice for whatever the judges might throw at her in the final round, the tedious task kept her mind from wandering.

It had been days since Tucker had come through for her. Days since she had delivered the DVD and the accompanying letter to Rachel's office. Had Rachel bothered to watch the footage? Had she read the letter? Griffin hadn't heard from her. Each day that passed with no word made it seem less and less likely she'd ever hear from her again.

I waited too long, she thought as she dropped a rump roast on the stainless steel counter. *I waited too long to tell her how I feel.*

She attacked the meat again. She winced when the knife sliced into her thumb. Blood gushed from the wound, which was deep but didn't seem to require stitches. She ran water over the cut, squeezed some antibiotic gel on it, and wrapped her thumb in a bandage from the first aid kit that hung on a nearby wall.

"Are you okay, chef?" Erica asked as Griffin pulled on a latex glove to protect her injured hand.

"I've been better."

"An injury in the kitchen is a sign of lack of attention," Erica said with a wink. "A wise woman taught me that years ago."

Griffin smiled through the pain. Erica had trotted out one of her favorite mantras. "So you have been paying attention."

"Only every second of every day."

Griffin placed the fresh cuts in the meat locker, cleaned the counter, then carefully cleaned her knives. By the time she dried them and packed them in a hard-shelled carrying case, she had come to a decision about her future.

"The kitchen's yours, chef. I couldn't leave it in better hands."

Erica looked up from the lamb chops she was marinating for tomorrow's lunch service. "Where are you going?"

"Home." She reached into her pocket and pulled out her cell phone. "Logan, does your offer still stand?"

CHAPTER TWENTY-FOUR

Griffin's adrenaline spiked when her nerves threatened to get the best of her. She forced herself to be patient as Kenny, a makeup technician in skinny jeans and a rhinestone-crusted *Cabaret* T-shirt, slathered her face with a mixture of assorted bases, creams, and oils. She had often accused Veronica of treating food like a science experiment; now she was being turned into one.

"Is all this really necessary?" she asked as the makeup tech reached for another brush.

Kenny put a hand on his hip. "If I had a face like yours, I wouldn't have to keep my plastic surgeon on speed dial. You don't need me to make you more beautiful, girlfriend. You need me to make sure you don't look like Casper the Friendly Ghost when the studio lights come on. How are you going to repay me?" He stepped back to review his handiwork. "You're going to give me your assistant's phone number, that's how."

Griffin cut her eyes toward the corner of the small dressing room, where Tucker was texting furiously and pretending not to be eavesdropping on their conversation. The hint of pink on his cheeks betrayed his knowledge of what was being discussed. He had often said he didn't have a "type," but the flamboyant makeup artist certainly seemed to have piqued his interest—if the Mona Lisa smile playing across his features was any indication.

"I think I'll let my assistant have the final say on this one."

Kenny tossed a powder puff in Tucker's direction. "He isn't going to be able to say anything with my breadstick in his mouth."

Tucker brushed makeup out of his curly hair. "You bring the bread; I'll bring the butter."

"Ooh, child." Kenny pulled Griffin to her feet. "Girl, get your ass out of that chair. I've got bigger fish to fry."

"I certainly hope you aren't referring to me," Veronica said. "If you are, we have a problem." The leather on the makeup chair creaked as her weight settled into it. She combed her stylishly tousled hair with her fingers. "I didn't mean to interrupt your hen party, Sutton, but I want to look my best while I'm kicking your ass in front of an audience of millions."

Dodging the barb, Griffin tossed one of her own. "Where's your Bunsen burner?" she asked after making a show of looking around the room. "I didn't think you ever left home without it."

"Good one, Sutton, but I don't need tricks to beat you." Veronica closed her eyes as Kenny began to ply his trade. "I'm still waiting on my apology, by the way."

"For what?"

Veronica broke into a grin. "Kissing you on national TV has wreaked havoc on my love life."

"It hasn't done wonders for mine, either." Griffin checked her phone, hoping Rachel would call or even send her a text. Something. Anything to let her know all had been forgiven. The phone remained ominously silent.

"Seriously, Sutton." Veronica opened her eyes. "I know we've had our ups and downs over the years, but let's put all the B.S. behind us for one night and focus on what's most important: the food."

"May the best woman win."

Griffin held out her hand. Veronica's grip was crushing.

"I intend to."

Griffin flexed her fingers as she walked out of the room. If Veronica's show of strength was meant to intimidate her, it accomplished quite the opposite. Now she was even more determined to win.

For her, tonight was about more than bragging rights. She didn't just want to win. She needed to. If she won, she could leave New York feeling like a success instead of a failure. On the practical side, she needed the money. When her contract ended in March, she'd be out of a job until La La Land opened its doors. The $250,000 winner's check would help bridge the gap. In more ways than one, her future was on the line.

At the moment, though, she didn't care about any of it. None of it mattered without Rachel.

She peeked through the curtain that separated the set from the backstage area. She scanned the faces in the audience while one of the technicians fitted her with a microphone and battery pack. The eliminated contestants milled around in front of their reserved seats in the front row. Kathleen and Ava sat nearby. Most of the other seats were already filled. Most of them. The ones that corresponded to the tickets she had left for Rachel were empty.

She let the curtain fall back into place. It was finally time to face the truth. She and Rachel were over.

❖

Rachel and her parents found their seats just before the floor director began counting down the remaining minutes before the broadcast went live. Rachel was so nervous she could barely sit still. She would have preferred to watch from the privacy of home so she could chew her fingernails in peace, but she had to be here. She had to see Griffin one more time.

Rumors were circulating Griffin was leaving Match when her contract was up to return to Newport Beach and open her own restaurant. The one she and her brothers had decided to buy while they sat around a bonfire on the beach. The night Griffin had taken her to the scene of her first kiss.

Rachel remembered the smell of the ocean breeze and the feel of the salt water when they had stood under the pier and she had said, "Tara gave you your first kiss. I want to be the one who gives you your last one."

That night seemed so long ago. Was it really less than three months? They had known each other only since December, but it felt like a lifetime.

"Is that Elinor Davies?" Rachel's mother asked as Elinor, Stewart Sands, and the evening's guest judge took their places at the front of the room. "She's even more beautiful than she is on TV."

"Mmm," Rachel said noncommittally. Elinor was a looker, all right, but she wasn't who Rachel had come to see. Rachel sat up straighter when the finalists' sous chefs marched in.

Erica Barrett led Griffin's team onto the set. The rest of the staff followed. If the rumors were true, the group would soon be reporting to Erica full-time. She looked ready for the challenge. Rachel hoped she would be able to say the same about Griffin. Griffin had come so far and fought so hard. She had sacrificed so much for this competition. She didn't deserve to go home empty-handed.

"Ten, nine…"

The floor director's countdown to airtime reminded Rachel of Griffin's New Year's Eve party. Flirting with her while they sampled exotic spices. Kissing her while the band played "Auld Lang Syne."

"…six, five…"

Rachel still remembered the feel of Griffin's lips and the taste of her tongue as she had sampled both for the first time.

"…two, one…"

The On Air sign overhead lit up in bright red letters.

Elinor Davies addressed the audience in the studio and the one at home. "Ladies and gentlemen, welcome to this season's final episode of *Cream of the Crop*." The Applause sign flashed and the audience clapped on cue. "We're a couple of minutes away from beginning the final elimination challenge," Elinor said when the noise died down. "Let's hear it for the two talented chefs who will be competing for the chance to be called the cream of the crop."

Rachel led the cheers as Griffin and Veronica took their positions behind their respective prep areas. Shielding her eyes with her hand, Griffin tried to see into the audience. The lights shining in her face were so bright she probably couldn't see past the first few rows.

Rachel's mother nudged her in the side with her elbow. "She's looking for you."

Rachel raised her hand in a tentative wave. She had hoped to remain incognito until the competition was over. She didn't want to be the distraction that cost Griffin a prize she seemed to value above everything else. Or was she already too late? Griffin looked anxious. Her body language was tense. She looked nothing like the relaxed, confident chef she had proven herself to be. She didn't wave back.

"She can't see you," Rachel's mother said. "You have to do something more dramatic to get her attention."

"Yeah? Like what?"

"Something like this."

"Uh oh." Rachel's father dropped his head and covered his eyes. "Here she goes."

Rachel's mother stood up, put two fingers in her mouth, and whistled so sharply dozens of heads whipped in her direction. As Rachel tried to drag her back into her seat, her mother cupped her hands around her mouth and yelled, "Griffin, she's up here!"

"Mom!" Rachel covered her face with her hands, fairly certain she was about to discover if it was possible to die from embarrassment.

Her mother resumed her seat with an air of triumph. "It worked, didn't it?"

Rachel peeked between her splayed fingers. Griffin was grinning from ear to ear.

❖

"It sounds like we have some enthusiastic fans in the audience tonight," Elinor said with a laugh.

Her comment prompted a round of cheers for both contestants. Griffin could barely hear them over the beating of her heart.

Fighting her instincts, she hadn't contacted Rachel since she delivered the package to her office. Instead, she had given Rachel the time and space she needed to make up her mind without any external pressure. The tactic had used up every ounce of her patience, but it had worked. Rachel was here.

She rubbed her palms together in anticipation, then gathered her team around her. "No matter what happens tonight, guys, always remember what I'm about to tell you." She looked at each of their eager faces. "You're the best group I've ever worked with and I love every one of you." The words that had always been so hard suddenly came so easily she had to say them again. "I love you, guys. Now let's have some fun."

"Yes, chef!" they said in unison.

"Tonight's challenge will test the limits of our contestants' imaginations," Stewart Sands said, his shaved head gleaming under the bright lights.

Two volunteers brought out large wicker baskets and placed one in front of Griffin and the other in front of Veronica. Griffin inhaled deeply to try to guess what was inside but couldn't detect any distinctive aromas. She laughed when she saw Veronica doing the same thing.

"The competitors have no idea what's in those baskets," Stewart said, "and as you can tell, they're chomping at the bit to get inside them."

"Chefs, after you open your baskets, you will have one hour to create an appetizer, an entrée, and a dessert," Elinor said, reminding everyone of the rules. "You must incorporate all the ingredients in your baskets into your dishes. You will also have unlimited access to the items in the pantry to your left. The clock starts…now."

Griffin and Veronica opened their baskets and began to remove the contents: a watermelon, a block of feta cheese, a carton of strawberries, a pack of portobello mushrooms, and a bag of prosciutto.

Her hands on her hips, Griffin stared at the ingredients and tried to formulate a plan for a three-course meal.

"What am I supposed to do with this?" she said under her breath.

Veronica echoed her sentiments but much more colorfully. "Shit on a biscuit." The crowd tittered as the tiny microphone pinned to Veronica's chef's coat broadcast the epithet all over the studio, though the network's thirty-second delay probably prevented it from going out over the airwaves.

While Veronica struggled to plan a menu, Griffin pulled out a pen and quickly created one on the fly. She gathered her team around her once more. "Here's what I'm thinking," she said, showing them what she had written. "I want each course to lead to the next one. A summer salad followed by a hearty fall main course and, to finish, a chilled soup that acts as a harbinger of spring." She turned to her line cook. "Ben, take point on the first course. Do you remember the watermelon salad I made for my Fourth of July barbecue?"

"Watermelon, feta cheese, radishes, peanuts, scallions, prosciutto, olive oil, lime juice, and mint." He rattled off the list so fast it was as if he had memorized the answer to the question.

"That's your dish."

Ben swallowed hard. "H-how many servings?"

Griffin put a steadying hand on his shoulder. "Four. Three for the judges and one for me. I'm starving."

Her joke lightened the mood. Ben visibly relaxed. "Yes, chef." He ran to the pantry to gather ingredients.

"Erica."

"Yes, chef."

"I want to focus on the entrée, so I'm putting you in charge of dessert." She winked. "If I screw up the main course, I'll need you to help me finish strong."

"You got it, chef."

Griffin gave Erica a high five. Her team ran like a well-oiled machine, in stark contrast to the train wreck on the other side of the room. Veronica's assistants looked skittish. As if they were afraid of making a mistake. No one wanted to be the scapegoat who cost Veronica a victory.

While Veronica's prep cook crafted a prosciutto salad with pears, feta cheese, and pecans, Griffin poured flour on the counter, hollowed out a circle in the center, and cracked an egg over the crater. She worked the ingredients until they formed a dough, pressed the dough flat with a rolling pin, then fed the dough through a roller. She set the first noodle aside and quickly formed another.

A reporter roaming the sidelines provided a running commentary. "Chef Sutton is cranking out lasagna noodles. Did someone order Italian?"

❖

Rachel stared at the monitor overhead that provided close-ups of the action taking place at the front of the cavernous room. If Griffin was making lasagna noodles, that meant her main course would most likely be mushroom lasagna. The dish that had brought her and Veronica together—and torn them apart.

"Please tell me she isn't doing what I think she's doing."

Griffin looked up as if she had heard her. "If I'm going down," she said with a grin, "I'm going down swinging." She checked on the salad preparation. "How are we doing?"

"Almost there, chef."

Ben had chopped the watermelon into cubes and sprinkled it with feta cheese. Torn pieces of prosciutto were waiting to be browned in the oven. Ben whisked lime juice and olive oil together to make the dressing. Griffin dipped a finger in the liquid to check the flavor.

"Perfect. Great job."

"Thank you, chef."

With forty-five minutes left on the clock, Erica grabbed tarragon, honey, orange juice, lemon juice, and a lemon from the pantry and began prepping the dessert course. She tossed the strawberries into a food processor and slowly added the liquids. Then she added the chopped tarragon while Griffin stirred. She offered Griffin the first taste.

Griffin lifted the spoon to her mouth and smiled. "Just what I was hoping for. Excellent, chef."

Erica covered the bowl of soup with plastic wrap and put it in the refrigerator to chill.

Calm and focused, Griffin seemed to know exactly what she wanted to do. Veronica, meanwhile, seemed at her wits' end. Barking orders at the top of her lungs, she implored her sous chefs to keep up with her.

"They call this a timed challenge for a reason, people. If we don't get it on the plate, it doesn't count." She tasted her saucier's offering and screwed up her face in disapproval. "You call that white sauce? It tastes more like paste." She brushed him aside. "Get out of the way. I'll do it myself."

"I wish I'd brought some popcorn," Rachel's father said. "This is better than a movie."

Rachel hated to say it, but Veronica's appetizer looked delicious. On the other hand, her dessert was simple but boring—the required watermelon and strawberries mixed with grapes and pineapples from the pantry. Her main course was, naturally, mushroom lasagna. Her version of the dish was going to go head-to-head with Griffin's.

I guess tonight's the night we find out once and for all who makes it better.

❖

Halfway through the challenge, Griffin put the finishing touches on her Béchamel sauce and slid her mushroom lasagna into the oven. With fifteen minutes to go, she helped Ben brown the prosciutto.

Sweat was pouring down her face, but she reminded herself to be patient. For her team, this wasn't a competition. It was a teaching experience. Ignoring everything she had riding on tonight's result, she allowed her staff to fix their own mistakes without stepping in to do it for them and offered gentle encouragement whenever possible. She felt like a mama bird watching her chicks prepare to leave the nest.

Even though she had often said she didn't want kids, she had essentially been raising them for as long as she could remember. Busboys, dishwashers, servers, line cooks, sous chefs. She had mentored them all over the years. She felt like a proud parent each time they moved to the next level in their careers.

Maybe it's time I gave the real thing a try.

She and her team plated the dishes with minutes to spare and exchanged fist bumps after Elinor called time. She sneaked a peek at Veronica's offerings. Despite her histrionics, Veronica had pulled off three spectacular-looking courses. Griffin hadn't expected anything less.

"I don't know if my dishes are good enough to beat yours, but it was a pleasure facing off against you."

"You gave me a run for my money, Sutton. Before either of us claims victory, though, let's see what the judges have to say."

They shared a weary hug as the audience gave them a standing ovation.

❖

The judges seemed to take forever to reach their decision, but it couldn't have been longer than a few minutes. Rachel rubbed her sweaty palms on her pants as Elinor and Stewart prepared to announce the verdict.

"Veronica," Stewart said, "your salad was to die for and your main course was close to perfect."

Not what Rachel wanted to hear.

"Griffin," Stewart continued, "your dishes showed surprising flavor and unexpected heart."

Of course they did. Griffin's food was a reflection of her— soulful, passionate, and complex. If she were fortunate enough to spend the rest of her life with Griffin, Rachel doubted she would ever uncover all of her many layers. But oh, how she wanted to try.

"In second place with ninety-three points out of a possible one hundred, let's hear it for…"

Elinor paused, letting the tension build. Rachel's heart rate climbed close to its maximum.

"Veronica Warner. Griffin Sutton, you are the cream of the crop!"

Griffin closed her eyes as relief washed over her face. Or was that validation?

Despite her obvious disappointment, Veronica was the first to offer her congratulations. "Well done, chef."

"Thanks, Ronnie."

Rachel, her parents, and the rest of Griffin's supporters leaped to their feet as Griffin and her staff met in a joyous group hug. Confetti rained from the ceiling while Elinor rattled off the list of prizes Griffin had just won. Rachel doubted the cash meant as much to Griffin as something money couldn't buy: the respect she had craved for so long. She had finally earned a spot in the upper echelon of the culinary world.

"Is there anything you want to say?" Elinor asked.

Griffin adjusted the oversized cardboard check one of the show's sponsors had shoved into her hands.

"I want to thank Veronica for being such a worthy opponent, I want to thank my team for doing such a great job, and I want to thank the fans for supporting the show as passionately as they do. None of us could do what we do without you. But, most of all, I want to thank Rachel Bauer for being here tonight. Rachel, I couldn't have done this without you. I couldn't have made it this far without you. And I can't imagine taking another step without you."

❖

"I'm sorry I misjudged you," Rachel said when they were alone. "If I had been paying attention when we watched the episode, I would have noticed your hair was wet one second and dry the next."

"We believe what we choose to believe sometimes."

"I should have chosen to believe you."

"It's water under the bridge, Rachel. Water under the bridge."

Confetti littered the empty studio, prolonging the evening's festive feel. Rachel could still hear the cheering, even though the rest of the audience was long gone.

"Veronica looked devastated by the judges' decision."

"Oh, I think she'll be okay."

Right on cue, Veronica strolled through the room with Elinor Davies on her arm. "What do you say, Sutton?" she called out. "Best two out of three?"

"Name the time and the place."

"Tomorrow." Veronica glanced at Elinor. "I'm going to be tied up tonight."

"Literally, I'm sure." Griffin turned back to Rachel. "Where are your parents?"

"Headed home. My mother wanted to congratulate you, but she couldn't wait to see herself on TV."

"I love your mom," Griffin said with a chuckle. "But I love her daughter even more."

Rachel stiffened. "Don't say that."

"Why not?"

"Because you're leaving. Don't say you love me if you're going to walk out of my life in a few months."

"I'm not leaving without you. When I said I can't imagine taking another step without you, I meant it. Every word."

"That sounds vaguely like a proposal."

"Only vaguely? Then I'm not doing a very good job of expressing myself. I love you, Rachel. All those things you want, I want. I want a family with you. I want a life with you. I want to be with you for as long as you'll have me."

Rachel's mind reeled as she tried to absorb the magnitude of what Griffin had just said. But Griffin wasn't done.

"In case you haven't heard, I'm going to be opening a restaurant next year. I could use a reputable accountant to keep me from losing my shirt. Do you know where I can find one?"

"You want me to work for you?"

"*With* me."

"I hate to play devil's advocate, but my practical side is begging me to. If the restaurant failed, it could drag us both down."

"Then it's my job to make sure that doesn't happen. Do you trust me?"

"Yes," Rachel said. "I do."

And she had never been more certain of anything—or anyone—in her life.

EPILOGUE

Rachel was excited but a bit anxious as well. Her carefully-planned life was suddenly far from it. And she couldn't be happier. Not about being three thousand miles away from family and friends—that part sucked—but an even larger family was waiting to greet her with open arms. And when things settled down, she and Griffin would start a family of their own. Provided, of course, they could find a place to call home. Logan had a long list of properties that met their requirements—something near the beach with two bedrooms, two bathrooms, and a large kitchen. When he found one they liked, they planned to fly out and take a look at it in person to see if the real thing was as good as the pictures on the Internet.

But that was weeks if not months from now. Today wasn't about the future or the past. Today was about coming full circle.

She had asked Griffin to let her plan the last leg of their culinary trip around the world. Griffin had happily acquiesced. Her eyes widened when Rachel led her through the doors of the restaurant on the corner of Houston and Ludlow. Rachel escorted her past the (in)famous table where Meg Ryan memorably faked an orgasm in *When Harry Met Sally*. They found seats in a recently vacated booth, rubbing elbows with locals and tourists who probably didn't know cornichons from Cornish hens. Looking at the expression on Griffin's face, Rachel could tell she had made the right choice.

"Welcome to Katz's Deli," she said after she ordered a pastrami sandwich for the two of them to share. At Katz's, the portion sizes were so large one sandwich could feed a party of five.

"You told me once that I represent New York for you," Rachel continued. "For me, nothing represents New York more than Katz's." She took a sip of her egg cream. "As we begin our new life together, I thought this would be the perfect point of departure."

Griffin rested her chin on the heel of her hand. "So I should cancel the trip to Italy?"

"Don't you dare."

Griffin had won the two-week, expense-paid trip while she was on *Cream of the Crop*. They planned to cash it in the following spring before they got bogged down in the last-minute details prior to La La Land's grand opening. Rachel had already reserved a room at a quaint bed-and-breakfast hotel in Tuscany. Griffin, of course, had booked tables in all the best restaurants.

"I can't wait to see the world with you," Rachel said. "What do you think our next adventure will bring?"

"I don't know." Griffin leaned forward and gently kissed her lips. "But I can't wait to find out."

About the Author

Yolanda Wallace is not a professional writer, but she plays one in her spare time. She has written three previous novels, *In Medias Res*, *Rum Spring*, and *Lucky Loser*. Her short stories have appeared in multiple anthologies including *Romantic Interludes 2: Secrets* and *Women of the Dark Streets*. She and her partner live in beautiful coastal Georgia, where they are parents to four children of the four-legged variety—a boxer and three cats. Yolanda can be reached at yolandawrites@gmail.com.

Books Available From Bold Strokes Books

Month of Sundays by Yolanda Wallace. Love doesn't always happen overnight; sometimes it takes a month of Sundays. (978-1-60282-739-4)

Jacob's War by C.P. Rowlands. ATF Special Agent Allison Jacob's task force is in the middle of an all-out war, from the streets to the boardrooms of America. Small business owner Katie Blackburn is the latest victim who accidentally breaks it wide open but may break AJ's heart at the same time. (978-1-60282-740-0)

The Pyramid Waltz by Barbara Ann Wright. Princess Katya Nar Umbriel wants a perfect romance, but her Fiendish nature and duties to the crown mean she can never tell the truth-until she meets Starbride, a woman who gets to the heart of every secret, even if it will be the death of her. (978-1-60282-741-7)

The Secret of Othello by Sam Cameron. Florida teen detectives Steven and Denny risk their lives to search for a sunken NASA satellite-but under the waves, no one can hear you scream . . . (978-1-60282-742-4)

Dreaming of Her by Maggie Morton. Isa has begun to dream of the most amazing woman—a woman named Lilith with a gorgeous face, an amazing body, and the ability to turn Isa on like no other. But Lilith is just a dream...isn't she? (978-1-60282-847-6)

Andy Squared by Jennifer Lavoie. Andrew never thought anyone could come between him and his twin sister, Andrea...until Ryder rode into town. (978-1-60282-743-1)

Finding Bluefield by Elan Barnehama. Set in the backdrop of Virginia and New York and spanning the years 1960-1982, Finding Bluefield chronicles the lives of Nicky Stewart, Barbara Philips, and their son, Paul, as they struggle to define themselves as a family. (978-1-60282-744-8)

The Jetsetters by David-Matthew Barnes. As rock band The Jetsetters skyrocket from obscurity to super stardom, Justin Holt, a lonely barista, and Diego Delgado, the band's guitarist, fight with everything they have to stay together, despite the chaos and fame. (978-1-60282-745-5)

Strange Bedfellows by Rob Byrnes. Partners in life and crime, Grant Lambert and Chase LaMarca, are hired to make a politician's compromising photo disappear, but what should be an easy job quickly spins out of control. (978-1-60282-746-2)

Speed Demons by Gun Brooke. When NASCAR star Evangeline Marshall returns to the race track after a close brush with death, will famous photographer Blythe Pierce document her triumph and reciprocate her love—or will they succumb to their respective demons and fail? (978-1-60282-678-6)

Summoning Shadows: A Rosso Lussuria Vampire Novel by Winter Pennington. The Rosso Lussuria vampires face enemies both old and new, and to prevail they must call on even more strange alliances, unite as a clan, and draw on every weapon within their reach—but with a clan of vampires, that's easier said than done. (978-1-60282-679-3)

Sometime Yesterday by Yvonne Heidt. When Natalie Chambers learns her Victorian house is haunted by a pair of lovers and a Dark Man, can she and her lover Van Easton solve the mystery that will set the ghosts free and banish the evil presence in the house? Or will they have to run to survive as well? (978-1-60282-680-9)

Into the Flames by Mel Bossa. In order to save one of his patients, psychiatrist Jamie Scarborough will have to confront his own monsters—including those he unknowingly helped create. (978-1-60282-681-6)

Coming Attractions: Author's Edition by Bobbi Marolt. For Helen Townsend, chasing turns to caring, and caring turns to loving, but will love take five steps back and turn to leaving? (978-1-60282-732-5)

OMGqueer, edited by Radclyffe and Katherine E. Lynch. Through stories imagined and told by youth across America, this anthology provides a snapshot of queerness at the dawn of the new millennium. (978-1-60282-682-3)

Oath of Honor by Radclyffe. A First Responders novel. First do no harm…First Physician of the United States Wes Masters discovers that being the president's doctor demands more than brains and personal sacrifice—especially when politics is the order of the day. (978-1-60282-671-7)

A Question of Ghosts by Cate Culpepper. Becca Healy hopes Dr. Joanne Call can help her learn if her mother really committed suicide—but she's not sure she can handle her mother's ghost, a decades-old mystery, and lusting after the difficult Dr. Call without some serious chocolate consumption. (978-1-60282-672-4)

The Night Off by Meghan O'Brien. When Emily Parker pays for a taboo role-playing fantasy encounter from the Xtreme Encounters escort agency, she expects to surrender control—but never imagines losing her heart to dangerous butch Nat Swayne. (978-1-60282-673-1)

Sara by Greg Herren. A mysterious and beautiful new student at Southern Heights High School stirs things up when students start dying. (978-1-60282-674-8)

Fontana by Joshua Martino. Fame, obsession, and vengeance collide in a novel that asks: What if America's greatest hero was gay? (978-1-60282-675-5)

Lemon Reef by Robin Silverman. What would you risk for the memory of your first love? When Jenna Ross learns her high school love Del Soto died on Lemon Reef, she refuses to accept the medical examiner's report of a death from natural causes and risks everything to find the truth. (978-1-60282-676-2)

The Dirty Diner: Gay Erotica on the Menu, edited by Jerry L. Wheeler. Gay erotica set in restaurants, featuring food, sex, and men—could you really ask for anything more? (978-1-60282-677-9)

Sweat: Gay Jock Erotica by Todd Gregory. Sizzling tales of smoking hot sex with the athletic studs everyone fantasizes about. (978-1-60282-669-4)

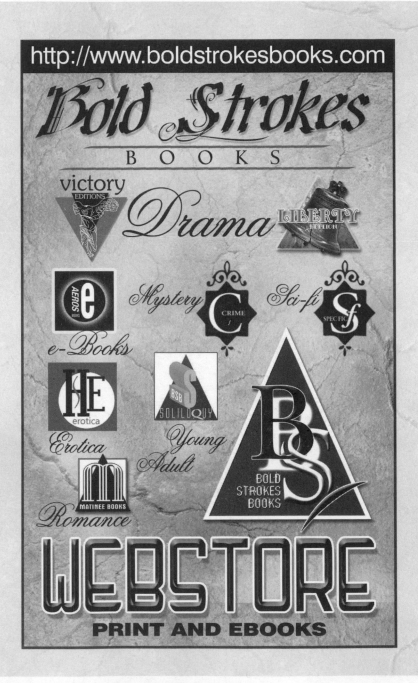